Beyond the
HORIZON

Beyond the
HORIZON

PENNY ZELLER

Dedicated to all who've been trapped in the throes of guilt,
then set free by the Lord's forgiveness.

*If a man have an hundred sheep, and one of them be gone astray,
doth he not leave the ninety and nine, and goeth into the mountains,and seeketh that which is gone astray?*
~ Matthew 18:12

Chapter One

Horizon, Idaho, 1895

FOR A MOMENT, SHE was the world-famous reporter, Ruby Shepherdson, author of the latest award-winning article.

Ruby closed her eyes and imagined seeing her name below the numerous articles and stories she submitted to Mr. O'Kane, the editor of *The Horizon Herald*. The editor from the prestigious *Boise City Chronicle*, who was just happening to visit his mother in Horizon, would peruse the pages of *The Horizon Herald* and become engrossed in one of Ruby's engaging articles. He would then invite her to submit a monthly story to his well-read publication.

But alas, such a fanciful dream would have to wait.

Ruby resumed scrubbing one of Papa's shirts on the washboard. There was no fictional editor from *The Boise City Chronicle* visiting his mother in Horizon. And until Ruby's shipment of her Smith Premier typewriter arrived from the R. Altman & Company in St. Louis, Missouri, she would continue to dip her pen in ink and handwrite each and every composition she submitted to the cantankerous man who'd become her boss just one year ago last week.

Not that she minded tending to every day chores, including laundry on Mondays, for she didn't. As a matter of fact, Ruby's highest aspirations were to marry someday and be a wife and mother. But until the Lord saw fit to allow a suitable gent into her life, she would continue on the path of writing.

Ruby hung the shirt on the line and proceeded with washing the next item when she noticed a buggy rounding the curve to their farm. She stood tall and placed her hands on her lower back to stretch the tightness from hunching over the washboard. A closer perusal indicated Wilhelmina, one of Mama's best friends, was paying them a visit.

Wilhelmina, a permanent smile on her round face, folded Ruby into a hug. "It's so nice to see you. Your ma and I are planning some new recipe ideas, but first, I was asked to deliver a message."

It didn't surprise Ruby that Mama and Wilhelmina would be experimenting with recipes. After the Bible, Mama's favorite book was *Recipes from Augusta's Kitchen*, a book she'd purchased when she and Papa first married. "A message?"

"Yes. Tabitha said to tell you that your special purchase has arrived."

The air caught in Ruby's lungs. "My special purchase? It has arrived?"

"That's what she said."

Not caring how unladylike it might be, Ruby let out an enthusiastic squeal, threw up her hands in excitement, and danced a little jig.

"Might be that you are thrilled to hear this news," teased Wilhelmina.

"Oh, yes. Not only thrilled, but exhilarated. I've waited forever for this momentous occasion."

"Congratulations."

"Thank you." Ruby plopped the unwashed clothes in a pile. She'd finish the daunting chore later, but for now, she'd seek

Papa's permission to take the wagon into town and retrieve the item that would change her life forever.

Wilhelmina put an arm through Ruby's, and together they marched to the house, albeit more slowly than Ruby would have preferred. She attempted not to be impatient as Mama and Wilhelmina greeted each other and acted as though they hadn't just spoken at church yesterday. Finally, Ruby was able to edge in a word.

"Mama, may I please borrow the wagon? My shipment has arrived at the mercantile."

Mama's eyes widened. "So soon?"

For Mama, it may be soon, but for Ruby, it had been an eternity since she'd sought a loan from the bank and ordered her soon-to-be prized possession.

"It's fine with me, but check with your pa and see if he'll need the wagon in the meantime. And would you mind gathering some provisions while you're there?"

"Not at all."

After Mama handed her a list, Ruby bounded out the door and to the farthest northern corner of the field to secure Papa's permission. She lifted her hem and ran, being sure to dodge the numerous muddy puddles from last night's rain. The spring breeze whipped her skirts and blew wisps of hair from her once-secure chignon.

"Ruby? Is there an emergency?" Papa stood from fixing the plow, concern in his eyes.

"Oh, no, I was just hoping to borrow the wagon to retrieve my shipment."

"I'm going to town tomorrow for some lumber. I can fetch it for you then."

"Thank you, but if it's all the same, I'd like to retrieve it today. Posthaste."

Timothy, her younger brother, shook his head. "What's the rush, Rubes? You've been waiting for the shipment for this long. One more day won't make a bit of difference."

"On the contrary, dear brother. It makes all the difference. Papa, please may I borrow the wagon? I fear Tabitha will close the mercantile for the day if I tarry."

"Judging from the sun's placement in the sky, reckon you have plenty of time," offered Timothy, whose favorite pastime was offering unsolicited advice.

"Not everyone is a dawdler, Timothy. I prefer not to lollygag as time is of the essence."

Papa chuckled. "You two and your squabbling. Yes, Ruby, you can take the wagon to town. Would you mind stopping by the mill for the lumber? It will save me a trip tomorrow. Vernon will load it for you."

"Yes, absolutely, I will stop by the mill." She waited two more seconds in case Papa had more to add. When he said nothing, she added, "Thank you, Papa. I'll be back as soon as possible."

She hitched the horses, and with her notebook, pencil, and Mama's list in hand, Ruby climbed into the wagon. She beckoned the horses and headed to town, excitement filling every part of her.

Once at the mercantile, Ruby gathered everything into a crate from Mama's list and stood in line behind three other customers, all of whom, while dear people, seemed to have a penchant for prattling on. Finally, she reached the counter.

"Hello, Ruby. You must have received my message."

"Yes, I'm here for my shipment." Her breathless words indicated her anxiety to secure her order.

"Jimmie will load it for you. It's a sizable crate." Tabitha's face lit. "You're well on your way to becoming an established journalist now that you'll be the proud owner of a Smith Premier. I noticed in the catalogue that there's even a new version now."

Ruby was content with the previous version, especially given the cost. Tabitha put Mama's items on her account and beckoned her husband to hoist the crate hidden in the back room.

"Say, Ruby, I thought you should be the first—well, second to know, seeing as I told Tabitha first—that I'm planning to run for another term as mayor."

"That's delightful news, Mayor Trabert."

"Thank you." He pushed the crate to the front of the wagon beside Mama's provisions. "I love serving this town. Perhaps you could write an article about my plans to run again."

"I'd be happy to ask Mr. O'Kane if he'd be amenable to me doing just that."

Mayor Trabert tipped his hat. "Tell your folks I said hello."

Ruby stopped next at the mill where Vernon loaded the lumber for Papa after assisting two other customers.

And finally, Ruby was on her way home.

All was well until an idea struck her for a story she hoped to approach Mr. O'Kane with. Since she knew that it would escape her overcrowded mind forever if she didn't stop to write down the thought, Ruby pulled to the side of the road, set the reins beside her, and reached for her notebook and pencil, which had fallen off the seat.

But there was one small problem.

In her haste, she'd forgotten to set the brake.

The horses advanced forward, jolting Ruby from her once-comfortable spot on the buckboard. The reins, also jolted by the sudden movement, slithered just beyond her reach.

Mud flew up on the sides of the wagon as the horses determined their route—a route off the road and into the muddy weeds.

"Whoa!" she yelled as the wagon bumbled along and the pieces of lumber rattled in the back. A cursory glance told her the typewriter remained secure, but some of Mama's provisions rolled throughout the wagon.

Ruby clamored again for the reins and finally secured them, but not before the wagon immersed itself in a thick patch of dark-brown mud. It screeched to a halt, propelling her forward.

Several minutes later, she righted herself and heaved a deep breath of relief. "Thank You, Lord," she gasped, noting she could have fallen headfirst beneath the horses or wagon and been trampled.

She may have emerged unscathed from her adventure, but the wagon had firmly rooted itself in the mud. Taking a minute to catch her breath, she determined she was halfway home, although far from the road.

Ruby had two choices. Attempt to dislodge the wagon wheels from the mud or walk home and fetch Papa and Timothy.

She could hear her brother's voice now. *"Reckon I'm not surprised it happened the way it did, Rubes. You can be such a knucklehead sometimes."*

No, she wouldn't walk home and seek Papa's and Timothy's assistance, prideful as it may be. Instead, she would endeavor to liberate the wagon.

Mud caked the hem of her dress as she attempted to pry the wheels loose with a piece of Papa's lumber. Her arms ached from the laborious undertaking, and after what seemed like hours, she paused and climbed back into the wagon.

Perhaps she would have to rethink her options and overlook and ignore Timothy's insolent admonishments.

Just as she'd uttered her fifteenth prayer for wisdom and was about to embark on the journey home, she saw a passing wagon. Help had arrived!

As ladylike as possible, Ruby stood on tiptoe and waved her arms. "Over here!"

The driver of the wagon peered in her direction. Would he stop?

Surely he would. The residents of Horizon, most of them anyhow, were kindly folks.

"Help!" she yelled again, her voice echoing on the vacant stretch of land.

The man reversed direction and drove his wagon toward her, and Ruby released the breath she'd been holding. He stopped on the road away from the muddy patch and disembarked.

"What seems to be the problem?"

While his hat was pulled low over his eyes so she couldn't see much of his face other than a scraggly and unkempt brown beard, Ruby was quite certain she'd never seen him before. As any perceptive reporter would do, she attempted to ascertain his age. Given there was no gray in his beard and his hands were not gnarled or arthritic, he must not be elderly. He wore a red plaid shirt stretched over broad shoulders. His tan trousers and boots indicated he was likely a farmer. Dark brown hair curled beneath his hat, and a portion of his neck was sunburned.

"Yes, I seem to have taken an accidental adventure by departing from the road and finding myself plumb stuck in the middle of a muddy field." She laughed, noting her voice sounded nervous in her own ears.

"I see that."

"Yes, well, I hadn't meant to. You see, I had this most amazing idea for one of my articles, and while I was reaching…"

"Miss, with all due respect, I'll just assist you and be on my way."

"Oh. All right."

He was obviously one of few words.

"I was attempting to use a piece of the lumber—"

But the man was not listening. Instead, he strode to his own wagon and reached for a shovel from the back. When he returned, he said, without so much as a lift of his head, "You might want to remove yourself and stand over there."

His voice was deep and clipped, and Ruby did as he requested. The man dug the wheels from the mud, coaxed the horses, and freed Ruby from her predicament in a matter of minutes.

"Thank you so much. I appreciate your help. Might I ask your name?"

"No."

How abrupt! Such a peculiar man. "Oh. All right. Well, thank you again."

"You should be able to continue to wherever it is you're going. Next time, I would suggest you mind yourself while driving the team. You're fortunate you weren't injured or worse."

"Oh, yes, sir. I will be more mindful in the future. You see, when these ideas hit me, I have to—well, never mind." The man likely would not care to hear her flimsy excuse for being so careless.

"If that's all, I'll be on my way." He tipped his hat and strode to his wagon.

Ruby tapped her chin as she watched the unusual stranger drive away. Perhaps Mr. O'Kane would allow her to investigate the man's identity. After all, who could resist a mystery?

CHAPTER TWO

JAKE JOLTED AWAKE, WILLING himself to catch his breath as he gasped for air. His shoulders heaved and sweat drenched him, his heart refusing to calm. He had to find Corbin. Had to warn him—demand he not ride that horse.

He flung aside the quilt and swung his legs over the side of the bed. Cool wood hit his feet as he stumbled toward the bedroom door's vague outline. The floor creaked and groaned, mingling with the phantom sounds of jangling tack.

Jake's chest tightened as he fumbled about the cabin, searching for the front door. He had to find Corbin. Had to tell him not to ride that horse.

No, not just tell him, but *command* his younger brother to listen to Pa's admonition.

"Corbin?" His voice echoed in the dark room.

But there was no answer.

"Corbin?"

Still no response.

Why wasn't his brother answering? He yelled Corbin's name twice more before running to the door, throwing it open, and staring into the night. "Where are you, Corbin?"

His heart pounded in his ears. "This isn't some game. Reckon you better answer!"

Sweat dripped down his back and the sides of his face, and his ragged breath caused him to beg for his lungs to obey his command to function.

A coyote's howl in the distance, crickets, and a noisy owl competed with the sound of his racing heartbeat. His eyes attempted to adjust to the murkiness of the night. The smell of a Russian olive tree floated on the breeze, and the sliver of the moon and plentiful stars greeted his upward glance.

He blinked. Where was he?

Then the realization hit him like a blow to the gut.

He wasn't at his parents' farm outside of Ingleville. No, he was at his own farm in Horizon. And Corbin wasn't disobeying Pa's rule not to ride Lucky.

Corbin.

Jake grasped the doorknob to steady himself before crumbling into the chair on the porch. A mosquito buzzed around his ear, and he swatted at it as the emotion engulfed him.

It had only been a nightmare, but while what he'd dreamed hadn't been real, there was a reality that would haunt him all the days of his life—his negligence in causing his brother's death.

Once upon a time, Jake might pray for God's help, but not now. After what happened, God was as disappointed in him as Pa was—if not more so. Jake peered into the nothingness, but in his mind, the memories played over again as if it all happened yesterday rather than several years ago.

Corbin rarely listened to reason. Pa said it was because he was immature for his age. Ma said it was because Corbin was like her older brother. Always thirsting for adventure.

Fearless, daring, and, in his mind, invincible. A wanderlust in his spirit that couldn't be satisfied with the day-to-day routines of working on a farm in Idaho. A personality that couldn't be tamed.

But Corbin's accident proved he wasn't invincible.

An accident Jake was responsible for.

He blew out a deep breath and settled his head against the house. The nightmares weren't as frequent as they had been right after Corbin's death, but they'd been regular enough to contribute to a lack of sleep and a guilt that crushed Jake worse than if he'd been crushed by an enormous boulder.

Jake closed his eyes as the horror again washed over him.

Ma, Pa, and Dinah Jo had gone to town for provisions and lumber. Just before they left, Pa had clapped Jake on the back, instructing him to watch Corbin and keep him from doing anything foolish.

It started off well enough with Jake and Corbin mending the fence near the corral. Jake had mentally checked off the things he had to do that day. His list hadn't included watching his brother die.

Corbin had assisted with the fence, but his thoughts were obviously elsewhere. Jake asked for the fencing pliers, but Corbin didn't respond. When Jake looked over at him, Corbin's attention was on Lucky, the quarter horse Pa had received in trade for some work.

"Sure wish I could ride that horse," Corbin had said, an unsettling glint in his eye.

No matter what Jake said, it hadn't mattered that Pa said no one was to ride the obstinate creature. Corbin hadn't cared that Lucky wasn't broke yet or that the horse had seriously injured his former owner. No, Corbin used the same argument he always wielded when attempting to ride a horse he shouldn't.

"How am I supposed to be hired by Buffalo Bill Cody himself for his Congress of Rough Riders Wild West show if I haven't had practice riding an untamed horse? If I'm inexperienced, he'll never hire me to tame the mustangs and broncos."

Jake hadn't told his brother that it was highly unlikely Buffalo Bill would hire Corbin anyhow because he didn't want to dishearten him and destroy the dream Corbin had since he was five. So instead, he reached for the pliers himself and continued working.

But Corbin refused to let the matter drop, and he continued to pester Jake about riding Lucky for the next hour, all the while grumbling that he was nearly a man and shouldn't have to obey Pa's ridiculous rules. Jake had stopped for a moment and stared at his brother. At fifteen, Corbin was a scrawny sort with gangly limbs, a thin stature, and a permanent scowl. With his large eyes and sandy blond hair, he resembled Ma's side of the family.

"Just a few minutes is all," Corbin had said. *"I promise."*

Jake refused.

Corbin persisted.

And then Jake relented. *"Fine, but only for a few minutes."*

Without hesitation, Corbin had leaped over the corral fence and ambled toward Lucky, his voice low and soothing. Jake had removed his hat, plopped it back on his head, removed it again, then asked the Good Lord to keep his foolish brother safe. Because in those days, Jake believed God was faithful. That He protected His children.

But Jake no longer believed that just as he no longer believed God answered prayers. At least, not his.

He tamped down the emotion that knotted in his throat as the memory of that day formed as vividly in his mind as if it could have happened just seconds ago.

Corbin was able to saddle Lucky and climb on his back for a mere three seconds. A pheasant's characteristic call had sounded as the bird ran just to the left of the corral. Lucky had spooked, then thrown Corbin.

Jake would never forget the cold rush of terror coursing through him as he bolted toward Corbin's still body.

He hadn't needed to see the blood or Corbin's crumpled form to know his brother was gone.

When Ma, Pa, and Dinah Jo arrived home, Jake was kneeling beside Corbin, crying out to God.

Pa ran toward them and dropped to his knees, expression puckering with anguish. *"Jake, what have you done?"*

What had he done? He'd allowed his brother to die.

CHAPTER THREE

RUBY PARKED THE WAGON at Reverend Marshall and Maribel's humble cabin. Each week, she commenced assisting the older couple in any way she could. When Ruby was twelve, Mama suggested Ruby visit and assist with everyday tasks. She unloaded a crate, which included provisions, sandwiches, carrots, and cookies for the noonday meal, and a glass bottle of Stedge's Tonic. She looked forward to Wednesdays each week—the day when she could spend time with the people who had become surrogate grandparents to her.

The cozy home was just large enough for the couple and boasted a small porch that Papa, Timothy, Albert, Landon, and Hans had built a few years ago. A wheelchair was positioned to the right along with a flower pot that Miss Greta had given to the retired pastor and his wife last summer.

Reverend Marshall opened the door before Ruby had a chance to knock. "Hello, Ruby, do come in." He waved a hand to the interior of the home.

"Thank you, Reverend. How are you today?"

"Doing fair to middling."

Ruby's heart jolted, as it always did, at the sight of Reverend Marshall. His stooped posture had reduced his formerly tall frame to a much shorter one. He relied on his walking stick to toddle about. His balding head with thatches of gray hair and his thick spectacles told of his age. Wasn't it just yesterday that he was preaching from the pulpit, his voice clear and methodical?

"Ruby!" Maribel pootled toward her with an unsteady gait and arms outstretched.

Ruby placed the crate on the table and embraced the older woman, mindful of her fragility. "It's so nice to see you both. Are you ready for our picnic, Maribel?"

"I am."

"And, yes, I'm ready for my nap." Reverend Marshall offered a good-natured grin. "You two have an enjoyable time, and I'll see you when you get back." He planted a kiss on top of his wife's disheveled gray hair. Any cynical person who might insinuate that true love didn't last forever need only witness the abiding love shared by the couple before her.

"Before we go, might you fix my coiffure?"

It was a special kindness Ruby did each week she came to visit and on Sundays before church as well. She'd brush Maribel's hair and fashion it into a braid or a chignon. "Yes, and I'm happy to say I found some Stedge's Tonic at the mercantile just yesterday."

"Stedge's Tonic?" Maribel's brow furrowed. "Not sure as I've ever heard of such a thing."

"It's supposed to be invigorating for the hair."

Maribel laughed. "Invigorating? I do declare."

Ruby shared in her amusement, applied the tonic, then brushed Maribel's hair before braiding it and winding it into a chignon. Maribel raised a gnarled hand to the base of her neck. "How does it look?"

Reverend Marshall took Maribel's hand in his. "You look as beautiful as ever, but it doesn't take a tonic to accomplish that."

Maribel blushed. "Oh, dear me."

Ruby watched the married couple's interaction for a moment almost feeling as though she was interrupting a cherished moment between the two. Her own parents experienced a loving marriage as well, but standing here with her two elderly friends, something stirred in Ruby's heart. Oh, but to have a love spanning a lifetime as Maribel and Reverend Marshall shared. To know that through the good and the bad, the fleeting days of youth to the changes the passing years brought, through it all the one you loved remained by your side.

Yes, Ruby Caroline, I do declare you are a sentimental sort.

She retrieved two sandwiches, several carrots, and three cookies from the pail in the crate and set them on the table for Reverend Marshall.

"Thank you, Ruby." He settled into one of the two chairs and took a bite of a cookie.

"Marshall," gasped Maribel. "After all these years you are still eating dessert before the main course." A glint shone in her eye and she batted at his arm.

Reverend Marshall swiped a crumb from his cheek. "At my advanced age, I don't think it's prudent for me to try to change my order of eating." His eyes twinkled, and he leaned forward and deposited a kiss on his wife's cheek. "These cookies are delicious if I do say so myself."

They both laughed in comfortable camaraderie, and Ruby joined in their contagious joy. "Is there anything else you need before Maribel and I leave?"

"Nothing this fine meal and a good nap won't solve. Take care of my beautiful bride, and I'll see you both in a short while."

They bid Reverend Marshall farewell. Ruby offered her arm, and she and Maribel ambled to the porch where the older woman took a seat in the wheelchair. Ruby pushed her down the wooden ramp.

"I so look forward to this day each week. Thank you, Ruby. You are such a blessing."

Maribel might consider Ruby a blessing, but the older woman had no idea what a blessing *she* was to Ruby.

Due to Maribel's pain with her rheumatism and arthritis, she couldn't walk beyond a few steps at a time. Ruby pushed her slowly in the wheelchair Albert and the elders at church purchased for her last year. Even so, the mode of transport bumped along the wooden slats of the boardwalk causing the older woman's thin frame to jostle with the movement. Maribel said hello to everyone they passed, and they often stopped to converse with the townsfolk.

Those in Horizon vowed to care for Maribel and Reverend Marshall in the days since their health had begun to decline. Ruby visited on Wednesdays each week and she and Timothy retrieved them for church on Sunday; Mama took Maribel to the sewing circle on Tuesdays; and Papa took Reverend Marshall fishing regularly during the summers. Albert and Velma, Mae and Landon, and Lucy and Hans frequently invited them for supper. Other members of the town delivered meals and stocked wood for their fireplace during winter.

They reached the river sometime later, and Ruby stationed Maribel's wheelchair on a clearing a safe distance from the edge. Willow trees dipped their branches into the rushing water, and three ducks loitered on smooth boulders in the center, their quacking competing with the meadowlarks. The tranquil babbling enhanced the serene surroundings, and the smell of pine, Russian olive trees, and purple dame's rocket flowers floated in the air.

Ruby supported Maribel's feeble steps to a wooden bench made two years ago in memory of one of Horizon's longtime citizens. She then dispersed a sandwich to both Maribel and herself.

"Oh, I love egg sandwiches." Maribel removed the lid of the sandwich. "And an abundant amount of butter too." Her hazel eyes rounded. "Thank you, Ruby."

"You are most welcome." Each time Ruby visited, she brought a noonday meal for the reverend and Maribel. She'd previously realized Maribel had an affinity for hard-boiled eggs sliced and nestled in butter between two pieces of bread.

After Ruby blessed the meal and they finished the sandwiches, carrots, and cookies, Maribel reached for Ruby's hand.

"Tell me how things are going for you, dear."

"Things are going well. I am writing articles for Mr. O'Kane although he is a challenging boss." She thought of the times he'd rejected the articles Ruby had gone to great lengths to write, and she was forced to pen another story on a tight deadline.

"For *Ruby's Horizon Happenings*?"

"Yes. He did hire another reporter, his brother's daughter, Lillian. She started working as a reporter shortly after I did, so there are three of us providing the news, including Mr. O'Kane."

Maribel patted her hand. "I've read each of those things you've written, and you are a talented writer."

"I do wish Mr. O'Kane thought so."

"But if he's publishing your stories, he must think highly of them."

Ruby stared at the bubbling water washing over the rocks. She'd kept every rejected story. Perhaps someday she could alter them and submit them again.

"So tell me, have you met any nice young men?"

Maribel's innocent inquiry interrupted Ruby's thoughts. "I don't think there are any such men available for courtship in Horizon."

"That could be the case. I recall not so many years ago thinking the very same thing before I met my Marshall."

"I did think I would be married with perhaps a child by now." The words of her heart slipped out before Ruby could stop them.

"All in the Lord's timing, dear."

But Ruby had resigned herself to spinsterhood even though having a husband and family had always been her greatest desire. Even more so than being a writer. Yes, she doted on her many nieces and nephews, but to be a mother herself... She shifted on the bench and faced Maribel. A question sat on the tip of her tongue—one she knew Maribel would keep in confidence. "Do you think God always gives us the desires of our hearts?"

"It does depend on those desires and if they are in line with His will." Maribel paused. "Psalm 37:4 promises that if we delight ourselves in Him, He will give us the desires of our heart. Are those desires for you to have a husband?"

"Yes, and to be a mother. Both Lucy and Mae have been blessed to have found godly men to marry. All of my friends from school have married." Ruby sighed. "I do so delight in Him and seek to glorify the Lord. I don't mean to sound impatient, but the Lord's timing seems awfully slow at times."

"Indeed it does. However, we must remember that in 2 Peter, we are told that one day with the Lord is as a thousand years and a thousand years as one day. He does not see time as we do. We see the tintype version, but He sees an enormous painting."

Maribel's wisdom always comforted her. "Yes, that is true. I just wonder if maybe it's not His will that I marry. And if that isn't His will, I pray I will be content in the life He has chosen for me. For I am ever so grateful for my family, my church, and my employment as a writer."

"There is nothing wrong with having desires of the heart, Ruby. One of the greatest callings on a woman's life is to be a wife and mother. Is that the calling He places on every woman's life? No, but I am confident that if He has chosen you to remain a spinster, He will give you the contentment you are praying for."

Ruby swallowed the ache in her throat. "I know you are right."

"I will join you in prayer for God's will. Sometimes He has a way of surprising us."

They changed the topic then to other ongoings in Horizon, and as Ruby sat with Maribel, another prayer of gratitude overflowed in her heart.

Her appreciation for a grandmother like Maribel.

Chapter Four

JAKE PLANTED HIMSELF IN the old rocking chair on the porch of his cabin. The former owner, an elderly man who'd passed shortly before Jake arrived in Horizon, likely sat in the very same chair and immersed himself in the amazing view of the fields bordering majestic mountains in the distance.

The man had been in ill health before his passing, and as such, the farm deteriorated. But Jake had always relished a challenge and set about restoring the neglected acreage.

Jake drained the last bit of coffee in his cup and feasted his gaze on the sunrise. In his mind, few things could compare to an Idaho sunrise. Not that he'd been to any other state, for he hadn't.

Samson, his black-and-white collie, propped his forefeet on Jake's lap. "We did well for ourselves here, didn't we, Samson?" he asked, petting the dog's head.

The dog angled his head to one side as if contemplating his owner's words. "Not that I ever imagined I'd make my permanent home in Horizon," Jake mused.

A few short years ago, he figured he'd always reside in Ingleville right next to Ma and Pa. Farm the land. Have a family of his own. But now such plans, disrupted and tossed aside by an unforgivable action, seemed so far in the past they might never have been his objective in the first place.

Samson batted at Jake's leg. "I know, boy. Just a few more minutes, then we'll head to the fields. There might be a squirrel or two for you to chase or some rock chucks to pester." The dog sat on his haunches as if to silently agree and patiently wait. Samson had been a faithful companion since Jake found him as a stray in Ketchum last year.

And, really, the dog was the only companionship Jake needed. Samson was loyal, forgiving, gracious, and liked hamburg steak almost as much as Jake. While the last item lacked importance, one would be hard-pressed to find the first three traits in people.

People like Pa who hadn't and never would forgive him for his role in Corbin's death.

That's why Jake had to leave home.

But Horizon?

After Corbin was laid to rest in Ingleville, Jake kissed Ma on the cheek, hugged Dinah Jo, and told Pa this was for the best. Ma had begged him to stay, and he'd never forget the tears that streamed down her face. Dinah Jo began to sob and buried her face in Ma's shoulder.

Pa's expression remained stoic.

Had his father even cared that he was about to lose another son?

Jake then set out, just him, his horse, and seven possessions—his Bible, revolver, rifle, a change of clothes, bedroll, pocketknife, and a tin cup. He rode until exhaustion set in that first day without knowing his destination. He camped alongside the Snake River, the pain so embedded in his heart he could think of nothing else but the loss of his brother.

Even God was likely disappointed with him. For how could even a Holy God forgive such carelessness on Jake's part?

So he determined it better to run from the Lord as well.

Jake secured odd jobs here and there during his first year away from home. Farmhand, construction, and even a short stint in a mine before traveling through the beautiful and rugged Sawtooth Mountain Range and stopping in a small town named Ketchum. He easily secured a job as a freighter and hauled goods to the mines. He may have still been there were it not for his love of farming and his longing to return to the profession that he'd been born into.

And as Jake roamed aimlessly looking for a place to settle, a paper flapping in the breeze at the Horizon Mercantile told of a farm for sale. If Jake prayed as he once did, he might have sought God's guidance in purchasing it. But instead, he saw the farm and bought it the same day without a second thought. He'd saved up a tidy sum at his former jobs and now owed little on the banknote.

He knew the pain he'd caused his parents and didn't want to remind them of that pain each day they laid eyes upon him.

Things had changed since he'd left Ingleville and vowed never to return. His appearance was one of the most profound. Instead of his short, thick dark hair, he'd let it grow. He'd allowed abundant whiskers to replace a clean-shaven chin. He'd visited a barber only twice since leaving home. The rest of the time, Jake had trimmed his own beard and hair, albeit imperfectly. Not that it mattered anyway. There was no one to see him since he only occasionally went to town. His own scissors assisted in keeping his hair from going beyond his shoulders, but he knew he still resembled a mountain man.

Jake returned his cup to the house before preparing to start the work day. He had made plans for his own life without the Lord's help. And as he strolled to the vast fields, he reminded himself that this life he'd chosen was the perfect one for him.

Ruby had just returned home from an afternoon at *The Horizon Herald* and was unsaddling her horse when she heard some commotion outside. She peeked her head around the corner of the barn door. Timothy drove the wagon, and behind him, Papa drove a dilapidated buggy. The black folded top was weathered and faded, the red seat ripped in spots, and the wheels splintered.

Mama emerged from the house just as Papa and Timothy halted their respective horses.

Ruby had ridden in Mae's buggy a handful of times, but the Bennick mode of transport was new, clean, and of premier quality. Unlike the one Papa parked near the house. Was he repairing it for someone? Ruby unpacked her saddlebag and joined her family.

"So I thought it seemed like a decent trade," Papa was saying.

"Papa did some work for Mr. Dorsey and he traded this old girl for the work." Timothy patted the side of the buggy.

Mama tilted her head to one side. "Tyler," she said, fond disapproval in her gaze.

Papa slung an arm around Mama and pulled her to him. "I know, my love, that payment in cash is always preferable, but Mr. Dorsey didn't have the funds, and he was looking to part with this fine buggy."

Mama never could resist Papa's charming ways and she smiled. "All right, then."

"Besides, once I restore it a bit, it'll be of good use, especially since our farm could use something besides the wagon. Especially Ruby." Papa's blue eyes sparkled. Eyes he'd passed on to Timothy. "Might be beneficial so you can go hither and yon for your articles and such."

"Hither and yon and such while dragging her brother along by the ear," muttered Timothy.

Mama and Papa laughed, and Ruby playfully slugged Timothy in the upper arm. He pretended to wince. "You're utterly dramatic Timothy Tyler Shepherdson. You know full well that..." she held up her pointer finger, "that number one, I appreciate you for accompanying me, and two, that you'll receive lovely curtains for your new house, my tireless efforts at picking rock from the fields with you, and most importantly, my undying gratitude."

"She's right, son," said Papa. "You might have to escort her on her assignments, but you're receiving ample payment."

Timothy scratched his head. "Reckon so."

"We'll see about restoring this buggy to her former glory." Papa smoothed a hand on the ripped seat. "Might be the finest buggy in all of Horizon when we finish with it."

"And I'd be happy to see what can be done about the seat," added Mama.

Ruby hiked her skirts and climbed into the mode of transport. There was a lightness in her chest as excitement trilled through her. "I honestly don't mind driving the buggy as it is." It was her turn to smooth her hand along the tattered upholstery. "The slight defects give it character." She chewed her lip. "May I drive it now, Papa? For my next endeavor?"

"Timothy and I do have to fix one of the wagon wheels before it splinters further, but yes, if it's all right with your ma, it's all right with me."

"Mama?"

"Certainly. And I do believe you look quite regal in it."

Two days later, Ruby drove the buggy to town for the first time. Papa agreed just this once as he and Timothy had temporarily fixed the splintered wheels. She'd have to wait to permanently drive it until all four wheels were properly fixed and Papa had completed some other repairs.

No matter. Ruby would enjoy the opportunity today. As she rode into town and parked the buggy in front of *The Horizon Herald*, she imagined the joy of such a gift radiating off her.

Clutching her most recent assignment in hand, she entered the newspaper office. "About time you arrived," grunted Mr. O'Kane.

"Oh, dear, what is that dreadful mode of transport parked outside the business?" Lillian shivered.

"That dreadful mode of transport is my new buggy."

Lillian wrinkled her nose and tilted her head to one side. "You poor thing. Such an ignominy. Were you not dreadfully embarrassed to be seen in such an atrocity? I'm utterly surprised you arrived here without it malfunctioning."

"No, I was not embarrassed. Thrilled to have the privilege of driving it, in fact. And you might consider ceasing with the histrionics. It is a fine buggy."

"The audacity," seethed Lillian. "Histrionics, indeed."

Mr. O'Kane frowned at Ruby. "Miss Shepherdson, you'll do well to remember your place. Lillian was only concerned about your welfare. Now, do tell me what articles you have for me today and what ideas you have for the next assignments."

Ruby dreaded this part of the morning. She'd much prefer to keep her plans private lest Lillian take it upon herself to purloin Ruby's ideas and write the articles herself. Again.

Mr. O'Kane tapped his foot on the floor as he waited for her and Lillian to answer.

"You go first, Ruby. I insist." Lillian offered a saccharine smile.

There was so much Ruby wanted to say in response. So much she *could* say, but so much she *ought not* to say. She took a deep breath and prayed to be long-suffering and show forbearance. "My article idea is about the incident that happened two days ago between here and Varner City when two horses pulling a wagon tumbled over the embankment. Apparently the driver…"

"I was going to cover that article." Lillian jutted her chin. "Uncle Barnaby, I was already going to cover that story."

"Very well, Lillian."

Why was Ruby not surprised? "But, Mr. O'Kane, I'm the one who—"

Her boss waved her comment aside. "Now, what articles do you each have for me this week? Miss Shepherdson?"

With effort, Ruby hiked her shoulders to straighten her posture and presented the typed sheet of paper to Mr. O'Kane. She was proud of her story—perhaps the proudest she'd been of just about any article she'd written.

Her employer thumbed his nose and read the carefully typed words on the paper, his stoic expression evident failing to indicate his acceptance or rejection. "A story about Mr. and Mrs. Eddington and the deaf school. Hmm. There will be some changes that need to be made."

"Yes, sir." At least it wasn't a rejection.

"Lillian?"

Ruby's nemesis handed him her own sheet of paper. "You'll be most impressed to know that I was able to secure a story about how to ensure apple cider remains tasting sweet and flavorful. I traveled to Cornwall and interviewed Mr. Inman at the recent fruit fair. He offered a variety of exceptional suggestions." Lillian offered a satisfied smile.

"Once again, you prove to be efficacious in presenting a well-thought-out, well-developed article. Magnificent job, Lillian. Your father was always so articulate and dependable, just as you are."

A mixture of frustration, irritation, and dolefulness filled her, and Ruby fought the emotion stinging her eyes. Mama's words echoed in her mind providing some comfort. *Always remember, Ruby, there is only One we aim to please. When we please Him, everything else will fall into place.*

It wasn't that Ruby disputed Mama's words of wisdom, but it would be nice if for once Mr. O'Kane appreciated her efforts.

CHAPTER FIVE

JAKE PLOPPED ONTO THE hay and wiped the sweat from his brow. The newborn foal had made it into the world safe, and the mare, Goldie, was fine as well.

He stared at the foal as it attempted to stand on wobbly legs as her mother protectively watched over her. The foal closely resembled her mother with her golden coat and white mane. Another of God's creatures so perfectly designed.

Jake inhaled a sharp breath and raised his eyes toward the barn's ceiling. The Lord may be a magnificent Creator, but He'd likely hold Jake accountable for the untimely death of his brother for the remainder of Jake's days on earth.

An older brother—the responsible one—as he'd once heard overheard Pa refer to him—wasn't so responsible after all.

In those days after Corbin's untimely death, Ma and Pa had relied on the Lord for their comfort. But not Jake. Instead, he'd turned from his Lord and Savior. Safer that way than to think of how he'd not only broken the hearts of his parents but also his Heavenly Father.

There had been times in the past couple of years when something in Creation had reminded Jake of the intricacies of God's handiwork. There had been times when Jake started to open his Bible out of habit of spending time in the Word.

But then he'd reminded himself that it was best he turned his back on the Lord in addition to his family.

Better that way.

Or at least that's how he rationalized it.

He stretched his legs in front of him and removed his hat, keeping an eye on the foal as she stumbled toward the mare and attempted to suckle. He removed his hat and ran a hand through his dark hair. Ma would have his hide and then some if she saw his appearance. She'd tell him she hadn't raised her son to look like a disheveled hermit. Jake could easily ride into town and visit the barber for a cut and shave—might help his appearance some—but he lacked the motivation for such a venture.

He visited town for two reasons and two reasons only. To haul his crops to be shipped and to purchase provisions. Even then, he rarely spoke more than a word to those who sought to engage him in conversation. No sense in getting close to anyone. Not when they'd hightail it the other way when they discovered what kind of man he *really* was.

Of course, Jake hadn't banked on having to assist that featherbrained woman the other day. He never could resist someone who needed assistance, but he sure hadn't aimed to partake in idle chitchat. From the way she prattled on, he figured she was a chattering hen for certain. At least he'd done more than grunt and nod, mainly because she ought to have known the danger of lollygagging while driving a team.

He shook his head and recalled the redhead with her expressive green eyes and the prominent dimple in her chin. He would reckon she was a comely woman *if* he'd noticed.

But he hadn't. Someone like her was a danger to the rest of the folks on the road and those far off the road as well.

Daft woman anyway!

Jake tore his thoughts from the woman and a trip to town and again focused on the foal. What should he name her? When he'd purchased Goldie, she'd come with the name, unlike his other two horses.

The name popped into his mind unannounced.

Butterscotch.

Butterscotch? No man in his right mind names a horse Butterscotch. More like Thunder or Lightning.

But you can't name the foal Thunder or Lightning as you already have horses by those names.

Jake scratched his head. He was certifiably insane with the way he conversed with himself.

The foal stopped eating and released a whinny, her first. The sound brought a smile to Jake's lips. She was the color of butterscotch candy, Ma's favorite. He was taken back in time briefly to the Christmas when he and Pa found butterscotch candies at the candy store in Cornwall and brought them all the way back to Ingleville during a snowstorm.

He and Pa may have been tired and haggard by the time they arrived, but the prized candies were tucked safely in the crate with the other items, and the look on Ma's face that Christmas...

Jake swallowed the emotion that rose in his throat whenever he thought of his family. Did they miss him? Had Pa forgiven him? Would they ever want to see him again?

He chastised himself. No use in thinking of such things. Besides, it was likely that if he ever returned home, he'd just remind them of the son they'd lost due to Jake's irresponsibility.

If only he could turn back the hands of time. But he couldn't do that any more than he could return home.

"All right, Butterscotch it is," he said aloud, and one of the chickens clucked in response.

A breeze outside the barn door caused a dust devil to swirl, kicking up the loose dirt near the corral. The rooster crowed, a cow mooed, and a crow expressed his opinions on the matter. There was plenty here on his farm to keep him entertained and to keep him busy.

Why then did the niggle of loneliness embed itself firmly in his chest?

Going to town because his horse threw a shoe was not on his list of items to do today. Fortunately, few people engaged in conversation with a man who spoke few words and resembled a hobo.

That was fine with Jake. He hadn't moved to Horizon to make friends. He'd moved here in an attempt to escape the guilt. And farming, as his first love, far surpassed any of the other types of employment he'd temporarily held.

He still had a lot to do, and the unexpected visit to the blacksmith precluded him from fulfilling his plans. He didn't need a timepiece to know the afternoon was fleeing faster than a mouse being chased by a starving cat.

Jake pulled the brim of his hat lower over his forehead to shield his eyes from the late afternoon sun. As he crested the hill before taking a right to his farm, he came upon a curious sight.

A horse was tethered to a tree. But that wasn't the curious sight. No, the image that caught his attention was a woman standing at the top of an embankment that led to a ditch below. Her dress was covered in caked mud. Jake slowed his horse to a stop and stared for a moment before inwardly being reminded of his manners. Was the woman in danger? Did she need help? He squinted and took in the messy red hair.

It was the same woman who'd driven her wagon off the road last week.

He dismounted and noticed that she frantically peered from left to right while struggling through the weeds.

She was a peculiar one, all right.

"Need help?" he asked.

"Oh! I'm so glad you stopped. Yes, I do need assistance." She attempted to scrape some of the mud from her dress.

Did she need help with her horse? Was she lost? He waited for her to elaborate.

He didn't have to wait long.

"Have you seen my notebook? It boasts a raspberry-and-beige mottled marble cover with a raspberry-colored spine. I had it when I went to town and then to visit my sister, Lucy. I carefully packed it for safekeeping in the left saddlebag. Then low and behold, suddenly, unbeknownst to me, I was riding along without a care in the world when I noticed it was missing." She held a hand to her heart, and Jake contemplated responding, but before he could, she continued, her words rushing from her in a deluge of rambling nonsense. "It could be anywhere by now if I've perchance dropped it along the way. Such contemplation is most dreadful as the words within the pages are not for just anyone's eyes to see. Rather, if someone were to stumble upon my notebook, it would be most detrimental." Her eyes rounded and the dimple in her chin became more prominent. "I *must* find it. It has all sorts of secret information tucked within its pages."

The verbose woman wasn't even out of breath after speaking more words in a minute than Jake had spoken in two years.

"Have you seen it?" Desperation lined her features as her eyes darted from side to side. Mud crusted her left cheek.

"No."

Her shoulders fell. "I really must find it. I saw something in the embankment as I rode by for the second time, reversing course and returning from whence I came. I was hoping—praying—it was my notebook. But alas, it was not. And then when I attempted to leap across the ditch to the other side, my foot slipped and I plunged forward, facedown in the mud from last night's rain. It would figure that the year we have sufficient moisture is the year I find myself in all sorts of muddy adventures."

If she wanted to find the notebook before Christmas, the hopes of that diminished by the second. Jake waited to see if she'd say more.

And she did.

"So, have you seen it in your travels from town?"

"No."

The woman was certainly an oddity.

"I've felt as though I'm a Pinkerton detective with all the searching I've done. To town and back, then to town and back again. What if…"

A friend of the family once attended a theatrical presentation in Cornwall. He'd mentioned the actors performed the play with exaggerated words and motions. While watching the woman flail her arms about with her voice rising and lowering in pitch, Jake imagined she would do well at the theatrical presentation. If he was a man of more words, he might suggest it.

She peered behind her, around him, and then began walking along the road. "Would you mind assisting me in looking for it? It has to be along this stretch somewhere."

He wanted to ask how she'd narrowed down the exact location since town was nearly a mile from where they stood, but he wasn't sure he wanted to receive the earful that would likely follow. The woman paused, faced him, and stared, her mouth twisted to one side as she chewed on her lip.

"Well, all right then. Thank you all the same." She blew out an exaggerated breath, causing her cheeks and lips to expand. "Until we meet again," she quipped before continuing her search along the road.

Hopefully, there would be no next time.

She'd rambled unmercifully. The man likely thought her some sort of lunatic. A woman of unsound mind what with all of her ongoings about the notebook and how she'd somehow lost it. And why had she divulged such information to a stranger? A man she'd only met once before and that was because he'd kindly—albeit almost wordlessly—rescued her from her previous dilemma.

Still.

There would be dire consequences if the notebook was found by an unscrupulous individual. Her notes about upcoming stories and the serial she'd worked so hard to write whenever the words came to her would be lost forever. It wasn't as if she could again just conjure up the verbiage on a whim. Ruby had written at least enough installments for the serial for two months' worth.

She *had* to find the notebook.

Ruby trampled through the tall weeds, the stalks of grass whisking against her skirt. She'd not succumb to the thought her notebook was lost forever. Offering another prayer heavenward, she then peeked behind her to see the man standing near her horse.

Was he thinking of stealing it?

She hadn't thought of the fact that the unknown man could be an outlaw. A criminal on the lam. After all, Ruby didn't even know his name. She spun around and stalked back all the while noticing he was examining the saddlebag. She was about to object when he held up her prized notebook.

"Is this it?"

Her jaw slacked, and Ruby hastened her pace. "Yes! You found it! Where was it?"

"In the right-side saddlebag."

"Surely you are mistaken?"

"I'm not."

Hadn't she *thoroughly* looked inside the saddlebag? Well, the left side anyway.

"I do appreciate your help. You have saved me from a lifetime of misery, to be sure."

The man said nothing, only handed her the notebook before removing his hat, revealing an abundance of matted dark brown hair. He wiped his brow with his forearm. "If that's all, I best be on my way."

"Thank you again. I really appreciate your help."

But as Ruby mounted her horse and headed for home, she offered an unorthodox prayer. One beseeching the Lord that she might never again need the peculiar man's help.

CHAPTER SIX

THE LIEUTENANT'S SUGGESTION WAS an answer to prayer.

It was time again for Ruby to plan a fun adventure for her oldest nieces and nephews. Because she'd started this tradition two years ago, they'd come to expect that several times throughout the year, Aunt Ruby would gather them all and plan a festivity. She'd run plumb out of ideas until the Lieutenant offered an exemplary idea Ruby hadn't yet thought of.

"In which direction might I find the raspberry bushes?"

"According to my Greta, who said Wilhelmina mentioned it was Mrs. Kirkman who told her, who told Mr. Dixon, who told me, it's on Mr. Adler's farm about a mile or so from here to the north. It's not far from the road, and there's a grove of trees on the right-hand side and a broken-down fence that needs repair right next to the largest Siberian elm you've ever seen. I reckon your nieces and nephews would appreciate picking some raspberries." He patted his ample stomach. "And perhaps making some of your ma's famous raspberry jelly for starving townsfolk."

Ruby joined in the elderly man's laughter. The Lieutenant was far from starving, especially since he'd married Miss Greta a few years back, but Ruby wouldn't mention as much.

"My nieces and nephews would indeed revel in such a delightful trip, and yes, I'm sure we could can some delicious raspberry jelly for starving townsfolk." Ruby could just taste the fresh raspberries and the raspberry preserves they'd make to allow for the delicious fruit to be eaten in the cold winter months.

On Saturday morning, Ruby took her place on the buckboard beside Polly and Carrie. Hosea, Becky, Pansy, Simon, Sherman, and Little Hans climbed into the back. Only two of her nephews were too young to partake in such an adventure—Mae and Landon's youngest son, L.J., and Albert and Velma's newborn, Baby Albert. Next year they would join the others.

"I can't wait to pick raspberries," declared Carrie, who both spoke to Ruby and simultaneously signed for Polly at the same time.

To which Polly responded with her hands flying that they picked the fruit from the Bennick Horizon School for the Deaf grounds, but it wasn't nearly as fun as it was going to be with Aunt Ruby.

Ruby's heart soared. Oh, but to have a passel full of children someday! She and her husband, a handsome and dashing Godly man with thick blond hair and hazel eyes, would reside in their pleasant farmhouse not far from town. Ruby would write an article or two for the paper in addition to her wifely and motherly duties. They would have five or six little redheaded and blond children. Ruby would name her fictional husband Harrison for the sake of this particular daydream, and he would be a farmer and her a doting mother. He'd tend the fields while she started her day making breakfast and washing the bountiful laundry. She and their daughters would sing as they scrubbed the dirty clothes...of course, by then, Ruby would have one of those newfangled washing machines, so not nearly as much scrubbing would be necessary.

But I digress.

The bright sunny day and the birds chirping on their farm would make for the perfect...

"Can we, Aunt Ruby?"

The tapping on her shoulder and Sherman's voice drew her from her blissful daydream.

"Begging your pardon, Sherman, what were you asking?"

"If we could sing songs like we always do when we go places with you, Aunt Rubes."

Sherman was so much like his father. Albert loved to sing as well.

"Yes, that sounds like a delightful plan. What song shall we start with?"

Hosea stood in the back of the wagon and leaned into her vision, his hands forming the words. Ruby couldn't sign back as she was driving, so instead she nodded. They would start with *Old MacDonald Had a Farm*, followed by *Amazing Grace*, then the new song *Good Morning to All*.

Albert and Sherman weren't the only ones who loved to sing. Ruby did as well. She just didn't have the gift of carrying a tune as well as some members of her family.

No matter. As Mama always said, it didn't matter if you couldn't carry a tune, only that you sang for the Lord.

And indeed she would.

Jake rarely went to the far end of his expansive property. The never-ending chores hadn't allowed him to even fix the dilapidated fence near the raspberry grove. There would be time for that someday, but for now, his days were full with the crops and miscellaneous house repairs.

But today, he decided to ride the perimeter and check to see if the raspberry bushes were yet bearing fruit. He recalled Ma's famous pies—apple, raspberry, and pumpkin—and his stomach rumbled. Jake pushed the musings aside before he could allow nostalgic thoughts to overcome his mind.

He had a new life now.

No more reminders of Corbin and the fatal mishap. No more reminders of the pain etched on Pa's face or Ma's constant sobs. No more of Dinah Jo's continual questions about why Corbin wasn't coming in for supper.

Jake swallowed the lump that thickened his throat. If only it were that easy to forget.

He beckoned his horse along the road when he heard a noise. Singing perhaps? He stopped at the top of the hill and peered below. Sure enough, a wagon full of children was traveling along the road that edged his acreage. It came to a stop near the raspberry grove, but the singing didn't cease.

Their apparent happiness drew him in. They were joyful just like he'd been once upon a time with his family when they went on outings. During those times, the Lyntons didn't sing, but they did enjoy each other's company and make memories forever embedded in Jake's mind.

They finished singing *Amazing Grace*, then went immediately into singing *Good Morning to All*, a brand-new ditty Jake had only heard once before. Harmonious voices chorused as they repeated the song thrice more.

One particularly loud voice rose above the rest. While not an offensive voice—more so a pleasing one—it did garner his attention. It was clearly a woman's. From his view, he could also see that some of the children were partaking in sign language. He leaned to the right. A woman was driving the wagon. A woman with...

Red hair.

Could it be that same odd woman who'd found herself in two predicaments? He couldn't see her facial features from here, but he ventured to say he was right about his assumption.

The problem with the chattering hen of a woman wasn't that he'd had to rescue her twice, but that she was somewhat pretty.

And Jake Lynton had no time for pretty. And no time to be thinking of anything or anyone other than farming. Hadn't his thoughts, memories, and overwhelming grief already caused him enough heartache to last a century?

He watched as the children carried buckets to the raspberry grove. Were they helping themselves to his raspberries? Not that he minded, but shouldn't they ask first?

The grove obstructed his vision of the children and the woman, and he urged his horse closer. The Jake Lynton before Corbin's accident would tell them to pick all the raspberries they wanted—in exchange for some preserves or a raspberry pie. But he was not the Jake Lynton before Corbin's accident. He was a different man now and had no time for foolish trading of raspberries for tasty pies and preserves.

This was his property. Why couldn't everyone just leave him be?

The woman and the children didn't even hear him arrive as they were so involved in their singing and plucking the fruit from the bushes. He hadn't taken the lady, at such a young age, to have been a mother of so many children. He mentally counted eight of them. Who was the woman's husband and why was he never with her?

Jake dismounted, tethered his horse, and lurked at the grove's edge. Everyone seemed happy as they stole his raspberries. An unannounced memory flooded his mind of Ma taking him, Corbin, and Dinah Jo to the small orchard on their farm to pick apples in the fall. Ma would bake apple pie, can the preserves, and they'd enjoy the apples year-round—or at least until they'd polished off the jars of preserves, usually before spring the following year. In those days, all was right with the world. Pa would tease them that he had every mind to eat the entire pie all by himself. Jake and Corbin would beg him to save a sliver for them, and Dinah Jo would climb into Pa's lap and plant a kiss on his chin. Ma would drape an arm around Pa and whisper something in his ear. He would laugh, then suddenly decide perhaps he *would* share some of the pie with his children.

Oh, but to go back in time.

To make right the wrong that changed so many lives forever.

Jake continued his covert advancement toward the group and hid behind the trees. Some children appeared too old to be the woman's children unless she was older than he surmised her to be. Perhaps she wasn't close to his age after all.

The answer to Jake's question about the children came a few seconds later.

"Auntie!" squalled a tiny girl with two brown braids. "He throwed my bonnet in the twee!"

So the woman was the aunt. At least to one of the children.

Jake noticed that every word, even the songs the group sang, had all been signed in addition to being spoken. Even the little girl's frantic cries.

"Simon Albert Shepherdson, you can be sure your pa will hear about this shenanigan." The woman firmed her hands on her slim hips.

Jake couldn't see Simon's expression from his vantage point, but he figured from the way the boy's shoulders slumped that his father finding out would put the boy in a heap of trouble.

"Aww, I'm sorry, Pansy." Simon put an arm around the petite girl who was now crying, her own shoulders heaving.

"That was my favortist bonnet in the whole world."

"I just wanted to test my throwing skills. I've been practicing so I can play on Hosea's baseball team at the school benefit event."

One of the oldest girls, whom Jake could see the expression of, shook her head as she simultaneously signed the words. "Sure, Simon. A likely excuse if I ever heard one."

The other older girl signed something and then nodded in agreement.

"Now, Simon," said the woman. "Whatever your reasons are, it's never acceptable to upset your younger cousin in such a manner. Taking something that doesn't belong to you and throwing it beyond Pansy's reach is not how we should treat those we love. You owe Pansy an apology."

"You owe her an apowogy," agreed the smallest boy, who wore a miniature black bowler hat. He'd sidled next to Pansy and put a hand on her arm. "Don't worry, Pansy. You can have my hat if we can't get your bonnet back."

When the woman swiveled in his direction, Jake thought for a moment she noticed him, and he slid further behind the trees. She returned her focus to the tree and the fence then turned in the opposite direction again, kneeled, and enveloped the little girl in a hug. "Auntie will retrieve your bonnet. Now let's not allow this circumstance to ruin our outing. Continue picking raspberries, and I'll just…"

Her back was to him, but he watched as she tilted her head back and scrutinized the tree where bonnet strings flapped in the wind several branches up. Would she attempt to reach it? How?

The answer came within seconds when she grabbed a long stick and poked at the bonnet. When that failed, she marched to the fence and jiggled it, presumably to test its sturdiness.

The fence in need of repair.

That he hadn't yet repaired.

"Please be careful, Auntie." This from another of the girls.

"I will be."

Surely she wasn't seriously considering climbing the fence. If so, he'd have to put an end to such a featherheaded idea.

Jake was about to object when she hastily gripped the fence post and climbed on the first rung. She batted at the branches with the stick, attempting to dislodge the bonnet, her arms erratically waving about.

He released the breath he'd been holding. If she remained on the first rung, all would be well. It wasn't that far off the ground and the woman appeared to have decent balance.

The oldest boy signed something and pointed to himself. The woman shook her head. "Carrie, will you please tell Hosea thank you, but since I'm taller, I'll attempt to retrieve the hat?"

Carrie's fingers flew, and Hosea argued in sign language.

For a minute, Jake was mesmerized by the communication between them. He'd heard of the deaf school in Horizon but hadn't yet seen it. Jake peered at his own hands. Could such large hands and fingers learn the language?

It was in that brief moment when the signing between the children distracted him that Jake figured this was as good a time as any to both approach the family about the raspberries and alleviate the woman from potentially injuring herself or worse since she climbed up to the next rung of the fence, and then the top one. "You do realize you all are trespassing on private property." His voice came out far more brusque than he intended.

And it also surprised the woman who teetered and swayed, her blue skirt caught on the fence.

Jake sprang into action and in two lengthy strides, he was beside her as she tumbled into his arms.

"Auntie! You could have been broken!"

"Are you all right?"

"Who's that man?"

"What's trespassing?"

The children's voices loomed on the periphery of her consciousness, but something else drew her attention.

Strong arms held her against a broad muscled chest. She briefly closed her eyes, resting in the security and safety as her heart pounded at nearly taking a dangerous plunge from the fence.

Was this what it would be like for the lead female character in the dime novel she hoped to write someday? A handsome and dashing man would rescue her from imminent danger? He'd hold her tight, pull her to him, and comfort her in his embrace, reassuring her he'd be her hero forever. She'd gaze into his eyes and know he was the man God had chosen for her...

"Ma'am?"

Ruby's eyes fluttered open. Yes, just like her character, she was held in a strong man's embrace. Yes, just like in her future book, he'd rescued her. However...

She blinked as she peered into his blue eyes and—

"Oh!"

Her rescuer may be strong and he may have rescued her from a perilous situation, but with an abundance of facial hair and long scraggly hair on his head beneath a tattered cowboy hat...he was *not* handsome and dashing. Not in the least.

And what on earth was she doing having such ridiculous notions about her future book and comparing it to real life?

"I'd kindly request that you set me down," she squeaked.

"Gladly."

But his eyes remained locked with hers for a second longer.

Ruby brushed the dust from her skirt. Her unlikely hero remained standing beside her. She ought to thank him, especially since he was the same cantankerous man who'd rescued her twice before.

This was clearly becoming a habit. An unwanted habit.

"Thank you."

He didn't acknowledge her "thank you", but instead glowered at her. "And if you didn't hear me before, I'd like to know why you and the children are trespassing."

"Trespassing? Oh, we're not trespassing."

Several of the children shook their heads in unison. "Mr. Adler asked that we visit his property and pick as many raspberries as we'd like, so we did."

Nearly three of the pails were filled to the brim with the fruit.

"There's just one problem. This is not Mr. Adler's property. It's mine."

"Are you certain?" She realized the foolishness of her inquiry only after she'd spoken. Of course, the man would know where his own property was.

"Certain as the day is long."

"Well, that's most unfortunate." Becky's and Sherman's faces fell, and Little Hans hung his head. Perhaps the man would allow them to keep the contents of one of the pails for their raspberry pies. However, the way he stood, with his arms crossed over his thick chest and his mouth set in a grim line, did not offer her much hope.

The children were depending on her. This was their special day, and Hosea had mentioned he could almost taste the raspberry pie even before they'd set out from town. Ruby worked her throat through a sandy swallow. Would the man even consider the offer she was about to make? "We are sorry we didn't realize this was not Mr. Adler's property. Might you perchance allow us one pail of raspberries? In return, we'll make you a raspberry pie or perhaps some preserves."

A shadow fell across the man's face—one she nearly missed—before he spoke. "No to the pies and preserves." He waved a hand at her and the children. "Yes to the pails of raspberries. But next time, please ask."

"Thank you."

"Yes, thank you!" Several of the children jumped up and down, and Little Hans popped several in his mouth and smacked his lips before passing a handful to Pansy.

"These are nummy," Little Hans said, cramming far too many into his mouth.

"Mister, can you please get my bonnet?" Pansy asked.

An awkward moment of silence passed until the man agreed. "Yes. Reckon I'll see what I can do."

He was a large man, tall too, and it took little effort for him to reach the bonnet. He then turned to leave without saying another word.

Who was this peculiar man and why was she forever having to be rescued by him?

CHAPTER SEVEN

THE HORIZON HERALD WAS nestled between a vacant building and the bank on Main Street. The words "Horizon Herald" were printed in large lettering across the top of the building. Two hefty windows on each side of the door and several small decorative windows across the top indicated this was a fine establishment.

An establishment of which Ruby Shepherdson was a part.

Joy billowed in her heart every time she arrived at her place of employment. Her dreams had all come true the day Mr. O'Kane nodded his balding head, grimaced at her, and said, "All right. You've got the job."

Well, all my dreams except that of someday having a husband and family.

Ruby quickly pushed those thoughts aside as she parked the buggy. She glanced at the bank, its door still boarded up. Things had gone awry last week when outlaws robbed it—not a common occurrence for Horizon. She hoped Sheriff Zembrodt and his new deputy caught the robbers soon. And when they did, that would be a story she couldn't wait to write.

Oh, the things a bank robber could tell. The life he must have lived...

For everyone had a story.

Even criminals.

Ruby waved and smiled at the passersby. Nothing could go wrong on such a glorious day.

"Mr. O'Kane?"

"It's about time you arrived, Miss Shepherdson."

Was she late? Had he been expecting her? "I have the most marvelous article for this week's *Ruby's Horizon Happenings*. I can't wait for you to read it."

As usual, Mr. O'Kane tossed a lackluster look her way. "You always did have an exaggerated sense of self."

Ruby bit her lip. She hadn't meant to brag. She only wanted the approval of the dour Mr. O'Kane. "May I show it to you?"

"We have something far more important to discuss than your article idea."

We do?

"Yes, sir. And what might that be?"

"Come into my office."

It wasn't a request, but a command, and Ruby rushed past the two other employees to follow her boss into his dismal office. The apprentices kept their heads down and eyes averted.

This couldn't be good. At least Lillian wasn't here to gloat about any misfortune Ruby might experience.

"Sit."

Ruby obeyed Mr. O'Kane and sat in the uncomfortable chair that edged up against his desk. She watched as he paced the floor. Back and forth, back and forth. Glancing down, she noticed the faded wood floor, smoothed in certain areas from all of his pacing. "Whatever is the matter, Mr. O'Kane?"

Barnaby O'Kane shot her a brittle look and continued to pace. Back and forth, back and forth, his elbow nearly colliding with the edge of his weathered desk as he tromped the tight area.

Ruby stared at him with anticipation, fear, and curiosity, but mostly fear. Whatever she had done, it had caused her boss to be in an uproar. No one could accuse the man of having a pleasant demeanor, and Ruby had seen her share of Mr. O'Kane's harmless tirades. But never had Mr. O'Kane been quite so at odds as he appeared at this moment.

And all because of her. Or something she did.

Her legs shook, so Ruby folded her hands and pushed on them to stop their trembling. She must take her mind off the task at hand. *Lord, please help me with whatever might come my way.* Mr. O'Kane lowered his head and narrowed his eyes. He was losing hair quickly and would soon be completely bald. The generous fuzzy muttonchops growing from each side of his face and coming to two points failed to compensate for his lack of head hair. The poor man, bless his heart, had attempted to comb over a few long strands of hair with the hopes of covering the expansive bald spot on the front of his head. The remainder of the gray-brown hair lay in an irregular style around and behind his ears. Miss Greta at the boardinghouse insisted men became bald from years of wearing their hats too tightly on their heads. Was that what had happened to Mr. O'Kane?

Mr. O'Kane had a story to tell, all right. Probably an eccentric one at that.

Ruby had met Mrs. O'Kane only once. She and her husband matched as well as any married couple could.

Ruby then attempted to imagine Barnaby O'Kane as a child with more hair. When he had a tantrum, did his mother use his first, middle, and last names all at once in one long streaming sentence as Mama did when having to discipline her children? If so, what was his middle name? Ruby chewed on her lip and thought a bit. Perhaps his full name was Barnaby Norbert O'Kane. Or maybe Barnaby Manfred O'Kane. Ruby thought of a mother dragging out the entire name when Barnaby did something requiring discipline. Or maybe she'd just called him Barny?

Mr. O'Kane pinched his perfectly trimmed and waxed brown mustache, then pushed his spectacles up the bridge of his nose. "I can't believe you have done such a thing. This calls for your immediate dismissal!"

Ruby jerked her attention back to the present. "I beg your pardon?"

"It's not as though you have a family to support. As a spinster, you'll be fine continuing to reside with your parents and allowing them to support you."

Ruby took a deep breath and bit back the tears that threatened. Mr. O'Kane had said many rude things in her time as his employee, but none had hurt so much as hearing him call her a leeching spinster. Not that he'd said those exact words, but Ruby knew the context of them. "I'm sorry, sir, I don't follow."

"Your story for last week's *Ruby's Horizon Happenings* is not acceptable.

"Mr. O'Kane, you approved it before I prepared the typeset."

"I was having an arduous day and didn't have my wits about me. I have never seen such inferior reporting. I never should have allowed you to cover the story." He stooped to drum his fingers on the desk. "You're more suited to writing articles about the latest hats and women's fashions than responsible journalism."

Ruby wanted to interject that her column's two-part piece on women's hats and fashions had been quite popular among the womenfolk of Horizon. But she held her tongue.

"It's one thing to report the news, as you are to do. It's quite another to blatantly discuss the inferior job of our sheriff's deputy."

"Sir..."

"And to let everyone in Horizon know their money is gone. That juicy tidbit needn't have been discussed in the least."

"Sir..."

"I have had no less than four people in here demanding to know why you would write such a thing. Have you no common sense? You aren't to give the full details. No one desires to know they are now without the funds they placed securely in Horizon's bank. And no one wishes to know they have an inept sheriff's deputy helping to run the town!"

"Don't people want the..." *Truth?*

"I should have leaped from my chair at the barbershop and ran posthaste to the bank and covered the story myself. But for some reason, I figured you could manage it. How incorrect I was, and I shall live with that immense regret for the remainder of my life. There will be no future stories for you, Miss Shepherdson; therefore, take your article and be gone from my presence."

"Mr. O'Kane, may I please speak?"

"No!"

If her legs weren't shaking before, they sure were now. Her chest grew tight with panic and tears brimmed in her eyes. She hadn't known her article would cause such a scandal. "Mr. O'Kane, I only meant to tell the truth. People want to know that when they go to the bank, there will be no money to withdraw. Perhaps the law has caught up with the robbers by now and all will be well."

"Not everyone lives in your pleasant dream world, Miss Shepherdson."

Her pleasant dream world?

"And about the sheriff's deputy. I was only reporting that he accidentally allowed the one suspect to escape. I wasn't insinuating his ineptitude but rather alerting the public that an additional outlaw was on the loose. I meant no harm in my reporting, Mr. O'Kane. Please believe me."

Mr. O'Kane paused for a moment, his lips pursed and his beady eyes glaring through thick spectacles. Would he show Ruby mercy?

Lord, please help me. Give me the words to speak to rectify this matter.

"Please, Mr. O'Kane. I will write an editorial placing the entire blame upon myself. I'll apologize and tell the fine folks of Horizon I didn't mean to cause distress. I can make amends. Please. Give me this chance to make this grievous wrong into a right."

Mr. O'Kane continued to pace, his hands clasped tightly behind his back.

"You know I have a steadfast following, Mr. O'Kane. People in Horizon love my column. I can make amends. I know I can. If we've lost any readership, I'll see to it that I personally speak with those withdrawing their subscriptions about continuing their subscription to our fine weekly. Please, sir."

Ruby detested having to grovel. But what else could she do? Her job and, more importantly, her reputation were in jeopardy. She loved to write. It was an integral part of her life —one that she lived and breathed—one she couldn't live without. Her passion to share her words.

So what would she do if Mr. O'Kane stopped her from ever penning another word?

It wasn't as if Ruby could gather her things and move to another town. No weekly, or even daily, would hire her after her supposedly grievous errors. "I am so sorry." Her voice shook. Her legs shook. Her arms shook. For such a skinny and short man, Mr. O'Kane scared the bonnet off her.

"And what of the adverts I will surely lose from your irresponsible journalism?"

Irresponsible journalism? "If any such businesses no longer wish to place advertisements in the *Horizon Herald* because of my error, I will promptly pay them a visit and explain the entire situation."

Mr. O'Kane looked as if he didn't believe her. Then he pressed a hand to his chest. "My heart has elevated to un-necessary palpitations."

"I'm sorry for that too, Mr. O'Kane. I'm sorry for it all."

Even if she had only been doing her job.

"I suppose you do have some sort of favorable following in Horizon. Granted, most is by women, but then women are more apt to talk their husbands into buying the newspaper."

"Exactly."

"And I suppose you do have some sort of writing ability that does show its face at times."

"Yes, sir." *At times?* She hoped to someday be worthy of a compliment that she allowed her writing ability to be evident at all times. Of course, she'd always need to improve upon the way she strung her sentences together and provided proper grammar, but hopefully, at some juncture, Ruby would be considered a competent writer.

"And you have been an employee for nearly a year, much to my better judgment."

His better judgment? Ruby swallowed hard. It had only been by God's grace and much prayer that she had remained an employee for nearly a year. No one wanted to work for the critical and persnickety Mr. O'Kane. Two other writers resigned within two weeks of starting their new jobs. But he did have Lillian.

"I had so hoped to start writing interviews for my column, Mr. O'Kane. If you took a peek at my most recent article..."

"I'm about to have you dismissed, Miss Shepherdson. I highly doubt I'll be looking at your most recent article with much interest or that it would make nary a difference."

Ruby nodded. Best not to press her luck. She only wanted to use the gift of writing God had given her, but if Mr. O'Kane deemed not to allow her to continue as his employee, she'd find another way to use what she hoped was truly a gift. And she *could* get another job.

Even if she slumped into a deep melancholy for what might very well be the rest of her life.

Ruby brushed aside a tear that escaped. "Is there a hope of reclaiming my position here at *The Horizon Herald*?"

"The only way I'll allow you to return to my employ is if you uncover a sensational story that sells numerous papers. An interview with someone famous, perhaps. Or a true hero."

"The Lieutenant is a hero. He fought in the Civil War."

"Yes, and you've already conducted an interview with the Lieutenant—an interview I insisted you rewrite twice. I highly doubt the man has anything more to add that would necessitate a second article."

Ruby didn't personally know anyone famous, and few people of such high standing visited Horizon. Nor did she know any heroes besides the Lieutenant.

"No submitting any articles until you have one that meets that criteria. Then and only then will I consider rehiring you. Until then, *Ruby's Horizon Happenings* will not be happening."

If circumstances weren't so dismal, Ruby might laugh at Mr. O'Kane's play on words. Instead, her shoulders slumped, and her throat constricted. She could not meet those demands.

"That will be all." He waved a dismissive hand at her.

Her legs buckled as she stood, and she grasped the corner of Mr. O'Kane's desk. "Sir, should I speak to Deputy Shim about the situation?" She regretted that her voice quivered in her own ears.

"No need. It's best you don't mar the paper's reputation any more than you have."

Her boss—former boss—diverted his attention to his desk. "I trust you can see yourself out?"

"Yes, sir." Ruby knew her attempts at reasoning with him were futile.

Dragging herself from the office, she pootled to the front of the building when Lillian rushed through the door. "Oh, hello, Ruby."

Before waiting for Ruby to respond, Lillian, in her syrupy voice, announced, "Uncle? I have that article you asked me to write for *Lillian's Horizon Happenings.*

The article she'd hoped to present to Mr. O'Kane was moistened and tattered in her tight grasp. She was about to climb into the buggy when a familiar voice beckoned her.

"Ruby?"

She looked up to see Sheriff Zembrodt standing a few inches from her.

"Hello, Sheriff."

"Are you all right?"

"I am. I just…" her voice trailed. "Have you caught the outlaws yet?"

Sheriff Zembrodt shook his head. "Not yet, but we've had several sign up to join the posse, thanks to your article. We'll ride out tomorrow and see what we can find."

"I'm glad it was helpful."

"Are you sure you're all right?"

"It's been a challenging day. Mr. O'Kane didn't appreciate my article about the bank robbery." She hadn't meant to divulge that information. The words tumbled from her mouth before she'd had the wherewithal to stop them.

The sheriff rubbed his chin. "Can't see why he wouldn't appreciate your article. As you know, my wife insists we subscribe mainly for your column and the mercantile sales advertisements."

"He mentioned I discredited Deputy Shim."

"Deputy Shim did accidentally allow the prisoner to escape. He's new to the position and it was an honest error. Do you want me to speak to Mr. O'Kane?"

Sheriff Zembrodt had been a family friend ever since Ruby could remember. Everyone appreciated his tireless commitment to the town of Horizon. "While I greatly appreciate that, I will decline your generous offer." Her shoulders slumped. "I got myself into this mess, so I will have to see my way out of it."

"If you say so. But if you change your mind, let me know."

She nodded as the tears threatened again. Sheriff Zembrodt tipped his hat and strode down the boardwalk.

Leaving Ruby to wonder how she'd ever recover.

CHAPTER EIGHT

JAKE FINISHED FIXING THE fence, then turned toward the sun. It was about time for the noonday meal and given the fact that his stomach had started growling, he best commence preparing it.

"Come on, boy, let's get us some grub." He leaned down and scratched Samson's ears before turning the doorknob to enter his home. *His home.* Not his parents' home, not a boardinghouse, but his home. Far away from Ingleville, far away from the memories.

Far away from his father.

Jake fixed himself a sandwich, fed Samson some pieces of ham, and took a seat at the table. He positioned the copy of *The Horizon Herald* in front of him. He rarely read the paper and even more rarely shelled out a nickel for the privilege. Jake needed to save all of his money to rebuild the farm.

But when he'd gone to town for some necessary supplies, the headline in the newspaper caught his eye. Outlaws robbed the Horizon bank last week, and Jake had wanted to read all about it. Thankfully he hadn't any money to place in the bank so he hadn't lost any. His sympathies went to those who were affected by the thievery. If Jake still believed God could accomplish miracles, he would pray that the Lord would help the law to find whoever had stolen the money so the funds would be returned.

But with the past always crowding into the present, Jake had long ago realized that the Lord was no longer in the business of performing miracles and that some prayers went unanswered—like his prayer for Corbin.

He thumbed through the newspaper and read the *Ruby's Horizon Happenings* column.

Bank robbers robbed the Horizon Bank last Thursday. There was but one clerk, Mr. Sanders, in the bank at the time when the outlaws commenced with covered faces and pistols, demanding the full amount of money in the bank's safe. One of the outlaws engaged the clerk, who was at the wicket at the time, in conversation whilst the remaining outlaws gained access to the bank and closed and locked the door behind them.

No one in Horizon was the wiser. As this happened during the noonday meal, most folks were eating at Wilhelmina's Restaurant or at home. Apparently, the four outlaws had staked out the bank for some time before achieving their daring and well-thought-out plan. When the outlaws arrived in town is unknown.

In an interview, the saloon owner reported he had seen no unusual activity in his establishment prior to the robbery. "I ain't never seen no one suspicious or nothin' comin' through the doors of my business.

Don't mean there wasn't no one suspicious, just means I ain't seen them iffin' there was."

Mr. Sanders was tied up beside the safe, a gag in his mouth, but was otherwise found unharmed. "If only I had known what was about to happen, I would have been able to summon help. I feel right badly about how all this transpired. Be assured that the Horizon Bank has only been robbed one other time in all its history and that was years ago by the notorious Salter Gang."

Bandits not only took all of the money secured in the bank in the amount of $14,768, but they also stole numerous banknotes and papers. As such, until further notice, the Horizon Bank is closed.

The robbers made their escape on horseback, riding east of town and shooting their guns as they rode. Townsfolk were urged to take cover in the safety of their homes. Sheriff Zembrodt and his deputy, as well as numerous men from Horizon, formed a posse and pro-ceeded to follow the bandits. Sometime later, one of the robbers was apprehended and in the process of being brought to the jail by Deputy Shim. Unfortunately, the robber escaped. He reportedly had the banknotes and papers on his person. He has not been re-apprehended.

Deputy Shim regrets this error but was unable to give an interview at this time.

The four bandits remain on the loose and the public is advised to be on the lookout for suspicious activity. This would include unusually large purchases at town businesses and dubious and unknown men seeking boarding or food and able to pay for it with sufficient sums of money.

A posse has been scouring the area for leads and will continue to do so. If you would like to become part of the posse, please contact the sheriff.

Two of the men are described as having thin builds. One of the others is thick and heavyset, and the other is short and plump. They are all dressed in black and the heavyset individual is reported to have long black hair. Please advise the sheriff if you have any information leading to the arrest of these bandits.

Jake took another bite of his sandwich. He felt sorry for the bank clerk and the sheriff's deputy. But mostly, he felt for the folks of Horizon who'd lost their money to a wild bunch of bandits who'd never learned—or didn't care—that stealing was wrong.

Just another reason to stay away from town with all its activity. Much quieter here on the farm with only his thoughts and his work.

It wasn't often that Jake traveled to Cornwall, especially since his time away from his parents' home. When he was a young'un, they'd visit the city once or twice a year. During Jake's time in other parts of the state, he'd not been back to Cornwall.

And now, as he embarked on the lengthy journey from Horizon, thoughts crowded his mind.

Especially when he drove through the town of Ingleville.

He lowered his hat and slid down in the seat as he steered the wagon through the town he'd lived in nearly all his life. It had grown in the days since his youth and now was nearly the size of Horizon. As promised, the railroad brought new businesses, more residents, and caused the town's expansion.

Folks waved as he passed them, and Jake offered a slight nod in their direction. It was unlikely anyone would recognize him with his long hair, scruffy beard, and untidy appearance. And that was just how he wanted it. No sense in having some do-gooder report to his parents that they'd seen him.

The thought caused his chest to constrict. How would his parents reply to such a statement? Did they miss him as he missed them? Or did they, especially Pa, still consider it Jake's fault that Corbin was no longer alive?

The aroma of what smelled like mashed potatoes flitted from a new restaurant as he drove past. Jake's stomach rumbled in response. Would it hurt to stop and partake in a noonday meal?

The pail on the buckboard beside him reminded him needn't stop in Ingleville as he had nourishment beside him, even if it was just a bland sandwich he'd made before leaving home. So he forged ahead, reminding himself he could have ordered the new disc harrow he needed and had it shipped by rail to Horizon, rather than make the trip. Such a journey would cost him precious time he could be spending working in the fields.

But he'd pushed such notions aside after arguing with himself about it for over an hour. What would it hurt to travel to Cornwall and retrieve the plow and any other provisions he couldn't readily purchase in Horizon? What would it hurt to take some time away from his toil?

None other than when he left the town of Ingleville, Jake would pass right by his parents' farm on the outskirts.

Several minutes later, he passed the grove of willow trees on the left, then three farms, then his parents' farm on the right. Jake tilted his head slightly and his heart pounded. He noticed a man in the distance tending the land.

Pa?

He stopped the wagon, lifted his head a little higher, and squinted.

The man was tall and thickset like Pa, and the worn hat was just like his father's. A woman walked toward the man, a bucket in her hand. Ma? Jake swallowed to clear the knot of emotion in his throat.

He couldn't tear his attention from the couple, who now stood side by side, the man lifting a ladle from the bucket and taking a drink.

It surely had to be his parents unless they'd hired a couple to work the land, which seemed unlikely given Pa loved farming and they were too poor to hire a hand.

He'd once been their hand.

Jake shook himself into action and urged the horses along. Best he get a move on if he wanted to make Cornwall by tomorrow. No sense in watching his parents from afar and pondering what could have been.

For that would never be.

Jake had meant to purchase the meager cabin near his parents' property to start his own farm. He'd saved a bit, and Pa offered to sign the loan as well if it helped secure it. He focused his attention on it as he rode by. Someone else had purchased it now, and a little girl ran through the yard, a bouquet of flowers in her hand.

A wooden sign greeted him on the outskirts of Cornwall the following day. Someone had painted flowers beside the words *Cornwall, Pop. 3,542.* Wagons and horses vied for room on the crowded main street. The city boasted a train depot twice the size of Horizon's, and numerous streets branched in different directions. People moseyed up and down the boardwalk, and businesses, including a sizable hotel, several restaurants, a department store, a barber, several millineries, and more lined either side, many a couple stories tall.

It reminded him once again why he preferred small towns.

However, entering Cornwall where no one knew him brought about unexpected relief. He could talk with people and be just another face in a crowd of many.

The Vanchev and Son Implement Company was about a mile from town near the South Fork of the Cornwall River. Two farm wagons with high sides to keep crops contained were parked near the building. To the left, three plows, a reaper, and a threshing bee machine awaited purchase. To the right was a variety of surreys, spring wagons, corn shellers, and buggies.

One piece of machinery caught his eye, and Jake smoothed his hand along the wheel of one of the two Aspinwall Potato Planters. He'd long hoped to grow spuds on a cleared space on his land. Such a machine would enable him to plant faster and easier.

"That there does the job of eight men." A voice drew Jake from his contemplating how he could someday afford such a device. "Name's George Gholston."

"Jake Lynton."

"Takes a bit to afford the planter, but it will soon pay for itself with all the time you save. Can plant nearly eight acres a day."

Jake whistled. The efficiency alone tempted him to purchase it, but without a loan, such a feat wasn't possible. It had taken him forever to save for the plow.

"It'll increase your yield and your profits as well."

"Thank you, but I'll be saving for it for a while yet."

"I understand. So what can I help you with today?"

The position of the sun indicated Gholston would likely be relieved of his workday soon. No sense in making the man stay longer. "I'm here to retrieve a plow."

After loading the plow, Jake paid for his purchase and was ready to leave for the lengthy return trip to Horizon when four children—three boys and a girl—rode up in a wagon.

They'd barely climbed from the wagon when a chorus of excitement filled the air. "Pa! Pa! Can we go fishing?"

Gholston put his arm around the two closest children, a chubby boy and a little girl with long red braids. "These are my children. Children, this is Mr. Lynton."

They greeted him, and the girl tugged on her pa's arm and whispered something in his ear.

"That sounds like a fine idea, Betsy. I wouldn't mind some trout for supper." He gazed up at the sky. "Reckon I don't see any storm clouds."

"Is Mr. Vanchev here?" asked the oldest boy, a tall, lanky sort who strongly resembled his father.

"He left about an hour ago. Do you remember what he said about borrowing his canoe?"

"Yes, sir, we do." This from the second oldest, a boy thicker than the first with an abundance of orange hair. "He said be sure to return it to the barn when we're finished. So, can we, Pa?"

"You have to promise to take care of the younger ones, especially Betsy."

"We will, Pa. Anyhow, the river looks calm today. Besides, Mr. Strain is out there fishing."

Gholston lifted a hand to a man in the distance, and the man returned his greeting. "So he is. But Mr. Strain is always fishing. He's been on the water since early this morning."

"Please, Pa?" It was the oldest son's turn to try his best to persuade their father.

"All right. I'll wave you back in within the hour."

The youngest boy folded his arms across his chest. "Aww, Pa. So soon? How can we catch us a fish that fast?"

"Yes, that soon. It's already getting late."

"Yes, sir."

"All right then, let's retrieve the canoe."

Watching the youngsters reminded Jake of all the times Pa took him and Corbin fishing. Many times one of them would catch a fish that would later escape. Each time the story was told the fish's size increased. Jake chuckled to himself. It was doubtful anyone hearing the story of that "mighty" fish believed it. "Do you need any help?"

Gholston regarded him. "Much obliged for that. I injured myself the other day, so I'm taking it easy with the back.

The two older boys and Jake easily carried the canoe to the river, and the younger boy and Betsy retrieved fishing poles from their wagon. "Are you joining them, sir?" Jake asked.

"Naw. I never could keep those children off the water. They're like their ma that way." Gholston shrugged. "I've never been able to swim so I never took much to fishing unless necessary. You fish, son?"

Jake and Gholston stood on the shore watching as the older two rowed the boat onto the clear blue water.

"I do. Haven't done so in a while what with chores demanding all my attention." A gust of wind rustled through the nearby trees. "Seems it might get windy."

Gholston's brow creased. "Hope not. I'm always hesitant to allow them to fish this late in the day. Weather can change at any moment, but seems more apt to in the afternoon."

Jake could leave at any time, but something held him there, watching the children laugh as they attempted to catch a fish or two. Betsy reminded him of Dinah Jo with her shy demeanor. A swell of homesickness enveloped him, and with effort, Jake shoved it aside. It wouldn't do to ruminate on things that could never be.

"I forgot to ask them if they were finished with their chores," said Gholston. "There's been a time or two when the youngest ones worm their way into fishing before their toil is done."

Jake recalled many times when Corbin would insist his responsibilities were complete, only to have Pa find out later that such was not the case. A raindrop fell from the sky, followed by another. He lifted his gaze to the sky. Dark storm clouds brewed in the distance, and the wind increased, bending the branches of the trees and blowing Jake's hat off his head.

Gholston waved at the children, motioning them to return to the shore. "Right now!" he yelled as he began to flap his arms to garner their attention. "Why aren't they returning to shore?"

Jake's own heart thudded in his chest. "I think they're trying to, sir," he yelled over the sound of the roaring gusts. "They're fighting the wind."

He watched as the canoe bobbed on the tumultuous waves before capsizing and throwing the children into the water. "No!" Gholston cried as he started into the water. Even above the commotion, Jake could hear the man's shrill cries and frantic breaths.

There was no time to waste. Jake ran to the river's edge and charged in.

Rain pelted him as he started to wade through the water, the temperature shocking him at first before his body acclimated. Normally, he would ease into it slowly before a swim, but today's plight didn't afford him that luxury. So instead, Jake rushed as quickly as he could, ignoring the chill and its tug on his clothing. If only he had one of those cork vests he'd once read about that a man who swam the Niagara

River used. While the man had to be revived after becoming unconscious, he'd survived the feat.

But Jake wasn't thinking of himself. He was only thinking of the children.

No man should lose a child, and it was up to him to ensure that didn't happen again.

The wind whipped his hair into his eyes, the stringy strands temporarily blinding him. Jake blinked and swiped the hair from his face and tucked it behind his ears, providing a reprieve and enabling his unobstructed vision to return once more. He scanned the area in search of the four children.

The rain turned to hail, small pieces of ice plunking the churning water and stinging him as it hit his face.

It was then that he noticed one of the children clinging precariously to the edge of the overturned canoe. *Hang on. I'm coming!* His feet grappled along the river floor until the earth below suddenly disappeared. In an instant, he raised his hands overhead, leaned over, kicked his feet, and swam through the tumultuous waters.

The slow process frustrated him as he pushed against the current. Years of hard work prepared him for this moment. An upper body with impressive strength and numerous times swimming in the lake near home as a youngster made swimming through the churning river easier than if he'd never endured hard labor or swam in those earlier years.

Swimming with Corbin. Racing him to the shore.

Corbin.

The memory threatened to distract him and halt his progression, and with effort, he shoved aside thoughts of him and Corbin splashing each other, swinging from the rope and letting go into the waters below. In those days, he never realized one day Corbin would be gone.

Because back then, childhood lasted forever and those hours after chores created fond memories never to be forgotten.

Corbin.

And you let him die.

The haunting realization threw him off course again, and for a minute, Jake gasped for breath, unable to continue as the pain in his chest worsened.

But not pain from physical exertion. Pain from breaking his parents' hearts.

No, the pain wasn't because he lacked the lung capacity to expertly swim far distances, for he did possess that ability—but because every guilt-ridden thought of Corbin threatened to steal his breath and drown him in a sea of remorse. A sea much more dangerous than the waters of the South Fork of the Cornwall River.

"Help!"

The child's cries reminded him innocent lives depended on him, and his dismal recollections were better left behind.

No matter how difficult a feat that might be.

Jake reached the boy on the canoe, took him to shore, then rescued the two other children.

Gholston waded through the water. "Go back!" Jake yelled, his voice competing with the howling wind and hail hitting the water.

"My daughter—she's still out there!"

That's right. There was another child. "I'll get her!" he yelled in response. Jake didn't need to rescue the father too, but he didn't have the advantage of waiting to see if Gholston heeded his command and returned to the riverbank. Instead, Jake peered through the inclement weather and spied the girl hanging onto a tree branch far in the distance.

"Don't let her die!" Gholston's voice carried on the wind.

The little girl wouldn't die if Jake had anything to say about it. He urged his arms to crawl through the water again as extreme fatigue demanded he rest.

If he was a praying man...

But he wasn't. Not any longer. Not since Corbin. God could have saved his brother. So why hadn't He?

The thoughts crowded his mind, clambering for his attention and threatening to withdraw his focus from the girl.

But somehow, Jake pressed on.

"Help!"

Her frantic screams sounded in his ears. He wanted to reassure her—to tell her he was almost there—but Jake knew he must conserve what little breath he had left. His lungs burned and his arms throbbed. His shoulders felt as though weighed down by lead, and his legs grew weak as he battled the exhaustion.

I'm coming. Just don't let go of the tree.

The snap of the branch and the ensuing crackle sounded, the noise reverberating as the girl was swept beneath the water.

No!

Jake forced himself to swim faster. To push through. To overcome the weariness.

Where was she?

Then he spied her again just before she vanished from his sight.

How could he reserve some of his breath and simultaneously reach her in time? Jake dove beneath the water, the sediment obscuring his vision. The girl sank to the bottom.

He could not. Would not. Return without her alive.

Jake folded his arms beneath her and thrust her to the surface. Swimming backward, his legs kicking, he dragged her along the turbulent waters. The wind raged harder, fighting him every second, and the current threatened to permanently submerge them both. Ensuring her head was above water at all times, he begged her to hang on. Just a little longer.

They were so close.

A streak of lightning lit the sky and thunder boomed. Hard smatterings of rain replaced the hail, stinging his eyes, the excruciating pain making it difficult to keep them open.

Finally, just as he was about to surrender, Jake reached the river's edge.

Jake pulled her ashore and felt for a pulse just as the little girl began to choke and gasp before sobbing.

Gholston was on his knees beside his daughter, his sobs filling the air as he clutched her to him. "Thank you, Jesus! Thank you for Your mercy!"

Jake gasped for breath and turned to the water again.

And that's when he saw the other man who'd also been fishing. So preoccupied with saving the children, he'd completely forgotten about him.

The man's head bobbed as he paddled through the water.

"Can you help him?" Gholston asked, his frantic tone spurring Jake to action, and he once again entered the water.

Twice his body resisted as Jake forged ahead, and twice he considered just allowing the waves to carry him. He was so, so tired. Just a few seconds of sleep was all he needed, then he could again propel his way through the water and save the other man.

He closed his eyes. He'd become accustomed to the water's cooler temperature, and he relaxed. Oh, but to catch some shut-eye. To rest after all the swimming he'd endured.

Something hit his arm, and he flung his eyes open to see a snake. He thrust it aside, rejuvenation overcoming him.

He'd never liked snakes.

And even less so when they swam beside him.

Jake pushed toward the man, a resurgence of energy launching him forward.

Only this time, he pulled a lifeless body to shore.

Chapter Nine

Fatigue entrenched him, yet he couldn't sleep.

After he and Gholston loaded the children into the wagon, he followed the man and his family to Gholston's house. A neighbor fetched the doctor, who said all of the children would fully recover. By the time the doctor left, four other people—close friends of the Gholstons who'd been told by the neighbor about what happened—had braved the stormy weather and arrived to offer comfort.

Both Mr. and Mrs. Gholston thanked him profusely for saving their children. But he couldn't stop thinking of the man who'd perished.

Mr. Strain, an elderly man who'd lived in Cornwall his entire life, would likely be missed by many. If only Jake had reached him sooner. If only he'd tried harder.

If only...

For at least the tenth time, Jake turned to his other side. When the Gholstons offered their barn for the night, he'd accepted their generosity. It was better than hunkering down beneath the wagon somewhere on the road outside Cornwall.

The smell of hay and horse feed filled his nostrils. The storm had since ceased, and Jake could see a sliver of the moon through the barn window on a dark night with few stars and an overabundance of clouds.

"Lord," he said aloud, his voice sounding brittle and broken in his ears.

One of the horses stirred.

"Lord, I'm sorry."

Silence greeted his words. First Corbin, then Mr. Strain. Hadn't he prayed for both? Begged God that they would both survive?

Emotional numbness knifed Jake's heart.

It had been a week since Ruby lost her job at *The Horizon Herald*, and the traditional family supper on Friday night was the perfect antidote to temporarily take Ruby's mind from her predicament. Time with her sisters and brothers and nieces and nephews would surely make her forget her conundrum, even if only for a few hours.

Conversation ensued after Papa led the prayer for the meal. Ruby loved it when her family met together each week for supper nearly as much as she imagined Mama did. The highlight of Ruby's week was to see everyone and catch up on weekly events.

She held Baby Albert while Velma ate her own supper. His bright eyes and perfect features gave testament to the detail of an amazing Creator. She snuggled him close, kissed him on the forehead, and inhaled his baby scent. If the Lord someday blessed her with her own child, she feared all household chores and duties would fall rapidly to the wayside while she cuddled her little one.

All too soon, she returned Baby Albert to his mother and commenced eating. Landon scooped some mashed potatoes onto his plate. "I think I may have another story idea for you, Ruby."

"Oh?" Ruby set down her fork and leaned forward to better hear Landon above the various discussions around the table. Landon had been the source of a couple of ideas Ruby had presented to Mr. O'Kane.

"When I stopped in Cornwall two days ago, I overheard some of the townsfolk talking about a Horizon man who saved the lives of four people."

That statement caused hushed silence.

"Someone from Horizon saved the lives of four people? How come we didn't know about that here?"

Landon shrugged. "Not sure other than to say this man saved them while they were fishing on the South Fork of the Cornwall River."

Ruby's heart raced with anticipation. This was the *perfect* story to approach Mr. O'Kane with in order to reinstate her job. "Do you have the name of the hero?"

"Just a first name. Jake."

"Do we know someone named Jake in town?" Mae asked.

Papa shook his head. "The only one I know of might be Old Man Jacob Bullard."

Mama passed the plate of bread. "Does he go by Jake?"

"He might."

"I'm not sure Old Man Jacob Bullard would be capable of swimming, let alone rescuing anyone," countered Timothy.

"Albert," said Papa, "You know a lot of the folks in Horizon. Have you ever heard of someone named Jake besides possibly Old Man Jacob Bullard?"

"Can't say as I've ever met anyone named Jake. Horizon has grown in the years since the railroad, so we have a fair amount of newcomers—not all of them churchgoing folks."

Ruby refused to allow her hopes to be dashed. "Do you recall anything else from the conversation, Landon?"

"They only spoke of this heroic endeavor by a man named Jake from Horizon. Apparently, there were four children and one man drowning when the waters turned turbulent due to an impending storm. He was able to save the children."

Mama gasped. "Children?"

"You really must write this story," coaxed Lucy. "Can you imagine what would have happened if this Jake fellow was not there?"

"Indeed," added Mae. "Praise the Lord the children survived."

Ruby's hands itched to write down the information she'd already procured from Landon. A courageous man who'd risked his own life to save children had a story worth telling, whether Mr. O'Kane agreed or not. The problem was twofold. She had to find out who this "Jake" was—and convince him to grant her an interview.

Ruby was nearly breathless when she bounded out of the buggy and through the door of *The Horizon Herald* on Monday morning, hoping to arrive before any of the other employees. She feared if Mr. O'Kane was a God-fearing man who attended church, she might have pestered him during the potluck on Sunday. But alas, Mr. O'Kane had never, to her knowledge, stepped foot inside the Horizon church.

Thankfully, Lillian was nowhere to be seen. That made things much easier.

She inhaled the smell of ink, one of her favorite smells, and took a minute to take in the sight of the business she had grown to love.

"Mr. O'Kane, may I speak with you for a moment?"

"What, pray tell, are you doing here, Miss Shepherdson?"

If her heart didn't stop beating so loudly in her ears, Ruby wouldn't be able to hear her own self speak when she explained her idea to her former boss. She took one deep breath, then another.

"I really haven't the time to tarry."

"Oh, yes. Sorry, Mr. O'Kane. I came to tell you—" She chewed on her lip. How best to say it? "I came to tell you—to ask you—well to first tell you about a story idea."

One of Mr. O'Kane's overly pointed eyebrows inched into his former hairline. "What is it?"

"We have a hero in Horizon."

"I doubt that."

"We do, and I aim to secure an interview from him."

This time Mr. O'Kane narrowed his beady eyes. "What kind of hero? Because if you're going to interview Leonel about knowing someone, who knew someone, who knew Jesse James, that's not a story about a hero."

"No, sir. It's something entirely different."

"I'm waiting."

"You see, Landon, my brother-in-law..."

"I'm aware of who Landon is. Please commence with this story as I have other matters to tend to."

Ruby bobbed her head. "Yes, sir. Anyway, he overheard about a hero—a true hero—and I am requesting your permission to interview him with the guarantee that if I am successful, I will earn the right to return as a reporter for *The Horizon Herald* with my *Ruby's Horizon Happenings* column."

Mr. O'Kane folded his arms across his puny chest. "You are aware that Lillian now has her own column known as *Lillian's Horizon Happenings*? Perhaps she would be best suited to interview this, ahem, hero."

"I would prefer to do so with the understanding of regaining my employment." If it were up to her, she would ever let Lillian steal another idea again.

Her former boss stared at her, his eyes unblinking. The seconds ticked by, their sound echoing in the quiet building. She was about to state her case again when he spoke.

"Who is the hero?"

"I only have a first name, but with a bit of investigating..." She hoped her answer would appease him. After all, if word reached Lillian about the name "Jake", Lillian would do her best to undermine Ruby and solve the mystery of the hero's full name herself.

"He lives here?"

"He does." *Oh, please let Landon have heard correctly!*

Mr. O'Kane twirled the curled end of his mustache with his right hand. "It would be better to have Lillian write this story rather than someone who is no longer employed at this prestigious newspaper."

Ruby didn't mention that, while she had loved writing her column for the newspaper, *The Horizon Herald* was far from prestigious. Best to keep that opinion to herself. "Though I believe I can accomplish this assignment with a resounding victory." Mae and Lucy would call her dramatic for certain if they were to hear her exaggerated words, but as the saying went, desperate times called for desperate measures.

Mr. O'Kane released a deep exaggerated breath. "This is far beyond my better judgment, but I suppose I could assign the story to you, if—and only if—you were able to secure a propitious—note I said 'propitious' interview with this person. If you were to do so, which I highly doubt, I would allow you to stay and continue to write *Ruby's Horizon Happenings*. But only if you secure an interview with him that meets my approval."

"I'll do that, sir." *I'll do just about anything, short of pairing up with Lillian for an article or traveling all the way to Antarctica for an assignment.*

"I'll give you a month to present the article."

"I'll do my utmost best, sir."

"Your utmost best will not suffice. You'll meet these requirements or you'll not write for *The Horizon Herald*. It will be delivered to me in exactly four weeks from today, and there will be no more negotiating whatsoever. Am I clear?"

"Perfectly clear, Mr. O'Kane." Apprehension flooded her. What if she was unable to fulfill her promise? But she had to. "I'll not let you down."

"See that you don't."

Now if she could determine who "Jake" was, locate him, and write his story.

CHAPTER TEN

ON MONDAY, RUBY BEGAN her search for a man named Jake. She'd always enjoyed a mystery, and what better way to solve a mystery than to find the hero who could potentially save her job?

She first stopped at Maribel and Reverend Marshall's to drop off the new curtains Mama had sewn for their window.

"Hello, child." Maribel reached for Ruby's hand with her own soft wrinkled one.

Ruby stooped and placed a kiss on her velvety cheek. "Hello, Maribel. I have your new curtains."

"Oh, they are lovely. Do come in. Marshall and I were just finishing the remnants of the scrumptious apple pie your mama delivered to us yesterday."

"It is delicious," agreed Reverend Marshall, as he forked a piece of the fluffy crust.

Maribel waved a hand at the remnants of the pie. Only one sliver remained. "Would you care for some, dear?"

"No, thank you." While she loved Mama's desserts, she couldn't very well eat the final smidgen.

"Your mama sure has certainly come a long way since those early days of her marriage when it comes to cooking," Maribel said.

"Indeed she has. Papa teases her now and then, and they have some secret code between them each time she makes eggs for breakfast. She didn't waste a moment in teaching Lucy, Mae, and me how to cook." Ruby draped the curtains on the worn sofa and took a seat at the table with Maribel and the reverend. While excitement buzzed through her at the thought that perhaps her adopted grandparents would know this Jake fellow and the mystery would be solved during her first attempt, there would be plenty of time to inquire of them. For now, they would catch up and enjoy each other's company. Just like grandmother and granddaughter.

Maribel smiled. "I suppose cooking took on a whole new importance to your mama. She's done a right fine job raising you children."

"Thank you. She would appreciate your kind words."

Reverend Marshall divided the last slice and distributed the larger piece to Maribel's plate. "Are you sure you don't want any, Ruby?"

"I'm sure, but thank you."

"We enjoyed services yesterday. Albert makes a fine preacher."

"He would be honored to hear your compliment since you served in the pulpit for so many years."

"Indeed. I miss it at times." Reverend Marshall's gaze met Maribel's, and she reached for his hand.

"You were a fine preacher, Marshall. Still are. The Lord is using you in other ways now."

"Reckon so. I've been meeting at the barbershop from time to time." He smoothed a hand on his sparse hair. "Not so much for a haircut but to meet with the men who frequent there. I've been able to share about the Lord from time to time."

Maribel's look of admiration for her husband warmed Ruby. Even in their advanced ages, the two had a profound love for each other.

"We not only enjoyed the sermon, but I was able to hold that precious Baby Albert. Velma and the boys visit weekly, but to hold that little one..." Maribel held a hand to her heart. "Wasn't that long ago that Mae's baby, L.J., allowed me to hold him."

"He just learned to crawl, so he's not allowing anyone to snuggle him these days," laughed Ruby. "He's quite the busy baby."

"Indeed. And..." Maribel leaned closer and lowered her voice. "Just between the three of us, I noticed that Freya Zembrodt was acting a bit flustered around our Timothy."

"Oh, yes, it's no secret Freya fancies him, but Timothy is an ornery one. He would like nothing better than to farm and eat cookies."

Reverend Marshall chuckled. "Give him time. I was once that way too. Well, not farming, but working in my position at a tiny church in the northern part of the state. Too busy to think about courtship until a beautiful woman walked through the doors one day and stole my heart."

Maribel blushed. "Such a handsome man Marshall was. And godly too."

The two shared an intimate glance as seconds ticked by, and once again, Ruby felt as though she was intruding on their special moment. She'd once heard Reverend Marshall preach about how the Lord intended a strong and godly marriage to be the most wonderful thing this side of heaven.

Her heart stalled. Perhaps someday the Lord would see fit to bless her with the kind of marriage Maribel and the reverend had and her own parents shared.

Several seconds later, Maribel returned her attention to Ruby. "So, dear, do tell me how your writing is going as of late. Wilhelmina bought a subscription for us, but we haven't seen *Ruby's Horizon Happenings* lately."

Ruby inhaled a sharp breath. "I messed up the bank robbery article something fierce, and Mr. O'Kane removed me from my position."

"I am so sorry to hear that."

"Thank you."

"I know you're disappointed. Give me your hands, child."

Ruby obliged and placed her hands in Maribel's. "Now," Maribel continued, spacing Ruby's right-hand thumb and forefinger only an inch apart, "This is what we see of our lives. Just a teeny bit." Maribel then spaced Ruby's hands as far as they could go. "And this is what God sees. He sees the entire thing, from beginning to end. He knows the hows and whys of it all."

Ruby nodded. "I suppose you're right, Maribel. Sometimes I just don't understand."

"We don't always understand His ways. That's what makes Him God and us mere humans. Think of what our Lord says in the Book of Isaiah: *'For my thoughts are not your thoughts, neither are your ways my ways, saith the Lord.'*"

Ruby loved how Maribel never held any condemnation toward her when she asked the elderly woman the hard questions. Rather, as a patient mentor, Maribel explained with grace all she knew about God's Word after so many years of walking with her Heavenly Father.

"Of course," Maribel continued, "God has a purpose for your writing or He wouldn't have gifted you with being able to string your words together in such a fashion. Have you given Him your writing?"

"Given it to Him?"

"Yes, ask Him to guide your every step and bring glory and honor to Him by what you write."

Ruby thought for a moment. "I have surrendered it to Him. However, I must admit I've been so focused on seeking approval, especially from Mr. O'Kane."

Maribel nodded, her white hair flowing with the motion of her head. "Ah, well, that could be a problem. You see, we need to seek approval from God, not man."

"But it's Mr. O'Kane who can fire me permanently or decide to rehire me."

"Only if it's God's will, child."

"True." Ruby bit her lip. Was it God's will that she no longer *ever* worked in the employ of Mr. O'Kane? She hoped not.

"For what it's worth, I thought the robbery article was well written," interjected Reverend Marshall. He swiped at a crumb in his mustache.

"Thank you, Reverend. Fortunately, I have been given a chance to return to my position as a reporter if I can write an article to Mr. O'Kane's standards about a hero."

Maribel's eyes widened. "A hero?"

"Yes. "Do you know someone in Horizon by the name of Jake?"

Reverend Marshall scratched his head. "I've had some parishioners by that name over the years, but to my knowledge, the only one who still resides in Horizon is Old Man

Jacob Bullard, although I'm not sure I ever heard anyone refer to him as 'Jake'."

Old Man Jacob Bullard was indeed on Ruby's list.

After she hung the curtains and bid Maribel and Reverend Marshall farewell, Ruby next inquired of Postmaster Kleiber. And while Ruby didn't give details about why she was searching for this individual—only that she was working on a story for the paper—Postmaster Kleiber wasn't much help. He too offered Old Man Jacob Bullard's name and a man named Jake who had long since moved to Northern Idaho.

Miss Greta and the Lieutenant were next. She found the Lieutenant outside fixing the boardinghouse railing.

"Hello, Lieutenant."

"Good morning, Ruby. What can I do for you?"

She proceeded to tell the Lieutenant about her quest to find a man named Jake when she noticed his attention focused in the opposite direction.

"Lieutenant?"

"Oh, sorry about that. I was just…"

Ruby followed his gaze to the garden where Miss Greta perused her recently planted vegetables. She waited for the Lieutenant to continue speaking, and within seconds, he continued. "Look at the way the wind has captured her lovely hair. Ah, but what a lovely woman she is."

Miss Greta's orange-gray hair did, indeed, tousle in the wind. "Yes, she is lovely."

The Lieutenant scowled. "She's more than lovely. She's the most beautiful woman this old man has ever laid eyes upon. In all my years—and there have been many—I've never seen a more handsome woman."

Ruby's heart warmed at the Lieutenant's sentiment about his wife. The two were far advanced in years, but he still found her to be pretty. Perhaps she ought to write an article about enduring love between couples. Mama and Papa, Maribel and Reverend Marshall, the Lieutenant and Miss Greta…

"Don't you think?"

The Lieutenant's words interrupted her plotting for a future article. "Begging your pardon?"

"I was just saying that it could only be the Hand of Providence that could bring such a fine woman into my life. Seems just yesterday I was gawking at her like a lovelorn fool. And now look, I'm married to her." The Lieutenant unfolded his stooped self.

"Congratulations on finding your one true love."

The Lieutenant waved her response away. "While she is my one true love, there's no need to get all sappy about it. Now what was it that you were needing?"

"You know most everyone in town, correct?"

The Lieutenant puffed out his chest. "Yes, I do. Why do you ask?"

"I was wondering if you knew anyone in Horizon by the name of Jake?"

Without removing his gaze from Miss Greta, the Lieutenant answered. "Can't say as I do. Only name that sounds familiar is Old Man Jacob Bullard."

It was the same answer she'd consistently received, and Old Man Jacob Bullard's image flashed in her mind. His gray trousers pulled up high, accentuating his rotund stomach, his abundance of gray hair sticking up at odd ends, and his thick spectacles inching their way down his narrow, pointed nose.

"You might ask my Greta. Could be that a man named Jake stayed at the boardinghouse before I moved here."

"I will do that. Thank you." Ruby strolled to Miss Greta's location in the garden. "Hello, Miss Greta."

But the woman was otherwise occupied. A broad smile crossed her face, and she offered a tiny flirtatious wave at the Lieutenant. "My, but isn't he the most handsome man you ever saw? His eyes are so brilliant behind those spectacles." She held a hand to her bosom and swooned. "Sometimes I have to pinch myself and remind myself that it's not a dream that I'm married to him. Such a dapper man!"

Ruby watched the flirtatious interaction between the two elderly townsfolk, looking from Miss Greta to the Lieutenant, then back to Miss Greta again. She hated to interrupt such an intimate moment.

Miss Greta primped and fussed and patted her coiffure. "Tell me, Ruby, do I look a fright?"

"Not at all. On the contrary, you look lovely." *Just ask the Lieutenant.*

"Thank you. It's not easy at times having lived so many decades to still look comely."

"The Lieutenant finds you very comely."

"He does?"

"Indeed."

Miss Greta blushed. "Well, he does have refined taste. Now, what brings you by today?"

"Do you know a man by the name of Jake or has one by that name ever stayed at the boardinghouse?"

Miss Greta firmed a hand on her ample hip. "The only man I know of in Horizon by that name is Old Man Jacob Bullard. I suppose Jake could be short for Jacob."

Ruby sighed. This mystery wasn't likely to be solved in the immediate future. And if it couldn't be solved, she'd never write the article for Mr. O'Kane that would save her job

Miss Greta must have realized Ruby's frustration. "But let me look through my files and see if I've ever had a guest named Jake. Do you have a last name?"

"Unfortunately, no."

The older woman leaned closer and whispered. "Is this an investigation for an article?" Her eyes widened and her sparse orange-red eyebrows lifted. Likely she was hoping for a tidbit of information.

"Yes, but I'm not allowed to provide any details as of yet."

"I see. Well, I'm always happy to help you as best I can. Don't care much for Mr. O'Kane and even less for that Lillian woman who's constantly putting on airs."

Ruby agreed on both counts. She followed Miss Greta into the boardinghouse where the woman perused her files.

"According to my records, the only man by that name is one who stayed here four years ago and was visiting from North Dakota." She tapped her chin. "Can't say as I remember much about him other than he was a stuffy man who complained about the room and left quite a mess upon his departure."

That didn't sound like a man willing to risk his life to rescue people who were drowning. Besides, Landon mentioned the Jake Ruby was looking for currently resided in Horizon, not another state. She thanked Miss Greta and bade her farewell before asking at the livery, the blacksmith, and millinery, and in passing with Sheriff Zembrodt, who assured her he'd never arrested a man named Jake. Nor was there a "Jake" on the wanted posters currently hanging in the sheriff's office.

Ruby next stopped at the barbershop, and that's when she saw him.

Old Man Jacob Bullard was sitting in the barber chair, a crusty expression on his weathered and pasty-white face. A white cape was fastened around his narrow sloping shoulders and he wore spectacles so thick that his eyes enlarged twice beneath them.

"And be sure to clip them hairs in my ears too," he muttered.

"Always do," said Mr. Bjorn, the barber.

A mirror sat propped on the counter, sharing space with several tonics, cups with brushes, and shaving cream. Old Man Jacob Bullard's peeved demeanor stared back at her.

"Excuse me," she said, sidling up alongside the barbershop chair.

Old Man Jacob Bullard narrowed his eyes at her. "You supposed to be in here?"

"Yes, sir, just…"

"Waiting on a haircut, is that it?"

At his remark, both he and the barber guffawed.

"No, not exactly, but I do need to ask you if you've been to Cornwall recently."

"What's that you say?" Old Man Jacob Bullard inclined toward her.

"I wanted to ask if you've been to Cornwall recently."

"You're gonna have to speak up, young lady. I've become hard of hearing in my later years."

Old Man Jacob Bullard had never heard well according to those who'd known him for years, but Ruby didn't say as much. She repeated her question.

"Is this some type of interrogation?"

"To the contrary. I'm working on an article for *The Horizon Herald*, and—"

Old Man Jacob Bullard shook his head, causing the barber to nick a little too much gray hair from the left side of his head. "Don't like that O'Kane none. Only difference between him and a gossipmonger is that he's a tale-teller who gets paid for it."

Ruby did her best not to disparage her boss to others, with the exception of mentioning to her family the man's lack of fairness and failings as an employer and his obvious favoritism of his niece. "As such, I'd like to know if you were by chance in Cornwall or the vicinity in the past week."

"You working for Sheriff Zembrodt these days? That sounds like a question he'd ask an outlaw."

Ruby chuckled to herself. She'd no more be an effective sheriff than Timothy would be a baker. "No, I'm not working for the sheriff. So, tell me, were you in Cornwall this past week?"

"Do I look like I could travel to Cornwall?"

A glance at his weathered and severely wrinkled hands, his leathery and sagging face, and the cane propped against the barbershop wall reminded Ruby of his age.

"In case you didn't know, I'll be ninety-four next week. Most often, I aim to stay here in town rather than go to Cornwall. Even with the rail now, it ain't too conducive for a man my age, especially with my rheumatism acting up and such. Does that answer your question, young lady?"

"It does, thank you."

Ruby bid him farewell and stepped out onto the boardwalk. She'd known from the outset that Old Man Jacob Bullard was not the one who rescued the children from the river. She had one more place to visit, that was if Tabitha's lengthy line of customers had eased at the mercantile.

She passed the bank. That was one place she *wouldn't* be inquiring about the mysterious hero. Just as she approached, crusty Mr. Sanders emerged. He glowered at her through round spectacles.

A teeny part of her wanted to be mettlesome. To greet him with a fake saccharine smile and bid him a good day. Or better yet, to ask if he'd met any outlaws lately.

But being petulant wouldn't be pleasing to the Lord, even if Mr. Sanders had rejected Papa's request for a loan to purchase additional acreage last month for no good reason. He'd also declined to assist Miss Greta and the Lieutenant when, in desperation, they'd sought a loan for repairs on the boardinghouse. Or his refusal to give a kindly couple in town more time to make amends on their outstanding balance after the husband grew ill.

At least the banker had agreed to Ruby's loan for the typewriter. Lucy had surmised that was because he was close friends with Mr. O'Kane.

Mr. Sanders glowered at her and stiffened his puny shoulders. Ruby was at least a full head taller than him and, even though slender, much wider.

No, while the man was a challenge, retaliating with false kindness was not the answer. Mama would tell her to be sure her kindness was genuine or else it was a lie. And she'd tell her never to repay unkindness with unkindness.

Oh, but it sure was tempting!

With effort, Ruby avoided Mr. Sanders' gaze and continued to the mercantile.

When she entered, Mayor Trabert and Tabitha were at the counter partaking in a discussion. Not wishing to interrupt, Ruby strode toward the sewing notions and pretended to examine the variety of spools of thread. But her mind was far from thread spools.

If she couldn't find out who Jake was—if she couldn't produce a worthwhile article to Mr. O'Kane—if Landon had incorrectly heard the hero's name—if the man *wasn't* from Horizon, but was from elsewhere—if...

"Hello, Ruby, how are you today?" Tabitha's voice interrupted her musings.

"Doing well, thank you. I've been attempting to locate someone and am hoping you can help."

Tabitha's eyes rounded. "Sounds interesting. I'd be happy to do what I can."

"I'm wondering if either of you know a man by the name of Jake."

Mayor Trabert scratched his chin. "Old Man Jacob Bullard comes to mind."

Ruby shook her head. "It's not him. I thought it could be at first, but after interviewing him, I immediately noticed he wasn't the one I was in search of for my article."

"I don't recall anyone by that name," said Tabitha. "However, I'd be happy to look through our accounts if that would help."

"Thank you so much. I would greatly appreciate that."

Ruby followed Tabitha and Mayor Trabert to the counter where Tabitha removed a brown notebook from a shelf.

She flipped through the lined pages. "Hmm," she mused. "Nothing here."

Just as Ruby was about to concede defeat, Tabitha pointed at something in the notebook. "Jimmie, do you remember this gentleman?"

Jimmie peered over her shoulder. "Jake Lynton." He stroked his chin and stared at the ceiling. "It's been a while, but was he the one who came in to purchase a shovel and a sack of flour?"

"Yes, I believe so. He's only come in a handful of times and paid for his purchases but wanted to set up an account in case he needed more provisions. He's a man of few words."

"I vaguely recall him, yes."

Ruby failed to hide her excitement. "Jake Lynton?"

"Yes. Peculiar fellow. Do you remember where he lived?"

Mayor Trabert blew out a deep breath. "I think he lives on the old Kountz property."

Ruby had heard of the place, and Papa would likely know exactly where it was.

"Yes, the Kountz property, that's correct." Tabitha closed the notebook. "That's the only man named Jake we have in our account book. Could he possibly be the one?"

He could very well be, but Ruby wouldn't know until she talked to him.

As she left the mercantile, she added a spring to her step.

Ruby Caroline Shepherdson just may be able to reclaim her position at *The Horizon Herald*.

Chapter Eleven

"Papa said the old Kountz place is just ahead two miles." Ruby tapped her pencil on her notebook. Her fingers tingled to write the notes that would soon become the article that would reinstate her position at *The Horizon Herald.* A twinge of nausea overcame her. Why would she be so nervous about this particular meeting when she'd conducted numerous interviews?

Perhaps it was the unknown, or more likely, the fact that if she *didn't* secure a story, her days writing *Ruby's Horizon Happenings* were in the past. Would Mr. O'Kane be informing his subscribers about why *Ruby's Horizon Happenings* wasn't happening?

Timothy flicked the reins. "Not sure why anyone would want to live on that old dilapidated farm. I'm not sure Mr. Kountz was tending to it even before he fell ill."

"I heard the house is atrocious and not even livable."

"Could be. Strange that anyone would want to live there."

"I'm pondering how an old codger with a hunchback was able to save four children from drowning."

Timothy's brow furrowed, and he jerked his head back. "Old codger with a hunchback? Did Tabitha or the mayor mention that?"

"No, just writer's instinct."

Timothy shook his head. "And my farmer's instinct tells me you look ridiculous in that frou-frou hat."

"It's not a frou-frou hat, dear brother. I'll have you know only those with the utmost fashion sense wear such lovely accessories. Why, Mae said when she traveled with Landon to Denver to see his parents last month, all of the women were wearing similar hats."

"And then Ruby Shepherdson realized she lived in Horizon, Idaho, not Denver."

She playfully punched Timothy's arm. "How do you ever plan to find your one true love if you don't understand the necessity for a woman to occasionally purchase something elegant?"

"Don't plan on finding my one true love. Ever. Farming is all I need. Farming and food."

"What about Sheriff Zembrodt's daughter, Freya? She's a sweet girl."

Timothy shook his head so fiercely Ruby thought he might lose his hat. "No, thank you. Yes, she's a nice girl, but for some other fellow."

"Suit yourself."

Ruby held on to her hat to keep the breeze from blowing it off her head. The hat may have been an extravagant and unnecessary purchase were it not for the fact that it had been damaged in transit, and Mr. O'Kane's fussy wife declined to purchase it after ordering it. Tabitha offered it for a nickel, and Ruby, knowing she could alter it enough so it would be presentable, indulged in purchasing it. Once home, she and Mama all but fixed the flattened and ruined hat.

Now the hat was adorned with festive ribbons, flowers, and a feather. No one would be the wiser that it had ever suffered devastation at the hands of a rough trip between Chicago and Horizon. Ruby fiddled with a button on her green dress. *Lord, please relieve me of any anxieties. Guard my tongue and, should it be Your will, might Mr. Lynton please be amenable to my story?*

Jake finished milking the cows, then started toward the fields. Given the hot sun beating down on him at this early hour, the day would get warmer. Best get the worst of the chores out of the way. Wasn't that what Pa always said? Do the hardest and most grueling chores first while the weather is still somewhat comfortable?

Pa. Jake missed him, especially at times like these when he needed his father's wise counsel. He kicked at a mound of dirt. What would Pa say now that Jake had also been unable to save Mr. Strain? Would he be proud of him for saving the children? Or would he remind Jake about Corbin?

Pa was a good man. A hardworking, godly provider who loved his family. That truth conflicted with Jake's concerns about Pa never being able to forgive him.

Jake adjusted his hat on his head and scanned the farm, mentally listing the items he hoped to accomplish. Thankfully, he was busy as all get out when it came to restoring the farm to what it might have been before the former owner's illness. That and his hopes of bringing in not just a decent crop, but an abundant one.

In his prior days, Jake would have prayed for the Lord's direction in all things. But instead, when he'd seen the advertisement for the farm, he'd heeded his own path, plunked down his hard-earned savings, and purchased the land. Hours later, he was the proud—or not so proud—owner of the Kountz farm. He renamed it the Lynton farm, but kept that to himself, just like all things these days.

Oh, he'd briefly met the mercantile owner and had established an account just in case he should need it in the future. And he'd briefly conversed with the newspaperwoman. Other than that, he'd spoken to no one other than a grunt here and a word there. To his recollection, no one in Horizon knew his name, save for the mercantile owner, whose name Jake couldn't recall.

It was better this way. While loneliness often set in, Jake was so busy rehabilitating the place that there wasn't ample room for lonely thoughts. He worked day and night, rarely going into town. Going to Cornwall hadn't been on his agenda.

With effort, he shoved the thoughts of Mr. Strain's lifeless body from his mind. "Come on, Samson. We have work to do."

Samson ran to the oak tree, found a stick, and looked expectantly at his owner.

"You want to play fetch, boy?"

Jake chuckled when Samson seemed to nod his head. What would he have done without the injured stray? Probably talked himself crazy. "All right." Jake threw the stick and watched Samson bound after it. He repeated the game several times over, each time giving Samson a healthy pat on the back for retrieving the stick.

On the final time, Jake heard the sound of someone coming down the lane. "Feel free to drive on past," he said aloud.

However, the visitors paid his demand no mind. A buggy drew nearer. *A buggy?* He craned his neck to the side. *What on earth?* He squinted at the couple who'd stopped in front of his house, one of whom was a woman with an unsightly frou-frou hat.

He folded his arms across his chest, and Samson barked. Perhaps they were lost. Maybe they were relatives of the late Mr. Kountz. Likely they'd be on their way soon.

"Well, here we are." Timothy stopped the buggy and unfolded his long legs, came to the other side of the buggy, and assisted Ruby.

"I saw a man in the distance. Perhaps he's the farmhand. He might be able to assist us in locating Mr. Lynton."

Writer's instinct told her that Jake Lynton, the old homely codger, was likely in the house reclining away from the early morning sun, his back bowed and his vision failing. Mr. Lynton, unable to scuttle, would dawdle the meager distance from one side of his house to the other, his right foot dragging due to an injury from working on the railroad. At sixty-eight, he was completely bald on the front of his head, and his thinning hair grew to his collar in the back. His wrinkled and weathered skin gave testament to years of working outside partaking in grueling labor. An odor emitted from his filthy skin, a result of not taking his once-a-week bath before church services, which he attended in Varner City.

How he'd managed to rescue four children was nothing short of a miracle.

"Rubes?"

She blinked and brought herself back to reality in response to her brother's voice. "Yes, Timothy?"

"The farmhand is heading this way. Reckon we should attempt to get his attention or go to the house and ask to speak with Mr. Lynton."

Ruby squinted into the sun. The farmhand looked vaguely familiar with disheveled dark hair protruding beneath his hat. "I believe the better approach would be to go to the house. After all, the man in the distance is just a farmhand, and Mr. Lynton is inside the house."

"And you know this how?"

"Writer's instinct. Mr. Lynton is older than the man strolling this way."

"Ah, writer's instinct. Of course." Timothy offered Ruby his arm and together they started for the farmhouse.

Ruby stepped up to the front porch. One single old rocking chair had been placed on what could, with a little work, be quite a nice and inviting porch. The view of the green fields spread far into the distance and beneath the roof overhang, the shady porch beckoned one to sit and rest awhile. Why wasn't Mr. Lynton lounging comfortably in the cool sanctuary of the porch? At his age, farming wasn't as easy as it had once been. A noonday nap rectified the weariness in his aging bones.

Ruby turned briefly to see the farmhand walking toward them. It immediately occurred to her the identity of the man. He was the curmudgeon who'd assisted her on two occasions. So, he was Mr. Lynton's farmhand? *And* he owned the land with the raspberry bushes?

Did she detect a crusty expression on his face? Ignoring the thought, Ruby raised a hand to knock on the door. She giggled to herself. How could she ascertain if he had a crusty expression or not? The man had more facial hair than she imagined Methuselah in the Bible had.

Her knock received no answer. "Perhaps we should ask the farmhand if Mr. Lynton is sleeping. Those in their later years of life need more sleep sometimes, especially Mr. Lynton since he's been working since sunup."

Timothy shook his head but said nothing.

Ruby pivoted and gracefully sashayed down the porch stairs, mindful of keeping her hat firmly on her head.

Even beneath the mangy beard, she noted the scowl on the farmhand's face. Perhaps a little kindness could assuage his gruff demeanor.

It was certainly worth a try.

"First of all, thank you again for aiding me during my times of distress. And once again, I do humbly apologize for the raspberry debacle. Are you a farmhand for Mr. Lynton as well as working your own farm where the raspberry bushes are?" She sounded like a chattering hen in her own ears. When he said nothing, she continued. "How are you today?"

"What do you want?"

Such an untidy appearance and snarly demeanor! Apparently, the attempt to placate his surly disposition was for naught.

"Do you happen to know where we might find Mr. Jake Lynton?"

The man drew closer until he was only a few feet from Ruby and Timothy. His plaid sleeves were rolled to the elbow exposing muscular forearms. Stunning blue eyes stared back at her. A somewhat handsome man beneath a hairy façade. Ruby felt the heat climb her face.

"Who wants to know?"

"I beg your pardon? Who wants to know what?" she squeaked.

The farmhand was clearly not amused. "Who wants to know where to find Mr. Jake Lynton?"

"Oh, dear me. We would like to know." Ruby pointed to herself and Timothy.

"I recognize you. But why do you want to speak with Mr. Lynton?"

"I write the column, *Ruby's Horizon Happenings* for *The Horizon Herald*." Ruby wished she could say that with more confidence. But not with her job in jeopardy as it was. "This is my assistant, Timothy. And who might you be?"

Such brazenness. What would Mama say?

"Mr. Jake Lynton," he growled.

"I beg your pardon?"

"Mr. Jake Lynton," the man repeated.

"I'm sorry, I must have misunderstood. We're looking for a recluse of a man, a man gaining in years who must recline after several hours of grueling work in the fields."

Timothy nudged her in the arm, and she offered him a crusty frown.

"I don't rightly know a Mr. Jake Lynton who is a man gaining in years and who must recline after several hours of grueling work in the fields. You must have the wrong man. Now, if you'll be on your way."

Ruby shook her head. "With all respect, sir, we were told we could find Mr. Jake Lynton here. Perhaps the…" she paused. "The source for the information detailing Mr. Jake Lynton's age and past contained errors."

Timothy snorted.

"This is my farm."

"Then you must be the man we have been searching for. Do forgive us for having incorrect details." Ruby readied herself and prepared to take notes should the sour man agree to an interview.

An awkward silence permeated the air. Should Ruby ask her first question?

"This place is looking mighty fine, Mr. uh, Lynton." Timothy perused the fields, corral, barn, and house. "Looks like you've nearly finished restoring the house and the fields look as though the place was never neglected."

Thank You, Lord, for Timothy. Always at the ready to make matters more comfortable. "Yes," said Ruby. "I agree with my…Timothy. My assistant, that is. This place has taken quite a different appearance since you've set your mind to rehabilitating it. Why, when I was on your porch, I surmised how nice it must have been to sit in that rotting rocking chair and gaze upon the lovely green fields. You have done a fine job, Mr. Lynton. The place was in such disrepair."

Mr. Lynton offered not even the slightest of smiles in response to Ruby's gushing about his farm. No matter. Ruby had experience with sour individuals. She worked for Mr. O'Kane, after all.

"What is it you want?"

"Are you perchance the Mr. Jake Lynton who rescued four children in Cornwall from drowning?" The words tumbled from her mouth. "You're a hero, and I *must* have your story on paper and share your bravery with others. Might I interview you for *Ruby's Horizon Happenings*?"

"Go away."

"I beg your pardon?"

"I said, 'go away'."

How could Mr. Lynton be so rude? It was almost the twentieth century and most folks were much more corrigible. Such an uncouth man. Had his ma taught him nary a manner?

"Are you indeed the Mr. Jake Lynton who saved a family in Cornwall from drowning?"

"Yes, and you'll need to leave."

"But I'd appreciate it if you'd allow me to interview you."

"I'm not interested in an interview."

"Perhaps we could meet another time. I can see you have work to do, and I'd be willing to return when your schedule is less robust."

Jake Lynton shook his head. "Never will my schedule be less robust, and never will I give you an interview."

Ruby's jaw dropped. Mr. Lynton was insolent for certain. The tears burned her eyes at his harshness. And the fact that she would never be able to retain her position at the newspaper if Mr. Lynton refused. "May I ask why?"

"No. And I have nothing else to say. I trust you both can see yourselves off my property."

Ruby pursed her lips. "Surely you will consider my request and change your mind?"

"No. Now please leave."

She stared at him a minute to see if he might soften a bit. But Mr. Lynton stood, arms folded across his broad chest and a glower on his face. The next words fell from her mouth—words that wouldn't likely secure an interview with the man anytime soon. "Come along, Timothy. It appears there will be no talking any sense into this ill-mannered individual."

A moment later, Timothy assisted her into the buggy. "Can you believe that man, Timothy?"

"I think you might have been more polite yourself if you're wanting an interview, Rubes. I'm sure he didn't appreciate being called a farmhand when he owns his own farm. Likely didn't appreciate being called ill-mannered either." He paused. "Isn't there a saying about catching more flies with honey than vinegar?"

Ruby hadn't asked for Timothy's opinion. She whipped her head to the side to peer at the passing scenery. As for being kind to Mr. Lynton, well, she'd tried. Hadn't she?

"Look, Rubes. Don't be vexed at me. The man is a grump, that's the truth, but it's his right not to give an interview. Some folks don't like being fussed over."

"Whose side are you on?"

"Yours. Always yours. Well, in the case of Mr. Lynton and you." He transferred the reins to one hand and patted her arm. "You could always take him some of your famous white ginger cookies. That might do the trick."

Ruby hadn't thought of that. Perhaps if she did come bearing cookies, Mr. Lynton would be so overjoyed to have a home-cooked delicacy that he'd grant her the interview posthaste. "That might work, Timothy. Thank you for the suggestion."

"Reckon that's why you consider me your assistant and all."

Timothy's lopsided grin warmed Ruby's heart. He needn't be the brunt of her frustration with Mr. Lynton. "You're an accomplished one at that. Not sure what I'd do without you. What say we pay the man another visit on Monday, ginger cookies in hand? That will give me some time to send up some prayers and prepare the best batch of cookies I've ever baked."

"If all else fails, Mama has that worn cookbook written by that Augusta woman you could refer to."

"You're right. This is a fail-proof plan, Timothy. So, will you accompany me next Monday?"

Timothy nodded. "Sure. How are the curtains for my house coming along?"

The curtains for Timothy's house had been slightly delayed but were coming along well. "They will be done soon," she promised.

Ruby welcomed the challenge her next visit with the hermit would bring. Next Monday couldn't come quickly enough.

Jake watched as his visitors left his farm. Ma would have his hide and then some for being an insolent cad as far as the newspaperwoman was concerned. Her exaggerated notions had nearly made him laugh.

Nearly.

Good thing he had a full face of hair or she might have seen the struggle he faced with not chuckling at some of her words.

However...if that nosy Ruby woman thought he'd give her words for her gossipy article, she was sorely incorrect. He'd never give an interview, especially not to a reporter for the newspaper. Sure, she was pretty and all with her lovely hair—albeit covered by that obnoxious hat—sparkling green eyes, and slender figure, but he'd not let her beauty dissuade him.

The buggy made its way around the bend, and Jake lost sight of it. Just as well.

A question lingered in his mind—how did the newspaper-woman find out about the rescue? Who had told her? The last thing he wanted was for folks in Horizon to know about his failures to save both Corbin and Mr. Strain.

Nothing was worth his failures being unveiled. He'd protect those secrets at all costs.

Chapter Twelve

THE FOLLOWING MONDAY ARRIVED quickly, although not quickly enough for Ruby. Early in the morning, she set to baking ginger cookies. Perhaps the delivery of the treats might persuade Mr. Lynton to reconsider his refusal to be interviewed.

Ruby reached into one of Mama's kitchen cupboards and retrieved a circular cookie tin. She'd been saving the tin for a special occasion such as this. Tracing the intricate artwork on the top of the tin with her finger, Ruby wondered who had painted the elaborate meshing of lavender, green, and rose-colored flowers. She then placed an embroidered doily inside the tin. She mused how her ability to plan for additional time to seek more information from her interviewee proved she possessed the necessary capability to achieve her writing goals.

She had writer's instinct for sure.

Holding the ornate container in her hand, she went outside to where Timothy hitched the horses to the buggy, yet another prayer on her lips about Mr. Lynton acquiescing to her request.

Timothy met her near the barn. "Ready?" he asked.

"As I'll ever be."

Timothy eyed the tin. "Did I mention a fee for driving you to Mr. Lynton's today? Again?" He held out his hand. "One for the way there, and one for the way back."

"You can have these cookies anytime."

Timothy snorted. "Does the fact that I'm half-starved make a difference?"

"Didn't you just eat breakfast?"

"Three hours ago. Farming is hard work." He patted his stomach. "Men have died of starvation eating far more."

Ruby pried open the lid and deposited two cookies into Timothy's hand. He devoured one without even chewing it. "I hope you marry someone who knows how to cook or I'll be one brother less."

Timothy gulped and started on the second cookie—the one supposedly reserved for the return trip. "I don't plan on marrying, Rubes. It's me, my farm, and numerous trips to Mama and Papa's for three meals a day."

"You say that now, but just wait until some woman captures your fancy."

They climbed into the buggy, and Timothy flicked the reins. "Won't happen. I'm too busy anyhow."

There were at least three women in Horizon who fancied Timothy. He didn't cotton to any of them, despite their persistent efforts to win his heart. His dream of farming came to fruition, and that demanded all of his time—with the exception of church, visiting with family, and eating. "Even though you have your own farm, there must be some inclination to marry someday."

"Someday. When I'm forty."

"Forty?"

"Look at Miss Greta and the Lieutenant. They were older when they married."

"I don't think you want to be *that* old when you fall in love. Besides, God may have other plans."

"Far be it from me to argue with the Lord, but reckon I'm doing just fine farming and driving you hither and yon."

How very different they were! Ruby would love to be married yet had no prospects. Timothy loathed the idea and had three prospects. "I do appreciate you driving me hither and yon, dear brother."

"And I appreciate the curtains, the help hauling rocks, and the occasional food donations."

"Occasional?" Ruby had spent the better part of several days measuring and sewing curtains for Timothy's cabin and stocking his shelves with canned goods she and Mama prepared from last year's crops.

"Say, Rubes, maybe you could explain the situation to Mr. O'Kane about how Mr. Lynton hasn't been willing to allow an interview." Timothy scrunched his nose—a nose he'd inherited from Mama.

"If I don't secure this interview, Mr. O'Kane has made it clear I will never write for *The Horizon Herald* again. He refuses to listen to any excuses, legitimate or not."

"You could get a job at Wilhelmina's or the mercantile."

Ruby traced the design on the tin's lid. "And I will if need be. Or I'll take in washing or sewing, but I have always dreamed of being a writer. It would challenge me to allow that dream to perish." She thought again about the Lord directing a person's path. Did God have something different in mind for her? It certainly wasn't marriage, given the lack of options. She recalled her recent conversation with Maribel. *"Do you think God always gives us the desires of our hearts?"*

"It does depend on those desires and if they are in line with His will. Psalm 37:4 promises that if we delight ourselves in Him, He will give us the desires of our heart."

What if the desires of her heart—to marry, have a family, and write—were not God's desires for her? Would He give her peace if she never attained any of those things?

When she and Timothy arrived at the Lynton farm, Ruby caught a glimpse of Mr. Lynton mending a fence. He didn't turn to greet them when they stopped on the road in front of his house. That didn't surprise her. Apparently, Mr. Lynton had few guests and she could figure out why. His disposition wasn't top-notch.

On the other hand, Mr. Lynton's dog wagged his tail and seemed thrilled for the company. Ruby handed the tin and her notebook to Timothy, then leaned down to pat the collie's head. "How are you today, boy?"

He wagged his tail all the more and licked Ruby's hand. She smiled and patted him again before returning upright. The animal reminded her of Mae's dog, Beans. Perhaps someday if the Lord blessed her with a family, she'd also add a pet.

The man finally pivoted, strode toward them, and faced Ruby and Timothy but said nothing. He narrowed his deep blue eyes.

Ruby pushed aside the thought of his deep blue eyes that reminded her of the perfect summer day when nary a cloud was visible in the sky. For surely they were the only handsome thing on Jake Lynton's bedraggled self.

Mr. Lynton looked warily from her to Timothy and then focused his gaze on her. She took a deep breath and pasted on her best smile. "I brought you some of my famous ginger cookies." She extended the tin to him.

He took it from her, a curious glance on his face. Was that the beginning of a tiny smile on his partially-covered mouth? "Thank you."

Ruby attempted to hide her shock. So the man did have some manners after all. "You're quite welcome, Mr. Lynton. I was wondering if you've given any further thought to allowing me to interview you about your bravery in Cornwall."

If it was a tiny smile that had started to sprout on Mr. Lynton's face, it quickly disappeared. "So you've resorted to bribery, have you?"

Timothy chuckled and she cast her best glower his way.

"It doesn't matter if you bring me five thousand tins of your favorite ginger cookies, I'm not going to allow you to interview me."

"Please reconsider, Mr. Lynton. This is of grave importance."

"All I see is a nosy reporter looking for a story that could negatively affect the life of another. Why would I agree to that?"

"I don't understand. Why would your story negatively affect the life of another? People nearly drowned. But you, Mr. Lynton, pulled them to rescue. How many others would do the same?"

"Every man I know would do the same and a better job of it at that."

"You saved four people from what I've heard. How can that not be courageous?"

"Who told you about me saving anyone?"

Ruby pondered his question. "My brother-in-law over-heard some people in Cornwall discussing it. Folks in Horizon would be eager to hear such a story of gallantry."

"I won't be giving an interview. Not now, not ever. Now please leave as I have work to do."

"With such a dour disposition, I'm not surprised you don't have more company."

"Who says I don't have more company?" Mr. Lynton looked Ruby straight in the eye as if they both agreed to a stare-down.

Timothy tugged on her arm. "Come on, let's go. Mr. Lynton has said he's not interested in an interview."

"Just a moment, Timothy. Mr. Lynton, I am not your enemy. I only wish for an interview."

"And I only wish for peace and quiet and for you to re-alize no amount of bribery will get you an interview with me. Reckon I should notify the sheriff of your constant visits and your continual efforts to pester me."

"You wouldn't dare."

Jake Lynton's eyes glinted. "I wouldn't?"

"The sheriff is notified when a crime has been commit-ted. Not when someone is paying a friendly visit to their neighbor."

"Are we neighbors?"

"My family lives just down the road, so I imagine so."

"Thank you for the cookies. I have work to do." The insolent man turned on his heel and walked away without another word.

Leaving Ruby to ponder what she would say when Mr. O'Kane inquired as to the status of her article with the cantankerous Jake Lynton.

After the annoying reporter left, Jake opened the tin and perused the contents. Perfectly shaped round cookies greeted him. The aroma filled his nostrils and his stomach growled.

Jake sunk his teeth into one of the cookies. He closed his eyes and savored the bite. How had the newspaper reporter known that he had a weakness for cookies? He recalled once as a child when he'd given in to the temptation to eat every single one of the fourteen cookies in the cookie jar on the table. Ma had spent most of the day baking for the church potluck. When she tended to Corbin, who'd just awakened from his nap, Jake saw an opportunity he could not refuse.

The plate of cookies beckoned him, and he climbed on the chair and perched on the table. Pa would have had his hide and then some just for the simple fact of reclining on the table cross-legged as though it were a chair. Jake devoured the cookies, leaving not even a minuscule crumb behind for the folks at the potluck. Ma had not been happy. Neither had Jake's belly.

Jake missed Ma. He missed his sister. He missed the camaraderie at supper. He missed working beside Pa in the fields. When he decided to leave that day, Pa said nothing and didn't attempt to stop him. Ma clutched his arm as tears shone in her blue eyes. *"Jake, please stay. Don't go."*

"I love you, Ma," was all he'd said in return before mounting his horse and riding away without so much as a second glance.

Seeing his mother's pain—pain he'd caused by leaving—felt like a knife to his heart. She hadn't known that he struggled to restrain his own tears.

What was done was done. Jake had hurt Ma something fierce with his choice to leave. And there was no going back and attempting to set things to right. Not with Pa after Jake's negligence with Corbin and not with Ma after his calloused goodbye.

He lifted his eyes to the mountains in the distance and a verse he'd memorized as a young'un came to mind. *"I will lift up mine eyes unto the hills, from whence cometh my help. My help cometh from the LORD, which made heaven and earth."* The psalm lodged in his throat as he whispered it aloud.

For many years, he believed his help came from the Lord. But now?

Jake shook the thoughts aside. To allow such ponderings only allowed invited to settle into his heart.

With effort, he returned his thoughts to the cookies. A whiff of ginger filled his nostrils, and he inhaled deeply. He casually peered behind him, but only a waning plume of dust remained from the buggy where the newspaper reporter and her assistant had driven away once he'd rudely dismissed them.

He blew out a deep breath. Ma hadn't raised him to be anything but gentlemanly, yet he'd been anything but with the attractive woman who'd insisted he tell his story. Perhaps if he'd met her in town, at a barn dance, or at church, he might have welcomed the opportunity to talk with her, to get acquainted with her. She was easy on the eyes and despite the fact her featherbrained idea to get his story annoyed him, he did appreciate her determination and spunk.

Jake took a bite of another cookie and allowed it to melt in his mouth before starting on a third. Samson pawed at his leg. "What do you think of this whole mess, boy?"

Samson wagged his tail and eyed the tin of cookies. The dog seemed to like the newspaperwoman, but then Samson liked everybody. "I reckon she's a pesky one. Pretty though." He offered a small bite to Samson, who devoured it and begged for more.

Had Jake's life been different—if he'd been different—Jake might have shown interest in the woman. He might have someday asked her father for permission to take her for a ride along the meadows that edged the river. Jake might have relived the hope of someday having a wife and children. A good woman to love and to love him in return. One with whom to share his life. Likely that woman wouldn't be the one who'd graced his doorstep seeking a story, but whoever it was, Jake would love her the way Pa loved Ma.

But Jake wasn't different and there was no changing the past.

The only thing he had to be sure of was that Ruby of *Ruby's Horizon Happenings* didn't expose the past he wasn't proud of.

CHAPTER THIRTEEN

RUBY TAPPED HER PENCIL on the small desk in her room. She perused the things she'd written in her notebook about Jake Lynton.

All of one scant paragraph.

She had no story. Only a few notes as the number of days to be able to save her job dwindled.

The words "hero" jumped out at her from her notebook page. Mr. Lynton *was* a hero. His remarkable and sacrificial story of how God used him to save the lives of others demanded attention within the pages of *The Horizon Herald*. In such a bleak world with so much pain and suffering, a story such as this offered hope. So why wouldn't he oblige? It was the question that plagued her not only in her waking moments, but also when she ought to be sleeping. After all, how often did someone save not one, but four people from drowning?

Yesterday Ruby asked a few folks in town about Mr. Lynton, and she reached the same conclusion—of the few who even knew of whom she spoke, they all said the same thing. That he lived a life of solitude on his farm and rarely visited town except to procure the necessary supplies. Ruby had never seen Jake Lynton at church, and as inquisitive as she was, she would have noticed.

In desperation, she'd prepared three other story ideas for Mr. O'Kane. All failed to entice her former employer to rehire her. She'd prayed, sought God's wisdom, and talked to Mama, Papa, and Maribel about it.

Ruby folded her hands and closed her eyes. *Lord, please show me what I ought to do. Should I proceed? Accept that the job at* The Horizon Herald *is no longer Your will, but was for only a time? If that is the case, I pray for contentment in whatever You may have for me now. Father, I also pray that You would search my heart and know my thoughts. I pray for a pure heart and an unselfish motive in seeking this story. May all I write be for Your glory. In Jesus' Name, Amen.*

She tapped her fingers on the desk. Perhaps there was no way to convince Mr. Lynton to allow her an interview. The constant asking hadn't worked. The ginger cookies hadn't worked.

What could she do? Visit him one last time and beg and plead?

Lord, please guide my steps.

Jake wiped the sweat from his brow. While farming was strenuous work, he wouldn't trade it for any other occupation. He ladled water from the bucket just as Samson barked. Not the usual bark if he saw a rock chuck or heard a coyote at night, but an ongoing yelp combined with a growl.

A man and woman in a buggy stood near the barn.

A man and a woman Jake did not recognize.

Who had found him now?

They didn't appear to be peddlers, and from the sounds of Samson's nonstop barking, he was as thrilled they were there as Jake was.

Jake contemplated flattening himself and hiding behind the cornstalks, but the couple had already seen him.

The woman waved. "Hello!"

Samson growled, and with a frustrated sigh, Jake trekked their way.

"Are you Mr. Lynton?"

"Who's asking?"

"Well, I am, of course." The sloe-eyed tall and slender woman was somewhat attractive with her black hair, pale face, and fancy clothing. She fluttered her eyes at Jake, provoking a glare from her male companion.

Jake gave a clipped nod in the man's direction. "And you are?"

The man extended a soft hand and did his best to offer a handshake that was nothing but weak.

"I am Mr. Kuchel and I manage The Horizon Hotel, and this is Miss O'Kane, a reporter from *The Horizon Herald*."

"Yes, I write *Lillian's Horizon Happenings*. You might have heard of it."

"Not interested." Jake prepared to turn back from whence he came to finish tending to his chores.

Miss O'Kane pursed her lips in exaggerated fashion. "How do you know the purpose of our visit?"

"If you're a reporter from the newspaper, you're either selling a subscription or wanting to interview me. Neither of which are of interest to me.

Mr. Kuchel narrowed his eyes. "Perhaps we are here on hotel business. What then?"

"Same answer. Why would I care about staying at your hotel when I have a place to live right here?"

The woman stepped closer. "They were right about what they said about you."

"And that is?"

"That you're a mountain man. A hermit. Hiding something."

Mr. Kuchel harrumphed. "Hardly a mountain man when he lives in the valley."

"I am merely requesting an interview from you regarding saving the people from the Cornwall River." She opened a notebook and poised her pencil as if ready to write his answers.

"Just like I told the other newspaperwoman, I'm not interested in giving an interview now or ever."

Miss O'Kane's dark eyebrows raised into her hairline. "The other newspaperwoman? You must mean Ruby." She crinkled her nose and tucked her chin slightly in disgust. "Well, suffice it to say, she is not an authentic reporter but rather a woman hoping to make a name for herself." She lifted her chin and fluttered a hand just beneath it. "I, on the other hand, am an award-winning reporter who has earned the trust of Horizon residents near and far."

At this, the man jerked his head in agreement. "Indeed you are, Lillian."

The woman leaned toward him as if to share a secret and lowered her voice. "Did you really tell Ruby you wouldn't allow her to interview now or ever?"

Jake briefly pondered why that was important to her. "Yes, and I'm saying the same thing to you. Award-winning or not, I won't be giving you an interview."

Miss O'Kane inclined her head sideways. "But you told Ruby you wouldn't be giving her an interview, correct?"

"Don't be daft, Lillian, that's what he said," hissed Mr. Kuchel.

The woman glowered at her companion, then opened her mouth as if she might say something more to Jake but thought better of it.

Samson toddled over to her but didn't wag his tail.

"Go away, dog. I don't want your messy paws on my dress." To Jake, she added, "If you're sure you won't change your mind…"

"I'm sure. I have work to do, so if you'll excuse me. Come on, Samson." He touched the brim of his hat, and Samson followed Jake back to his chores.

A disconcerted thought lodged in his mind. How many people now knew he'd saved the four children?

Ruby hoisted some rocks into the back of the wagon then arched her back to relieve the stiffness. The sun blazed down and she briefly removed her bonnet and patted her dampened hair. She was thankful she'd tugged on a pair of trousers Timothy had outgrown to assist him with hauling rocks today. Skirts and blistering mid-day Idaho summer days did not mix. Nor were they conducive to bending, lifting, and trudging through the dirt and sagebrush. Tearing her skirt and subsequently tripping over it was a real concern.

She lifted her gaze to heaven and allowed the warmth of the sun to rest on her face for the briefest of moments before replacing the bonnet and tying the strings beneath her chin. She then reached for the ladle and drank the refreshment.

Timothy removed his hat and dumped a ladleful of water on top of his head. "Reckon it's a hot one today. Much obliged for your help, Rubes. When we get this section cleared, there'll be plenty of room for planting." Timothy stood taller, pressed his shoulders back, and deepened his voice. "As Papa always says, 'Never waste a usable portion of land.'"

Ruby laughed. "You sound just like him. And you're welcome." She'd assisted him numerous times since spring so his dream of planting every available field next year would come to fruition. She veered her attention to the rock-covered ground. They'd made progress, albeit slowly. "And thank you for accompanying me to interviews."

"Glad to do it."

Ruby only needed him when interviewing menfolk at their homes if they had no wife or their wives weren't present, but in an effort to pen as many articles as possible, the number of those interviews had increased to an impressive number. Or at least she thought it was impressive, although Mr. O'Kane would surely disagree.

She released a deep breath. Now if only Mr. Lynton would accede to her request.

"Thinking of Mr. Lynton?"

"How'd you guess?"

"Farmer's instinct?"

Ruby laughed. "Well, you're right. I only wish I could write this article and be done with it. That Mr. O'Kane would consider it well-written enough to rehire me."

"Do you plan to ask Mr. Lynton again?"

"One more time and then..." Ruby's voice trailed. And then, barring another idea, she'd have to settle with finding another job so she could assist Mama and Papa with expenses and pay off her loan on the typewriter. She envisioned the diminutive, ill-mannered Mr. Sanders attempting to lug her prized possession down the board-walk and into the bank where he'd auction it off to the highest bidder in an attempt to recoup his losses. It still amazed her he'd given her a loan at all. It could have had something to do with the Lieutenant standing behind her that day with a deposit from Miss Greta's with a scowl on his face because things were taking longer than he'd like.

Ruby forced her thoughts back to the present. "Do you think I should forego asking Mr. Lynton one more time?"

"No harm in one more time. I know you're fixing to get discouraged, but maybe you could find someone else to interview who'd be just as good. Mr. Lynton is a hero and all, but he hasn't taken kindly to your pestering."

She tossed a pointed look at her brother. "Pestering?"

"Badgering?"

Ruby elbowed him in the ribs and Timothy chuckled. "All right. Coercion. With the cookies and all."

"Timothy Tyler Shepherdson, it was not coercion."

But Timothy slapped his thigh then bent over and howled with amusement. He snorted a few times, then raised the pitch of his voice and planted a hand on his waist. "Here,

Mr. Lynton, have a ginger cookie. Have two. Have an entire tinful. Just tell me your story."

Ruby dipped the ladle in the bucket and flung the water his way. It hit its target.

"Hey!" Timothy reached his grimy hand into the bucket and slashed her back.

The water war continued until they'd emptied it.

Ruby flopped onto the edge of the wagon and patted her wet sleeves. "You do realize we'll have to return home if we get thirsty."

"I'm thinking we'll be done soon anyhow. Isn't it time for the noonday meal?"

"We already ate the noonday meal."

"We did?" Timothy rubbed the back of his neck. "I don't rightly recall. Are you sure?"

"I'm sure."

"All right then. The afternoon meal."

Ruby shook her head. "Says the one who could eat all the food in the house and the cellar and still be hungry. Where do you put it all?"

Timothy patted his puny stomach. "What can I say? I have a bottomless pit. Besides, I'm growing."

"In height maybe, but not width. You're still a lilliput-ian."

"A lili what?"

Ruby did her utmost best to keep a straight face, but Timothy's furrowed brow made it impossible. She tittered for several seconds before regaining control. "A lilliput-ian means diminutive, dinky, pint-sized. It also means underfed..." Ruby clutched her stomach and giggled. "But you are clearly not underfed."

They traded a few more good-natured jests before Timothy sobered. "If you want, I'll go with you to ask Mr. Lynton
one more time. I'm tuckered out and could use some time
away from the farm."

"Today?" Hope filled Ruby. Would Mr. Lynton finally say
yes?

"Sure, but you might oughta change into a dress."

Ruby's heart raced faster than normal, and she tapped her
notebook against her knee as Timothy parked the buggy
near Mr. Lynton's home. Apparently, the man was inside
because he was nowhere to be seen in the nearby vicinity.

"I'll see if he's home," Ruby said as Timothy assisted her
from the buggy.

Timothy nodded and leaned his tall, thin self against the
buggy. "You're sure this won't take long?"

"I promise it won't take long."

With one hand, Ruby lifted the edge of her skirt and
confidently strode toward the front door, all the while looking about for her interviewee. She knocked and waited. *Mr.
Lynton, please don't ignore me.* However, due to the time of
day and the extensive farmwork he would undertake, it was
likely Mr. Lynton would be in the fields working rather than
reclining in his home.

She rubbed a clean spot on the filthy window with her
palm, pressed her nose against it, and peered inside. Most
everything was in its proper place, she'd give him that, save
for a few cups and plates stacked near the sink. The room

contained a round wooden table with spindly legs and four chairs, a cook stove, and a shelf with a meager collection of assorted dishes. A rock fireplace lined the wall near the kitchen. She squinted. It appeared a Bible was atop the mantle.

He needed curtains on his windows. What a character he would be if she were writing a fictional story!

But alas, Ruby was writing a story of truth and whether the peculiar man had curtains or not was of no concern to her. She shielded her hands over her eyes and scanned the fields for Mr. Lynton. She chewed on her lip then flipped open her notebook to the page she'd need for the interview, should she convince the man to agree to an interview.

Ruby took a step back and scribbled in her notebook: *home is typical of an unmarried man, which due to prior investigations, I believe Mr. Lynton to be. His house is free of clutter and overt disorder but is not dusted or mopped. Appears Mr. Lynton has lived here for some time.* What on earth did this information do for her story? Maybe nothing. But she wouldn't know until she began to piece together the words for her column.

"Uh, Ruby?" Timothy's voice sounded behind her. Without turning around or taking even the smallest peek at him, she waved him away with her free hand.

"Not now, Timothy," she hissed.

She closed her eyes and struggled for the correct words to write, then balanced the notebook on the window without pressing too hard, and wrote: *Why is Jake Lynton in Horizon? Where is his family? What is he hiding?* Ruby giggled. Her questions sounded more like a mystery dime novel than an article for *Ruby's Horizon Happenings.*

"Ruby!" Timothy called her name again, but she chose to ignore him. He couldn't possibly understand the implications of interrupting a writer while she was in a thought.

Jake Lynton lived a very ordinary life. A farmer who devoted his life to his crops, he had no idea his life was about to change the day he came upon four people in need of rescue. No one would have suspected someone like Mr. Lynton to be a hero. He was a scruffy sort with matted brown hair and a beard long ignored. A grown ragamuffin, if you will. But appearances can deceive, and...

The words came quicker than she could scribble them.

"Rubes!"

She did not turn around and continued to write while simultaneously imploring her brother to exercise patience. "Ssh. I'll be but a moment, Timothy. I don't plan to lollygag any longer than necessary, but I do need to conduct some research."

"But..."

Ruby scribbled more words.

"Ruby Caroline..."

Timothy *never* used her middle name. She nearly pivoted to see what was the matter, but she best not be too impetuous or she'd lose the thoughts completely. Writer's instinct told her to write while she could—and all that she could—while the words flowed freely. *It was an ordinary day, but unbeknownst to Mr. Lynton, the Lord had plans for him to make a difference in the lives of others.* That was true, right? Perhaps if she was vague enough in her story...

"Uh, Ruby?"

"Timothy Tyler. I have neither the time nor the fortitude to argue with you. I am trying to uncover important details."

Her brother did not respond, and Ruby continued pressing on the notebook and writing any random musings that came to mind. She interrupted herself with a prayer thanking the Lord he only blessed her with one younger brother, then penned more words on the paper.

"Ma'am?"

Her breath caught and her lungs squeezed. That voice was not Timothy's.

Ruby closed the notebook and turned ever so slowly around to face Mr. Lynton.

"Was going to tell you that you might want to skedaddle," said Timothy, not in the least being a helpful sort at present.

Mr. Lynton had removed his hat and had pressed it against his leg. His brow furrowed. "Ma'am, might I ask what you are doing?"

"Well, I—"

"Was snooping around my place?"

"Not exactly *snooping*. You see, I had a thought and figured it best to pen it, even if this was an inopportune time."

Mr. Lynton set his hat on the nearby chair and held out his hand, palm up. "I'd like to see what you wrote."

"I'd rather not."

The man gestured for her to hand it to him. "Since it's about me, I'd appreciate seeing if it's accurate."

Ruby hesitantly handed the notebook to Mr. Lynton, open to the page she'd been writing on.

Mr. Lynton studied the page. Ruby cringed at what he'd think about what she'd penned, and Timothy took a step forward. "Sir, please forgive her for the words she's written. You see, she can be a flibbertigibbet sometimes."

Ruby elbowed Timothy in the ribs. "You're not helping."

"Ouch!"

"I'm not a flibbertigibbet, Mr. Lynton."

"Well, Ruby, you kinda are. Or maybe just a birdbrain at times."

Ruby pressed her lips together and gave her best glower at Timothy. When she'd collected some of her pride, she said to Mr. Lynton, "I am merely a reporter who aims to share truthful stories with the folks of Horizon."

She doubted he was listening because he gazed intently at the page and read aloud—"*He was a scruffy sort with matted brown hair and a beard long ignored. A grown ragamuffin, if you will.*" Mr. Lynton looked up and stared at her. "A grown ragamuffin?"

"Not a ragamuffin. Perhaps that's the wrong word. Maybe just disheveled?"

"Or unkempt?" he offered.

Ruby squeezed her eyes closed. If only she'd waited to write her thoughts. If only she'd listened when Timothy attempted to secure her attention. She searched her mind for the words to say that would alleviate some of the horrific embarrassment she was enduring at present. A few hopefully valuable words came to mind when she heard a low rumble. She flung her eyes open to see Mr. Lynton's eyes crinkling at the corners. His mouth, so dreadfully obscured by facial hair, opened and a rumble of a laugh emerged.

The perplexed expression on the reporter woman's face was priceless. The dimple in her chin ever more prominent and the way her eyes rounded and her mouth formed an "o" caused Jake to laugh even harder. While he didn't cotton to being called a grown ragamuffin or a scruffy sort with matted brown hair and a beard long ignored, it *was* true.

"Sir, I don't understand," she squeaked.

He handed the notebook back to her.

He'd not admit it, but she drew him in with her beauty and feistiness, even if she refused to leave him alone. He needed to sober before she realized she'd managed to break through his tough exterior. "Ma'am—Miss Ruby—"

"Yes?"

"While your description of me is amusing, I won't be relenting and giving you or that other woman an interview, no matter how many times either of you stop by for a visit."

"The other woman?"

"Yes, the one who dropped by here the other day."

Ruby bit her lip. "Might I ask for a description of her appearance?"

"Black hair, pale face, fancy clothing."

The woman drew a sharp intake of breath. "Lillian?"

"I don't rightly recall her last name."

"Lillian O'Kane." The newspaperwoman pursed her lips and clutched her notebook tightly against her chest. "Why was she here?"

"Wanted an interview."

"This isn't her story."

Jake wanted to reiterate that it was no one's story but his own, but he could see Ruby was a bit festered from hearing the other reporter paid him a visit.

"Who accompanied her?"

"I suspect it was her assistant, much like your assistant."

This time, the skinny young man frowned. "Doubt I'm anything like Lillian's assistant."

"Was the assistant approximately the same height as Lillian with swooped reddish hair, a ruddy complexion, and a spindly build?"

The woman was obviously a writer. "Reckon he was. I believe his name was Kuchel."

"Mr. Kuchel. Oh, yes." She thumped her toe on the porch. "The audacity of them both."

Jake could see she was seething. "Ma'am, you have no worries because I won't be telling her my story either."

"Ruby is much obliged for that. Come on, let's go." The young man whom she'd called Timothy pulled gently on her arm. "Mr. Lynton, thank you for your time and all, but we best go."

The woman acquiesced and allowed Timothy to assist her to the buggy. As he watched them leave, Jake contemplated her reaction to him telling her about the other reporter. Was the other woman attempting to undermine Ruby's job at the newspaper?

He took pity on her and almost waved them back so he could answer a few questions, but then he thought better of it. There were numerous other people Ruby could write about.

Jake smoothed his beard. Did she really think him disheveled and unkempt? And why did it matter?

CHAPTER FOURTEEN

RUBY CHORUSED HER "AMEN" after Papa prayed. Family supper with those she loved most was one of her favorite events. Gratitude filled her heart as she looked at each one of her family members. All around the table, all praying together, all sharing about their lives.

"And how is the interview going with Mr. Lynton?" asked Mae as she cut up pieces of the meatloaf for Pansy.

A sigh escaped her lips. "He still hasn't agreed."

Lucy tossed her an encouraging glance. "I'm sorry, Rubes. I know how much you'd like for him to agree to the interview."

"And how many times we've been to his farm and asked him," added Timothy with a shake of his head.

"Only a handful of times, mind you, but this last time was my final attempt."

Mama passed the potatoes to Papa. "Unless..." a sparkle gleamed in her eye,

When Mama had an idea, it was always worthwhile to sit up and take notice. "Yes?" Ruby chirped, unable to hide the excitement that trickled from her lips with just that one word.

"Why don't you and Timothy travel to Cornwall and interview the parents of the children Mr. Lynton saved?"

Ruby nearly knocked her cup of milk over in her enthusiasm. "Yes. That's a marvelous idea."

"The parents could very well agree to be interviewed." Velma held Baby Albert in her arms. He rested peacefully, the commotion not causing him to stir at all.

Landon set his fork on his plate. "I'll supply two train tickets."

Timothy leaned back in his chair. "And yes, Ruby, I'll accompany you."

"Thank you, Timothy. Thank you, Landon. And thank you, Mama, for the idea. This just might work."

If Mr. Lynton wouldn't allow her to interview him, then Ruby would interview the ones he'd saved. After all, there was more than one way around this debacle, and Ruby was determined, if not tenacious. She would succeed at this endeavor and reclaim her job no matter what it took.

On Tuesday morning, she and Timothy sat aboard the train awaiting its departure. Her heartbeat accelerated as the train's whistle blew, and she closed her eyes for a brief moment and rested against the back of the seat. Enthusiasm rippled through her, and although travel by rail was significantly faster than by horse and wagon, she couldn't arrive in Cornwall soon enough.

The train jolted, then chugged down the tracks. Ruby flung her eyes open and waved at Mama, Lucy, and Mae, who had come to see them off. Timothy shook his right knee as he always did when in an exciting or anxiety-provoking situation. She stared at her younger brother's profile. He resembled Papa so closely with the dark hair and blue eyes, and with Mama's snub nose, no one would miss the fact he was a Shepherdson.

And Ruby didn't know what she'd do without the brother who faithfully assisted her on her myriad of assignments. "I really appreciate you coming with me, Timothy, what with the crops."

"Happy to help."

Yes, Timothy could be ornery and irritating at times, but his loyalty, dependability, and generosity more than made up for it.

"I know you're nervous about this, Rubes, but it will all work out."

Spoken just like a man who always saw the brighter side of things. Yes, he may strongly resemble Papa, but he didn't have the tendency to borrow worry like their father sometimes did. "Thank you, Timothy. I hope we'll be able to locate the children who were rescued without too much effort." She thought of how they'd arrive in Cornwall early that morning and leave several hours later for the return trip to Horizon. It didn't leave much time. They'd have to be efficient.

"Surprised you're doubting your investigative skills."

"My investigative skills might be exceptional at times, but obviously my persuasive skills are not as Mr. Lynton won't budge on his denial for an interview."

"He likely has his reasons."

"True."

Timothy squeezed her upper arm. "It's not like you to give up, Rubes."

She had almost conceded several times. But to admit defeat would mean she'd never write for the paper again, even if it was a newspaper owned by a demanding boss. So Ruby persisted, although feelings of doubt often bombarded her. Was it really so important to write for *The Horizon Herald*? Was it really God's plan for her to be a reporter or was she attempting to be God's assistant and plan the future only He could orchestrate?

"Rubes?"

"Just thinking. The what-ifs have crowded my mind ever since Mr. O'Kane relieved me of my position."

"Understandable, but worrying about it rarely helps."

"Now you're sounding like Albert."

Timothy chuckled. "I am getting wiser in my older age."

"You are archaic." She leaned into him. "Thank you, Timothy, for coming with me and being willing to help. I know you have a million other things you could be doing."

"Although you can be a real pain sometimes, I am happy to oblige. Besides, I reckon there's some good food in Cornwall. Landon said the restaurant we'll be visiting has the best pork and beans."

"Ahh, the real reason Timothy Tyler Shepherson accompanies his sister on her journey for the truth." She elbowed her brother.

"That was one of the factors in helping me decide."

Ruby laughed. Timothy may be a nuisance but she couldn't do this job without him.

Ruby was grateful Landon had given them free tickets as this venture could prove to be a pricey one. If she retained her job, it was all worth it. Even if Timothy ate everything in sight at the Cornwall Bakery and Restaurant.

It was a challenge to wait until after they'd finished eating to ask the waitress about her knowledge of the near drowning. But the woman was nearly frantic at serving the sudden influx of customers, and Ruby did not want to add to her distress.

Timothy ate his entire meal with haste as if he hadn't eaten in days rather than mere hours. "You gonna eat your meatloaf, Rubes?"

She gaped at the generous portion of meatloaf, boiled rice, salad of watercress, and coffee. All worth the cost of twenty-five cents for each her and Timothy. However...she didn't necessarily have it in her budget since Mr. O'Kane still hadn't paid her for two articles from before he fired her. With a struggle, Ruby pushed the thought aside. This wasn't the time to have doubts. She was in Cornwall, Landon had paid for the tickets, Timothy had agreed to accompany her, and there was a strong chance she'd have an article for Mr. O'Kane that would allow her to keep her job.

Ruby pushed the rice around with her fork. Truth of the matter was, she just wasn't hungry.

Her stomach was tied in knots and her appetite was nil. She sipped her coffee. "No, you go ahead." Ruby nudged the plate toward Timothy.

Instead of being overjoyed at her benevolence, frown lines etched between Timothy's eyes and he shook his head. "Just joshing you, Rubes. You can have your meatloaf and the rest of it too."

"No, really, Timothy. You can have it if you'd like. It shouldn't go to waste."

Her brother regarded her, his characteristic pointy right eyebrow edging into his hairline. "Not to sound like Mama, but you do need your nourishment."

"There'll be plenty of time for nourishment after I secure an interview with the family."

After a few seconds of hesitation, Timothy shrugged. "Suit yourself." He cut the meatloaf into pieces and inhaled it.

"I sure hope Lillian doesn't convince Mr. Lynton to allow her to interview him."

Timothy gulped a bite, finished chewing quickly as if forgetting to savor it, and spoke. "Doubtful. He didn't sound too impressed by her. Not that anyone is, except Mr. O'Kane, that is."

"That's only because she's his brother's daughter, and he's obligated to like her."

"You're probably right." Timothy took a bite of the rice. "If Mr. Lynton isn't giving you an interview, he's not going to give her one either, and he said as much."

"Well, she is pretty."

Timothy wrinkled his nose. "Not really. She's not homely, but she's not pretty either."

"Mr. Lynton might think she is."

"Why would you care if Mr. Lynton thinks Lillian is pretty or not?" Timothy had stopped eating, and his pointy eyebrow arced again.

"I *don't* care. I was just saying that Lillian is pretty, and Mr. Lynton might think she's pretty, and therefore would acquiesce to giving her an interview."

"Well, she's not pretty, and I don't think Mr. Lynton cares about a person's appearance. He's irritable most of the time we've spoken with him."

Timothy had a point. Ruby doubted Mr. Lynton would be easily convinced, but still... "Lillian does have a way of hornswoggling people into doing what she wants." Why had Lillian attempted to interview Mr. Lynton in the first place when that was Ruby's assignment? "Something about her is suspicious. She has enough articles to write. Why would she try to take the one task that could return me to Mr. O'Kane's good graces?" If Ruby ever was in Mr. O'Kane's good graces.

"She's the queen of skullduggery if you ask me."

Ruby laughed at Timothy's statement. Lillian did present herself as dishonest, although Ruby tried to see the best in everyone, including her nemesis.

Several minutes later, their harried waitress asked if they wanted dessert. Ruby declined, but the look of anticipation on Timothy's face at the mention of boiled apple pudding was one she could not deny. She wondered where her brother stored all of the food he constantly ate. With his lean build, no one would guess he ate as much as Papa and Albert combined. "Go ahead," she said in answer to his unspoken inquiry. Without his help, she wouldn't have been able to make this trip, so even if she had to pay less on her typewriter loan this month, she'd do so to ensure he was adequately fed.

When the waitress returned with the dessert, Ruby saw this as an opportunity to ask her question. "Excuse me, ma'am, but do you know anything about the four children who were rescued recently from the South Fork of the Cornwall River?" Surely in the same restaurant where Landon heard the news, this waitress would know. And news likely traveled fast in Cornwall.

Ruby pushed her chair from the table and flipped open her notebook in preparation of any useful notations.

"Just that they were rescued by a man who jumped in after them."

"Do you by chance know the family's name?"

"I believe it was Mr. Gholston from the implement."

Ruby wrote the words in her notebook. "Do you know where I might find the implement?"

The waitress offered haphazard instructions. "I've never been there," she said, pushing a strand of blonde hair from her eyes. "But I know it's in that part of town not far from the South Fork."

"Thank you. Was Mr. Gholston present at the time?"

The waitress shrugged. "I'm not sure. All I know is a man from Horizon saved the children. You might find out some information at the newspaper office."

Ruby perused the fancy lettering on the window and gasped. Timothy nearly ran into the back of her. "Some notice before stopping suddenly might be nice," he said.

"My sincerest apologies. But look at that…"

"Another storefront. How interesting."

"Not just another storefront, dear brother, but the offices of *The Cornwall Courier*."

From Timothy's bored expression, one might have thought she mentioned it was a quilting circle. "I really must step inside, not only to see if they have any information about the children's rescue but also to see a *real* newspaper office."

"As long as it's brief. I believe you mentioned we were on a schedule. Your exact words were, 'It wouldn't behoove us to miss our return train home!'" Timothy raised his voice and flailed his arms about.

Ruby was not amused at Timothy's portrayal of her. "Pshaw. We've the time if we're efficient. It may be the only way we find out more information about where to find Mr. Gholston and the implement."

"The waitress already told us where to find the implement. Folks there will know where to find Mr. Gholston."

"But the newspaper may have written a story about the rescue. That would be most helpful to talk about with the reporter." She paused and sucked in a deep breath. "Besides, can you just imagine all the creativity behind that door? *The Cornwall Courier*...bringing the latest news to citizens of this fine town and beyond."

"And then he realized how dramatic his sister was."

"Not dramatic. Just overjoyed that we happened upon this way and that I'll be able to step foot inside *The Cornwall Courier*."

Timothy prattled on in disagreement, but Ruby was mesmerized by the fact that she would be stepping inside the newspaper business. Nothing could squelch her excitement. "I best go inside. Perhaps you could visit the..." she swiveled from left to right. "The millinery?"

"Funny, Ruby. Men don't visit millineries."

Several passersby ambled along, some nearly bumping into them, and Ruby stood to the side and faced the opposite direction, reluctantly removing her attention from *The Cornwall Courier*.

"Ooh! Look, Timothy. It's a tea shop. Perhaps you would enjoy spending time there whilst I'm in the newspaper office." Her broad grin did nothing to persuade her brother.

"I don't drink tea!" His Adam's apple bobbed double time with his declaration.

"You could always become someone who drinks tea. What is it they say? Broaden your horizons?"

Timothy's stubborn bent to his jaw told her he would not be broadening his horizons by drinking tea anytime soon.

"They likely have crumpets there as well. Just be careful with the fine china." Amusement rippled through Ruby at her brother's expression. She doubled over and squealed with laughter.

Meanwhile, Timothy was clearly annoyed. He scowled, "Poppycock, Rubes," before he patiently waited for Ruby to gather herself. Tears streamed down her face, the release of humor refreshing her soul. When she finally collected her wits, he continued. "And what's more, if we stand here while you chatter on about sending me to the millinery or tea shop, it'll be suppertime."

"You just ate the noonday meal. You're in no danger of starvation." She poked him in the stomach. A stomach that was as firm and flat as someone who ate far less than he did.

"A man such as myself needs sustenance. Often." Timothy scrutinized the line of businesses as folks bustled on either side of the street and numerous wagons and horses traveled along the dirt road in front of them.

"Is that a Stetson shop I see across the way?" Ruby asked.

Timothy squinted. The poor guy needed spectacles, but telling him so usually provoked an argument. "I think so," he finally said. "I'll meet you back here in ten minutes."

"All right." But neither she nor her brother had a time-piece, so ten minutes might as well be thirty. And while she needed to be efficient so as not to miss the train, she may need all of those thirty minutes inside the newspaper shop just to behold the amazing place where so many articles came to life.

Ruby bid Timothy farewell and wasted no more time opening the door of *The Cornwall Courier* and stepping inside. The delicious odor of paper and ink greeted her. A woman sat at the desk and numerous other workers partook in various duties. She angled her head to see two doors at the back of the business. Likely one led to the linotypes or multiple linotypes. Could she just remain here forever? For it truly was a writer's dream habitat.

"May I help you?" A woman in her forties with a stylish Gibson Girl coiffure asked. Suddenly Ruby felt plain in her everyday attire.

"Oh, yes, dear me." She straightened her posture. "I'm Miss Ruby Shepherdson. Might I speak with the owner of this fine establishment?"

The woman looked down her nose at Ruby. "He's preoccupied at the moment, but if you'd care to take a seat, I'll let him know you're here. May I ask what this pertains to?"

"Yes. A story."

The woman arched a thick dark eyebrow, her interest clearly piqued. "Well, Mr. Tupper always appreciates discussing stories."

"Thank you."

Ruby took a seat on a stylish green couch with a tasteful wooden table to the left of it. A stack of newspapers sat open-faced on a desk adjacent to the table. She did her best to abstain from allowing her prying eyes and overt curiosity to peruse the newspapers. Perhaps she could ask if she might take a gander at the contents while she awaited her meeting with Mr. Tupper.

She approached the woman at the front desk and presented her inquiry.

"I suppose you could surveil some of the papers." The woman sashayed over to the desk, snatched a healthy stack, and deposited them in Ruby's open arms.

Ruby thanked her and again settled on the couch. It was as if she'd entered a dream as she flipped through the pages. So thick. So full of information. Brimming with creativity. Advertisements, sales, help wanted ads, obituaries, and plentiful news articles crowded the pages. *The Horizon Herald* paled in comparison. She scanned the pages and deliberated on what it might be like to write for such a paper.

A headline in the second newspaper caused her to take a second glance. *Parts of Two Idaho Counties Combined to Make One By Henry Murphy.*

She read it again. If it was written by a Mr. Henry Murphy, why then did it sound suspiciously like an article written by Lillian? Paragraph after paragraph attested to the fact that this story and the one written by Lillian and published by *The Horizon Herald* were similar, if not identical. Which could only mean one thing. Someone had copied.

Ruby scanned the top of the page. This issue was published on March 19, 1895. She searched her memory for when Lillian's had been printed. Was it after March 19? Time hastened by too quickly these days, but it could have only been a few months ago.

It had to have been after March 19.

"Miss Shepherdson?" The woman at the front desk interrupted her musings, and Ruby returned the newspaper to the stack of other papers. "Mr. Tupper will see you now."

The woman led Ruby to an office in the far back of the room where a man in a tweed jacket sat behind a desk. He rose to a height similar to Ruby's five-foot-four inches and appeared to be in his early fifties. He had plentiful black hair swooped to one side and horizontal wrinkles permanently etched on his pale forehead. His far-spaced brown eyes blinked rapidly.

"Miss Shepherdson?" His mouth twitched and he rubbed the back of his neck with an unsteady hand. "Have a seat."

"Yes, sir. Pleased to meet you. Thank you for taking the time to see me."

Mr. Tupper took a seat again behind his desk and immediately began shaking his leg, causing the desk to tremble with the movement and the coffee to slosh over the side of the cup. He hastily wiped it with a cloth before returning his attention to her. "What can I do for you, miss?"

Ruby pondered whether to reveal her credentials, but surmised it would afford her a better opportunity to secure information if she was forthright. "Mr. Tupper, I am a reporter for *The Horizon Herald*."

"Oh. It was my understanding you had an idea for a story." He cleared his throat, reached for his pencil, and tapped it on the desk. "So you're employed by Barnaby then?"

"I am."

"Been some time since I spoke to Barnaby. How does he fare?" Mr. Tupper set the pencil down and began to pick at his fingernails.

"He's fine, sir."

"Did Barnaby send you?"

Ruby pressed the wrinkles from her skirt. Would the nervous Mr. Tupper provide her with any information? The only way to know was to ask. "No, I came of my own accord, although I am on assignment with *The Horizon Herald*." An assignment that meant more than merely seeing her investigation in print, but she didn't tell Mr. Tupper as much.

Mr. Tupper's mouth twitched again. "I see. What kind of assignment?"

"An article about the children who were rescued from the South Fork of the Cornwall River by a Mr. Lynton."

"Ah, yes. I remember that story." He cleared his throat and spoke so quickly that Ruby had to devote her full attention to his words. "Mr. and Mrs. Gholston agreed to a short interview, but the information provided was rather lackluster. My best reporter, Mr. Henry Murphy, was, unfortunately, unable to convince them for a second or more thorough interview. We could not secure one from Mr. Lynton."

That sounded like the Mr. Lynton she had come to know. "Might I examine the article?"

Mr. Tupper tapped his fingers on his desk in a rhythmic fashion. "Yes, yes, I do believe that is around here somewhere." He scooted his chair back and faced a table behind him cluttered with numerous newspapers. "Ah, yes, here it is."

Ruby scanned the words. Indeed, the paltry article offered no more information than what Landon had shared.

Four Children Rescued and Doing Well by Henry Murphy

Mr. and Mrs. Gholston's four children were rescued from drowning in the South Fork of the Cornwall River when a Mr. Jake

Lynton from Horizon jumped in to save them. The children have all recovered and are doing well.

She attempted to hide her disappointment. There were no other details other than the children recovering well—for which she was grateful—because she already knew the surname of the parents and the name of the rescuer.

Ruby handed the paper back to Mr. Tupper. "Thank you, sir."

"You're welcome."

"One other question...might you point me in the direction of the implement?"

Mr. Tupper pointed out the window. "Follow the boardwalk until you reach Fifth Street. Then take a left there. Follow it to the end where you'll find the implement. It is near the river."

"And the Gholston home?"

"Turn right at the mercantile to Idaho Street. It's a yellow home on the right."

"I appreciate your assistance, Mr. Tupper."

The man nodded twice. "You're welcome, Miss Shepherdson, although I'm not sure you'll be effective in securing an interview. If Henry cannot acquire one, I daresay no one can."

When Ruby emerged from *The Cornwall Courier,* Timothy had his arms folded across his chest and a glower on his face. "What happened to ten minutes, Rubes?"

"My deepest, sincerest apologies, Timothy. It took longer than I anticipated. However, I do have directions to both the implement and the home of Mr. and Mrs. Gholston."

An hour later, Ruby and Timothy stopped in front of a pale yellow two-story house. Three younger children played in the yard, and a woman hung clothes on the line. Ruby took a deep breath, prayed for guidance, and grasped her pencil and notebook.

Timothy slung an arm around her shoulders. "You'll do fine, Rubes." He paused, then added, "Hopefully."

"Thanks for having confidence in me."

Her brother tossed an ornery grin. "Always."

But even though Timothy prided himself on joshing her, truth was she couldn't do this without him. The woman pinning a shirt on the clothesline regarded them and trundled in their direction. "May I help you?"

"Are you Mrs. Gholston?"

"I am." She wiped her hands on her calico skirt.

"I'm Ruby Shepherdson from *The Horizon Herald*, and this is my assistant, Timothy. Mrs. Gholston, may we ask you a few questions about your children's rescue from the river?"

The woman, a petite lady in her thirties with auburn hair and almond-shaped brown eyes, hesitated a moment before allowing her attention to drift to the children playing tag in the yard. "We did already speak to someone from *The Cornwall Courier*.

Ruby placed a hand on the woman's arm. "I promise it will only be a few questions."

The woman sighed. "Perhaps a talk with my husband would be fine. While we are abundantly grateful for the

Lord's protection, it was a traumatic experience and one we don't wish to revisit, especially with the younger children."

"I completely understand. We will focus on the man who rescued them."

"We don't know much about him, but if you'll give me a moment, I'll fetch my husband. He's in the barn."

Mr. Gholston, a tall, thin man with brown hair graying at the temples, invited them to take a seat in the chairs on the narrow porch while he settled into a chair himself and clasped his hands. His knuckles turned white and he wet his lips before crossing his arms across his chest. "My wife said you had a few questions about the rescue?"

"Yes, sir." She again introduced herself and Timothy. "We do appreciate your time and promise we won't overstay our welcome."

"I'm not one to want to talk about that day." He pinched the bridge of his narrow nose. "Don't get me wrong, I'm much obliged to Lynton for saving our young'uns. If he hadn't been there..." Mr. Gholston squeezed his eyes shut and lowered his voice. "If he hadn't been there, we would have lost all four of them."

Ruby held her pencil midair. She regretted paying a visit to the Gholston home and asking about the rescue. It was clear that it stirred up painful memories. Her belly knotted, and she focused her attention on her worn tan boots. She regretted all of this hankering to procure an interview and prove herself to Mr. O'Kane. It wasn't worth continually pestering Mr. Lynton, and it for certain wasn't worth stirring up painful recollections for Mr. and Mrs. Gholston.

She shifted her gaze to the children still playing tag in the yard. Four young lives could have been stolen in the blink, but God had seen fit to preserve them using a man named Jake Lynton. Mrs. Gholston continued hanging laundry on the line, but at a slower pace and in between continual glances at her husband.

A heaviness settled in her chest and she closed the notebook and held it to her chest. "Mr. Gholston," she said, as the ache moved down her throat. "I'm sorry. I realized I don't need an interview after all. Please forgive me for interrupting your day."

Shock unhitched Timothy's jaw.

Mr. Gholston blinked.

And Ruby rose. "Thank you for your time, Mr. Gholston."

Their host rose as well and braced himself on the recently-painted porch railing with a shaky hand. "Every day when I awake and many times throughout the day, I thank God for the miracle of my children's survival. It could have gone so differently."

"Indeed, sir, and we praise the Lord with you that He protected your precious children."

"Just surprised you didn't continue the interview," Timothy was saying as Ruby stared out the train's window at the blur of passing scenery.

"I realized it wasn't worth it to cause the family turmoil. I ascertained they were grateful to Mr. Lynton for his courage in saving the children, but the pain..." She couldn't rightly explain the change in her desire to write the story. It wasn't just to assuage her guilt of being a bothersome reporter and not relenting even when she ought to have done so.

It was more than that. So much more than that.

The story didn't matter, not really. "Most times it's baffling to figure out the Lord's will on something, but this time I'm confident that interviewing both Mr. Lynton and Mr. Gholston isn't what the Lord would have me do."

The rumble of the train over the tracks competed with the copious amount of thoughts rambling through Ruby's mind. If Mr. O'Kane didn't rehire her, then she would be all right with that. Truly. Because people were more important than articles.

Even articles that ought to be written.

CHAPTER FIFTEEN

RUBY AT FIRST THOUGHT the knock on the door in the middle of the night was a dream, but when she heard Papa saying he'd hitch the horses to the buggy, she awoke with a start. Ruby swung her legs over the side of the bed and reached for her wrap.

Hushed voices and Mama crying softly greeted her.

Something wasn't right.

Ruby stumbled through the darkness. Albert stood just inside the door, shoulders slumped and his hat in his hands.

"Is it Velma?" Ruby croaked.

Mama rested a hand on Ruby's arm. "It's the baby. I'm going to Velma."

Ruby's heart pounded in her ears. "The baby?"

From the expression on Albert's face, seen clearly even in the candlelight, something was wrong.

Very wrong.

Mama dabbed at her eyes. Papa closed his own, likely in prayer.

Thoughts of the worst possible thing that could have happened to the baby lodged in her throat. "I'll bring the boys back here while you tend to Velma."

Papa opened his eyes and nodded. "That would be a good idea." He reached for Mama's hand and squeezed it. "I'll be riding my horse and will bring you back tomorrow evening, Paisley. Ruby, that way you can bring the boys here in the buggy. Timothy is preparing to ride to Varner City to fetch Velma's parents."

Tears streamed down her brother's face. "I don't understand why this happened."

Papa put his arm around Albert. "Reckon some things we don't understand." Papa's voice broke, and Ruby saw a tear in the corner of her father's eye.

The next few minutes passed in a blur. Ruby dressed, then prepared to meet Mama in the buggy. She stopped by Mama and Papa's room where Mama gathered items into a carpetbag. Mama paused, her back to Ruby, and slipped to her knees and folded her hands. Her voice trembled as she pleaded, "Father, heal their broken hearts."

Ruby swallowed through the overwhelming grief as moisture clouded her vision. There were often times when she didn't understand the Lord's ways.

This time was one of them.

The drive to Albert and Velma's took longer than usual. Or maybe it seemed that way because, while it wasn't mentioned, Ruby and Mama both realized the situation's gravity. Papa led the way on horseback, and Mama's hands shook as she flicked the reins. She and Papa had lost a grandbaby.

Albert reached his home first and barely took the time to tether his horse before bolting inside.

Ruby carried Mama's carpetbag, and together they followed Papa.

In the house, Doc sat at the table while Velma slumped in the rocking chair, Baby Albert in her arms. Her sobs infiltrated the humble home. Albert was beside her on his knees, providing comfort.

Mama rushed to her. Velma handed the baby to Albert and collapsed into Mama's arms. "My sweet girl, I am so sorry." They sat down on the worn sofa someone from the church donated to Albert and Velma years ago, and Mama rocked Velma in her arms.

Ruby stood motionless, the sorrow closing her throat. The boys huddled together in the corner, their sadness crushing her. She needed to retrieve them and take them to the farm, but her body felt leaden and her feet refused to move. Ruby clutched the table's edge and begged the Lord to pour out His peace and comfort on her brother and sister-in-law.

Beside her, she heard Papa's and Doc's muffled voices. "I suspect that his heart wasn't strong enough," Doc was saying.

Was it just the other day that Ruby held Baby Albert in her arms, and he'd peered up at her and cooed? Was it just the other day she commented how he had Velma's small squinty eyes and round cheeks?

And now...

She collected herself and plodded along the floor to Velma. "I'm so sorry."

Velma bobbed her head once before closing her eyes and resting on Mama's shoulder. Albert gripped his wife's hand in his. "Thank you, Rubes."

"I'm going to…to take the boys now." Her gaze traveled to the lifeless little one in Albert's arms. One last time to hold him before the funeral and then not to see him again until the Lord called them home.

With effort, Ruby tore her eyes away and trudged to where the boys were. "Simon and Sherman, would you like to come with me to the farm?"

Simon rubbed his eyes. Sherman's lip quivered.

"I'll make—" she paused in an attempt to catch her breath. "I'll make us pancakes for breakfast. And eggs too." It was doubtful the boys would care about food at a time like this, but she had no other words.

Ruby lowered herself and opened her arms. The boys flew into them, and she held them close. Simon's muffled question interrupted her continual prayer. "Can I have twenty pancakes?"

"Yes," Ruby whispered hoarsely. She'd make Simon a hundred pancakes if it helped ease the agony.

A half-hour later, Ruby steered the buggy down the road. Home seemed farther than usual today, and her hands shook as she held the reins. The bright orangey hues of the sunrise shone in the distance—the dawn of a new day upon them. God's mercies were new every morning, but on this agonizing day, a baby boy had died. *Where is Your mercy, Lord?*

She wasn't usually one to question the Lord's will.

Please, Father, please help Albert and Velma. Be with them. Please give them comfort.

Emotion burned the back of her throat, and she struggled to see clearly through the blinding tears. Beside her, Simon's thin shoulders shook and Sherman bit his lip. "Did our little brother go to heaven, Auntie Ruby?"

His voice quivered. Ruby transferred the reins to one hand and swiped at the tears that dampened her cheeks. She pulled the buggy to one side and slid in between her nephews. Wrapping an arm around each, she held them while their three voices chorused in sorrow.

"I loved our little brother," sobbed Simon. "Why did he have to die?"

Sherman leaned his head against Ruby's shoulder. "Ma said he wasn't breathing. I was hoping it was a bad dream. Why did he stop breathing, Auntie Ruby?"

Ruby had no words in response to his inquiry, for she didn't know why the Lord had taken a baby home so soon after he'd been born. Now Albert and Velma would never know the joy of seeing him grow into a man. He would never run and play with his older brothers, learn to ride a horse, celebrate birthdays, or throw a baseball. He'd never go on outings with Ruby and the rest of her nieces and nephews.

An image of Baby Albert flashed through her mind. His small squinty eyes and round cheeks. He was a perfect mix of Albert and Velma. Such a sweet, sweet baby. So content. So precious.

And now he was gone.

Ruby wasn't sure how long she and the boys wept on that otherwise quiet day only a mile from home. She only knew that, once their tears started, they couldn't be stopped, even as she prayed for solace. They remained huddled on the buggy seat, and Ruby wished more than anything she could erase the pain from the hearts of those she loved.

Jake secured the logs in the back of the wagon and proceeded toward home. He'd found the wood on the farthest edge of his acreage and would chop the downed trees into firewood once the wood dried and things on the farm slowed a bit.

He reveled in the cool crisp morning. Samson sat beside him on the buckboard, content until he saw a rabbit or other varmint scampering alongside the road.

As he drove the wagon over the rise, something akin to crying caught Jake's attention. He stopped the wagon and inclined his ear. A buggy was parked on the road to the left. Did someone need help?

He beckoned the horses and, instead of going straight at the crossroads, took a left to the buggy.

The sight when he drew closer took him unawares. The newspaperwoman sat in the buggy with two young boys on either side of her. He put the brake on and climbed down. "Ma'am? Is everything all right?"

She glanced up at him as he sidled up adjacent to the buggy. "Yes, I mean, no." She returned her attention straight ahead and pulled the boys closer.

The boys cried, their small shoulders trembling as they leaned into the woman.

"With all respect, let me drive you home." He paused, noting how badly she was shaking. "You're in no condition to drive."

"What of the buggy?"

"I'll return to retrieve it."

He half expected her to argue with him, given what he knew about her. But the newspaperwoman bobbed her head and whispered to the children to climb in his wagon. They did as she asked, and Jake assisted her from the buggy, and she teetered, nearly falling into him. He righted her and held onto her upper arm. "Are you all right?"

"I just don't understand things sometimes."

He waited for her to say more.

"Have you ever lost someone you love?"

Her whispered words tore at him, both because it was clear she had lost someone who meant a great deal and because he thought of Corbin.

"Yes, I have."

She raised her gaze to his. Tears darkened her long lashes, and one slid down her right cheek. Without thinking, he raised a tender finger and wiped it away. She closed her eyes and tottered, and Jake again kept her from falling.

"Parents should never lose their child." Her squelched sob followed her words. Jake felt helpless witnessing her grief.

Ma's and Pa's faces lingered in his thoughts. They *had* lost a child. Their middle child. One who thought he'd someday ride with Buffalo Bill's Congress of Rough Riders. One who would likely still be alive if Jake had stopped him from riding a horse.

Yes. He knew what it was like for parents to lose a child, even though he'd never been a parent himself.

Ruby's shoulders fell and she stared at the ground. "I'm sorry," she said.

"No need to be sorry."

He took a step toward her in an effort to guide her to the wagon. Instead, she leaned against him. Jake didn't know this woman well but knew she needed any consolation he could provide. It wasn't like the time she'd driven a wagon off the road or had lost her notebook or had trespassed on his land to pick raspberries.

This time was different, and something inside him stirred. He opened his stance and she rested against his chest. Slowly, hesitantly, he put his hand on her back.

What child had passed? Was it one of those who'd been in the wagon the day of the raspberry picking? Was it her child? A brother or sister?

The woman fit perfectly in his arms, and she smelled of lavender—a scent that reminded him of summer.

Should he say more? Tell her he understood? Say nothing?

He swallowed the dryness in his throat and craned his neck to see that the boys were huddled in the back of the wagon amongst the logs. Jake needed to get all three of them home, wherever that was.

She placed a hand on his chest and took a step back. "I'm so sorry."

It was the second time she'd apologized. "Nothing to be sorry for."

Their eyes connected once again, and he thought of how even though the sadness was etched deeply in her face, the newspaperwoman was beautiful.

"I'll take you and the young'uns home."

This time she allowed him to lead her to the wagon. He effortlessly assisted her onto the buckboard.

"Continue down this road," she said in a voice so quiet he barely heard her.

Birds sang in the trees that lined the way to her farm. Birds who were oblivious to the pain and heartache of those in Jake's wagon.

After some time, she pointed to a house. "That's it right over there."

Minutes later, he assisted her and the boys from the wagon, then unhitched one of his horses. "I'll fetch the buggy."

She touched his sleeve. "Thank you."

Ruby watched as Mr. Lynton walked away. What had overcome her that she should allow herself to be folded into his arms? Odd as it was, she'd discovered comfort there, a peace of sorts. There had been genuine compassion in his eyes and a willingness to help her and the boys as there was no way she could have maneuvered the buggy home in her grief-stricken state. That he had come along when he had—once again—was a blessing.

She recalled the pine scent of his plaid shirt and the strength, yet tenderness in his arms. The cantankerous hermit had another side to his mysterious personality, and from his words, he too, had experienced the loss of someone he loved. Was it a wife? A child? Parents? A brother or sister? A friend? She'd wanted to ask. To know more about what had brought pain into his life.

He returned with the buggy sometime later. Simon and Sherman fell asleep in Timothy's old bed, and Ruby commenced making pancakes and eggs for breakfast. While nothing would remove the pain of losing their brother, if she could temporarily distract them, perhaps that would be beneficial.

Ruby put the plates of food on the table, wiped her hands on her apron, and stumbled outside.

"I'll unhitch the horses," he said.

"Thank you for retrieving the buggy. And thank you for..." her words trailed.

"Glad I could be of help. I'm sorry for your loss."

Ruby nodded mutely, for doing anything else would cause another flow of tears. Her heart broke for Albert, Velma, and the boys. If only she could take that pain from them. *Lord, I don't understand why You took Baby Albert home, but I do know that You love and care deeply for us and that we never walk through our heartache alone. Please comfort Albert, Velma, the boys, and all who loved Baby Albert.*

She returned to the house, eager to busy herself by continuing to prepare breakfast. Ruby set the syrup on the table, poured milk into the three cups, and put away the dishes she'd already washed. Mama's sign above the fireplace that Papa made for her last Christmas caught her attention.

"Although the fig tree shall not blossom, neither shall fruit be in the vines; the labour of the olive shall fail, and the fields shall yield no meat; the flock shall be cut off from the fold, and there shall be no herd in the stalls:

Yet I will rejoice in the Lord, I will joy in the God of my salvation.

The Lord God is my strength, and he will make my feet like hinds' feet, and he will make me to walk upon mine high places."

Papa had etched the words of Mama's favorite verse in the oversized rectangular piece of wood—words that consoled Ruby. She read the words again and whispered, "Although

Baby Albert is now with Jesus and we miss him terribly, yet I will rejoice in the Lord, I will joy in the God of my salvation. He is my strength. And though Albert and Velma mourn the loss of their child, Lord, You will be their strength in their time of sorrow."

"Auntie Ruby?"

Ruby kneeled and opened her arms. Sherman flew into them. She held him for a few minutes before he took a step back. His dark blond hair was ruffled from sleep and a small crusted drool in the corner of his mouth told her he'd slept hard in just that short amount of time. He offered a weak smile, revealing his two missing top teeth. "I smelled something and woke up."

"Yes, I made pancakes and eggs for our breakfast."

Sherman rubbed his stomach. "I like those. So does Simon."

"Would you care to wake your brother? After breakfast and chores, I have a surprise for you."

"A surprise?" His brown eyebrows reached into his hairline. "Simon and me like surprises. Is it candy?"

"It's not candy. It's even better."

Sherman's mouth formed a perfect "o" before he dashed from her and into Timothy's old room.

Ruby crept to the doorway and watched as Sherman took a flying leap onto the bed. "Wake up, Simon!"

Simon batted at him. "Go away, Sherman. I'm dreaming about catching the biggest fish there ever was."

"It's time to get up. Auntie Rubes made us breakfast and then after chores, we have a surprise waiting for us."

That woke Simon in a hurry, and he sat up in his bed. "I wonder what it is?"

"Not sure, but it's not candy. It's better than that."

After a hearty meal, Simon milked the cow, Sherman gathered the eggs from the coop, and Ruby washed the dishes. She was almost as excited about sharing the surprise as Simon and Sherman were to receive it. Ruby handed each boy a pail, and in her own, she packed several cookies.

"We're going on a treasure hunt," she said, handing Simon a pencil and piece of paper. "We'll pen all the treasures we plan to find today. For instance, a pine cone."

Simon wrote the words, and Sherman jumped up and down in the chair at the table. "What about a pillbug? Those are my favorite."

"They're easy to find too," said Simon, slowly writing each letter.

Ruby tapped her chin with her finger. "There are a lot of interesting leaves to be found. Maybe we could find one from an aspen, elm, maple, and birch."

"A bird nest. That would be my favorite treasure," said Sherman.

Simon wrote "berd nest" on the list below "mapel and aspin leaf" in his oversized unsteady handwriting. "This is gonna be fun, Auntie Rubes. We can fill our pails with treasures."

"And then we can eat cookies." Sherman licked his lips. "I'm Uncle Timothy's nephew."

Ruby patted him on the head. "Indeed you are. Timothy does love cookies."

And as they set out to search for treasures, Ruby prayed that in a small way, the boys would have a few hours of distraction before Papa returned them home and the loss of Baby Albert was again forefront in their minds.

CHAPTER SIXTEEN

JAKE UNFORTUNATELY HAD TO ride to town several days later to secure some necessary items at the mercantile. Thankfully, the only person who spoke to him was the mercantile owner when he stepped up to the counter to pay for his items. She did quirk an eyebrow at him and attempted to engage him in conversation, but Jake refrained from giving more than his usual practiced one-word answers.

Living the life of a hermit wasn't an easy undertaking, but Jake had no desire to become friends with folks who would judge him for what he'd done should they somehow find out.

The sky had darkened on his ride home, and gray clouds replaced the white puffy ones. Rain was imminent, and while he had things to do, Jake welcomed the moisture for his crops. He'd just left the outskirts of town when he noticed a man sitting beside the creek, face in his hands.

Who was the man and was he all right?

Jake sighed. Seemed there was always someone needing his help when he longed only to be left alone. He tethered his horse and watched for a moment. Maybe the man was asleep or had a headache.

Not everyone needs your help, Jake.

He shoved aside that realization. How could a man have a hankering to help people but at the same time yearn to be left alone? He took a deep breath and followed the matted path of weeds to the creekside. "Sir, is everything all right?"

The man, looking to be in his thirties, startled. He lifted his face and peered at Jake before rising from his place on a log. "Not sure I understand the Lord's ways sometimes," he said, extending his hand. "I'm Pastor Albert."

"Jake."

"Nice to meet you, Jake."

"You're a man of the cloth. How could you not understand the Lord's ways?"

Pastor Albert shoved his hands in his pockets. "Sometimes difficult events make us wonder things we wouldn't otherwise wonder. I don't doubt the Lord or His faithfulness. I don't disbelieve that He works all things for our good as He states in the book of Romans. I just fail to understand why some things have to happen." His brows dipped. "Have you ever felt that way?"

An image of Corbin after he'd been thrown off Lucky's back flashed through Jake's mind. His limp and broken body. The blood. The end of a life in the span of a few seconds. He drew in a jagged breath. Why had Corbin died that day?

No matter how many times Jake asked that question, there would never be an answer.

That the Lord worked things for good? That He was faithful?

How was Corbin's death a good thing? How was the Lord faithful in allowing a young man to die?

He wanted to tell Pastor Albert that he stopped believing in God's faithfulness after Corbin's death. That he wanted nothing to do with his Creator. But the dejected expression on the man's face reminded Jake this conversation wasn't about him. It was assisting someone in need.

Even if that need wasn't physical. Jake rolled his shoulders to alleviate some of the tension that had settled there. "Did something bad happen?" he asked.

Pain was written in the pastor's eyes, and his gaze settled on the trees in the distance. Perhaps asking such a question wasn't appropriate. Not that Jake was the type to talk about deep matters, for he wasn't. But he did want to ensure the pastor was all right before he continued on his way.

"My wife. She gave birth to our third son a month ago. We recently lost him." Sorrow flickered in his eyes. "Baby Albert. That's what we named him. So tiny and so perfectly formed by the Creator's hand. But…" Pastor Albert paused. "Doc said near as he could figure, the baby's heart was too weak."

Emotions were not something Jake handled well, whether his own or someone else's. He stared at the ground. "I'm sorry that you and your wife lost your son that way."

"Thank you. I'll never understand why the Lord took him home before he'd had a chance to live. His older brothers would have doted on him." Pastor Albert's voice trailed.

Silence ensued with the only sounds being the trickling of the creek water and the tap-tapping of a woodpecker in a nearby tree.

"I do know," continued Pastor Albert, "that our baby is with Jesus. He'll never feel the pain of this world. Never experience heartache or disappointment. Never be sick or injured or hungry." Emotion laced his words. "And I'm grateful for the Lord's mercy in that way. But the ones left behind…"

He raked a hand through his hair. "My wife, Velma. She's distraught and understandably so. We both are clinging to Jesus and to each other in this time of trial."

"I'm sorry, sir. I'm sorry for your loss."

"Thank you." Pastor Albert sighed. "And thank you for listening. I apologize for sharing all of that information with you. Reckon you caught me at a vulnerable moment. I'd sure appreciate your prayers."

Jake hadn't prayed since he'd begged God to allow Corbin to live. He could promise the pastor he'd pray, but it would be a lie, and no matter Jake's opinions about religion, lying was wrong. Or he could share with Pastor Albert that he wasn't a praying man. But to do so would only discourage the man more, and Jake had no intention of doing that. So instead he offered a curt nod. "Looks like we're in for a storm. I best be on my way."

Pastor Albert followed his gaze into the darkened sky. "I should be as well. Velma will be wondering where I've wandered off to. Do you live in Horizon, Jake?"

"I do."

"I don't believe I've seen you about these parts. Why don't you join us for church on Sunday?"

"Meaning no disrespect, sir, but I'm not a church-going man." Jake prepared himself for a lecture on the ills of avoiding church.

But none came.

Instead, Pastor Albert clapped a hand on his shoulder. "If you should ever change your mind, we'd welcome you."

Jake wouldn't change his mind, but there was no sense in sharing that with the kindly pastor. He bid him goodbye, mounted his horse, and headed for home.

The rain pelted him and lightning flashed across the sky before he reached the house. Jake tipped his head down, the rain pouring off the brim of his hat as the water seeped through his shirt. Samson awaited him on the porch, barking as if to tell Jake to hasten his steps and seek cover.

Jake put his horse in the barn and dashed to the house. Shaking the water from his hat, he stepped inside, Samson on his heels. After a change of clothes, Jake took a seat on the porch where he was shielded from the weather. The cool air invigorated him, and he stared out over the railing to the green fields. His thoughts returned to Pastor Albert and the loss of his child.

Jake didn't understand the Lord's ways, but he hadn't wanted to share anything with a man he'd just met. Such thoughts were personal. Better kept locked up inside. What did amaze him, however, was that the pastor hadn't turned from the Lord after losing his baby. Instead, he mentioned that he and his wife were clinging to Jesus.

Had Jake's parents clung to Jesus after Corbin's death? They were both devout believers. Jake hadn't clung to his Savior. He'd turned from Him and had gone in the opposite direction.

That realization pricked his conscience, and, with difficulty, he shoved aside the unsettling thought.

"Well, Samson, it looks as though our work this afternoon has been halted."

Samson wagged his tail then rested his chin on Jake's leg.

Contentment found him once again. For while the pastor may need to cling to the Lord, Jake did not. He was just fine here at his home with his dog, the chickens, horses, milk cow, and the plentiful acres of crops. He needed nothing and no one else.

Exhaustion tugged at every part of him, yet sleep would not come. Jake turned onto his right side, then his left. This was the second night sleep eluded him. Today he'd worked diligently to compensate for the lack of work the day before due to the rain.

Yet even though his muscles ached from the continual labor, he could not find rest.

The conversation with Pastor Albert continued to flit through his mind unannounced. How could someone who lost their child still have faith?

Had the reverend ever considered abandoning his belief in the Lord as Jake had done?

What kept Pastor Albert and his wife hoping, praying, relying on, and clinging to a Holy God who would take an innocent baby away from his parents?

Why hadn't they turned their back on Him?

Had Jake's parents forgiven God for taking Corbin?

Had they forgiven *Jake*?

Did they miss him? Or were they glad he was gone?

Why were these thoughts permeating his mind?

Jake had never been one to overthink things, but in the dark of the night with only the coyotes, crickets, and Samson's snoring, the near silence led him to ponder things he ought not consider.

All because he'd stopped to talk with Pastor Albert.

Jake swung his legs over the side of the bed and sauntered to the window. Samson slept right through the sound of the creaking floor. Good thing no outlaws saw fit to break in and steal Jake's meager possessions, for Samson would never hear them.

The full moon surrounded by stars greeted him when he stepped out onto the porch seconds later. The rough boards pricked at his bare feet, reminding Jake he needed to tend to some repairs around the farm when he had the opportunity.

Perhaps he ought to ride into town and ask Pastor Albert some of the questions weighing heavily on his mind. After all, the reverend seemed to be knowledgeable about such things. Were he and his wife doing better? He'd mentioned other children. How old were they and how had they handled their little brother's death?

Look how you've handled your little brother's death.

Jake ignored the contrary thought. Maybe asking Pastor Albert questions wasn't the best idea. Maybe he'd just check on the man and ensure he and his wife were fine. For the pastor to have discussed such private matters with a stranger must surely mean he struggled, even if he still maintained his faith.

But how could that be?

Wasn't God supposed to give peace to His children? If so, why hadn't He given peace to the pastor and his wife?

Jake gripped the railing, then leaned over and allowed the cool night breeze to tickle his face and blow through his hair.

Yes, he'd pay a visit to Pastor Albert, and if the man asked him to church again, Jake would kindly, but firmly refuse. He only needed answers, not a sermon.

Jake first stopped at the parsonage. A friendly woman with a weary countenance and dark circles beneath her eyes greeted him. After pleasantries, she told Jake that Pastor Albert was at the church working on Sunday's sermon. "Please feel free to stop there."

"It won't interrupt him?"

"Not at all. He welcomes his congregation to stop by anytime they need to speak with him."

Jake didn't mention he wasn't part of the congregation. "Thank you, ma'am." He paused for a moment, wondering if he should express his condolences for the loss of her baby, but then decided against it. He turned and walked to the adjacent church, his steps sluggish and faltering as he grew closer. Perhaps he should just return home. After all, he'd not entered a church since Corbin's funeral, and he resisted the thought of doing so now. Even if Jake's reasons to speak with Pastor Albert had nothing to do with his brother's death or himself for that matter.

Would God even welcome someone like him?

Jake stalled on the top stair. While in need of a fresh coat of paint, the church reminded him of the one in Ingleville. Small, white, a cross and a belfry, and three steps to the door.

Jake took a deep breath then entered.

He halted again at the back of the church.

Once upon a time, he'd sat in pews just like the ones here and attended church regularly each Sunday with his family. He'd lifted his voice in worship, listened intently to the sermons, and fellowshipped afterward. Potlucks drew him to stay long after services ended, and he'd counted many of his fellow parishioners as friends. Until some expressed disapproval and disappointment because of Corbin's death.

That's why it was imperative he kept to himself and not allow anyone to know about the rescue of the children.

He backed to the door, deciding he'd offer his sympathies to Pastor Albert another day.

"Hello, there. Jake, is it?"

Jake removed his hand from the doorknob and turned around to see the pastor standing before him. "Uh, yes. Hello."

The man's tired smile didn't reach his eyes. "Good to see you again. What brings you here today?"

Jake fidgeted with the buttons on his shirt. "Reckon I was just stopping by to offer up my sympathies for the loss of your child and see if there was any way I could be of help."

"Much obliged for that. Thank you. We're doing our best to rely on the Lord for His comfort, but it hasn't been easy. I wish I could take all of Velma's pain and hoist it onto myself."

Jake recalled Pa's arms around Ma as she sobbed. Tears had flowed freely down Pa's face too—the only time Jake had ever seen him cry. He speculated that Pa would have wanted to take all of Ma's pain upon himself as well.

Pastor Albert leaned against a nearby pew. "We trust in God's ways, but they are hard to understand at times. So thank you for your sympathies and for your offer to help. One thing that would be much appreciated is if you would help us whitewash the church. A group of men have planned to meet here next Saturday. Would you be willing to assist us? A noonday meal and supper will be provided."

Jake hadn't anticipated *that* sort of help. Meeting with other men was not on his list of ways to aid the pastor and his wife.

"The church has needed a fresh coat of paint for some time now. An anonymous donor paid for the supplies, for which we are grateful. Would you be able to commit to helping us?"

"I..." Jake rubbed his furry jaw. Would it be possible to arrive and work hard then leave without much conversing? He wouldn't have to say his last name. Although that Ruby woman from the newspaper may have mentioned him. If so, how could he keep curious folks from asking about the incident in Cornwall?

"Don't feel pressured to help. I'll understand if you have other commitments. Why don't you think about it and let me know?" The pastor looked askance at the small table at the front of the church. "I sometimes sit there to write my sermons. That way, if I have any visitors, I'll be sure not to miss them. Your visit couldn't have been timed better. I was struggling for the proper words for my sermon."

"Well, I best be on my way then. I'll think about Saturday and let you know."

"Thank you. Perhaps you could assist me with some thoughts for Sunday."

"With all respect, sir, I doubt I would be much help."

Pastor Albert was not deterred. "As my younger sister would say, 'to the contrary'." He chuckled. "Anyhow, are you familiar with the Parable of the Lost Sheep?"

Listening to the pastor's sermons in Ingleville seemed a lifetime ago. Jake was sure he'd heard that parable and had read it in his own Bible reading time. "Sounds somewhat familiar."

"Sometimes we wander away from the Lord. For some, it happens slowly. Perhaps life's obligations get in the way, and soon, our Savior is the last on a list of things to accomplish in a day. For some, it happens right quickly. Life can be painful, and we live in a fallen world. Grief and hard times can cause us to either draw closer to Jesus or pull away."

Jake felt the stab of emotion in his heart. He'd distanced himself from the Lord due to Corbin's death. He choked on the conviction and edged away slowly. No need to be reminded that he was once close to the Lord and now no longer was.

"When we are His, nothing can take us from His grasp." Pastor Albert's gaze connected with Jake's. No condemnation. No judgment. However, Jake was certain the reverend saw through to his soul.

"Have you surrendered your life to Christ?"

"Years ago, yes. I walked with the Lord until..." Jake choked on the words caught in his throat.

Several seconds ticked by. "Tell me, Jake, do you have cattle at your farm?"

"Yes, sir."

"A dog? Horses?"

"Yes, to both." Jake rubbed the back of his neck where sweat had formed. Should he leave while he could?

"And you do your best to care for them. To make sure they're fed and sheltered."

"I do." What was Pastor Albert insinuating? "Sir, with all due respect, I'm not much for sermons."

"Not a sermon as I save those for Sundays. Well, unless you count my boys. Sometimes they need a sermon—or rather a lecture—for their wrongdoing. They're young yet, so I keep it short." A smile lit the pastor's face, cloaked by the sadness that remained etched behind tired eyes.

"I have my reasons for abandoning my faith."

Pastor Albert tugged on the sleeves of his shirt. "It's not an easy world we live in."

Jake figured he was thinking about his baby. "I'm sorry for your loss. I can't imagine."

"As I mentioned before, I don't understand it. I was angry at God right after it happened. I thought I'd done everything right—I answered His calling to lead the flock, try my hardest to be a devoted husband and father, I follow His Word, and care for others." Pastor Albert shrugged. "I just didn't understand why. I still don't. But then as I was holding my sobbing wife in my arms, I realized that while I can blame God for what happened, I'll never know the peace I could know while being distanced from Him." His voice broke. "I don't ever want to be distanced from my Lord and Savior. Not now and not in eternity."

Disappointment needled Jake. He'd distanced himself from God. He'd never known peace after what happened to Corbin, and he wouldn't know that peace after Mr. Strain's death either. "But if God is disappointed in us for something we've done, why would He want us to draw close to Him?"

The reverend didn't answer right away. Instead, he stared straight ahead as if contemplating his answer. Or perhaps praying for guidance. "Our God loves us so much He sent His Son to die for us. He wants us to draw close to Him. If it's something we've done to create the distance, He wants our repentance and graciously accepts it and forgives us. If our separation from Him is due to grief, a calamity, or a letdown about what has happened in our lives, He wants us to seek

Him. There's nowhere better to be than resting in the Lord's arms. Reckon that's the safest place for us to be."

"But what if we've done something the Lord can never forgive?"

A line etched between Pastor Albert's brows. "There is nothing the Lord can't forgive. And when the one in need of forgiveness seeks it, there is much rejoicing."

Could it be that God truly would rejoice over Jake's repentance? Suddenly, he wanted to know more. To be reassured this was true. If so, maybe his Heavenly Father would forgive him for his negligence in keeping an eye on Corbin.

"Remember when I asked if you took care of your animals?"

"Yes."

"God cares deeply for us. He tells us in His Word that He will supply our every need. Not the things we selfishly want, but the things we truly need. When one of your animals or your dog wanders away and gets lost, do you leave them to fend for themselves? Forget about them? Allow them to be a victim of a potential predator? Starve?"

"Absolutely not." Jake thought of Samson and how he'd been left injured and neglected. He loved that dog and ensured he was properly cared for.

"Exactly. When one of God's children wanders away, He doesn't forget about them. He goes after them."

Was God seeking Jake?

"He would leave his ninety-nine sheep grazing on the hillside to search for the one who strayed. Our Lord cares much for those who are His."

Was Jake His? He'd committed his life to Jesus as a young'un. If what Pastor Albert said was true, he still was the Lord's. That nothing could take Jake from God's hand. Jake cleared his throat. "Reckon I allowed my brother to do something he ought not to have done. He died because of me."

"Did you do your best to convince him not to do what he did?"

"Yes, but Corbin was strong-headed. He went his own way." A flash of Corbin on the ground after being bucked off flashed in Jake's mind. Why could he not find rest from the horrible memory?

"Sometimes despite our best efforts, things go awry. People have wills of their own."

"But I promised Pa I'd take care of him. Promised him I'd make sure Corbin didn't ride that horse." Jake's voice cracked, and he struggled through the strain of contained grief.

"Can I pray with you, Jake?"

Less than an hour ago, Jake wasn't sure God would hear the prayers he himself prayed. But if Pastor Albert was doing the praying, God would surely hear him. Although the Lord hadn't saved the reverend's baby and undoubtedly the man had prayed for that. The mighty tug of indecision enveloped him. Pastor Albert waited patiently while Jake determined his answer. Finally, he nodded. "All right."

The reverend placed a hand on Jake's shoulder and bowed his head. "Lord, thank You for this day. For Your blessings. For Your grace. And for Your forgiveness. I don't know the full details of how Jake lost his brother, but I do know that You are mighty to forgive any of our wrongdoings. I know that when we wander from You, You come in search of us. That's the kind of Father You are. Please draw Jake to You.

Bring him back to You. Give him comfort over the loss of his brother and peace that You are still in control, even when events don't always seem that way. Give him a hunger and thirst for You and Your Word. In Jesus' Name I pray, Amen."

Jake lifted his weary head as tears stung his eyes.

"Come back and talk with me again," said Pastor Albert.

The reverend had given him much to ponder, and while the emotion lodged in his throat precluded him from answering, Jake knew he'd be back.

That Sunday, Jake slipped into the church and stood at the back. He observed the congregants greeting each other—just like the members of his church in Ingleville.

For a brief moment, the scene tugged at him. Some in Ingleville blamed Jake for Corbin's death and uttered disparaging comments. But others said nothing. Perhaps those folks hadn't thought him guilty of failing to stop Corbin from riding Lucky, and in doing so, causing his subsequent death.

Perhaps Jake had erred in leaving Ingleville. Leaving his family.

But no. There was still Pa to consider and the pain etched on his face and his voiced opinion.

Yes, Jake made the right decision in leaving Ingleville and settling in Horizon.

Pastor Albert made several announcements, including the upcoming whitewashing and other repairs of the church. Men nodded and some of the wives prodded their husbands.

Hymns followed. Jake recognized the words to all of them, but something stayed his tongue from singing.

True to his word, Pastor Albert's sermon was on the Parable of the Lost Sheep. Jake shifted, the words the reverend spoke again causing comfort and discomfort at the same time.

When Jake committed his life to Jesus at ten, he had no foreknowledge of what the future held. It had been relatively easy for Jake to follow Jesus and live his life for his Savior. But after Corbin's death, the guilt was too much to bear, and Jake knew he'd disappointed the Lord beyond redemption.

But what if he *was* like the one sheep who'd wandered away? What if the Lord *would* leave ninety-nine others to bring Jake back from his wanderings?

The newspaperwoman turned around then and her eye caught his. A slight smile shown on her face. She was the only one besides Pastor Albert who'd noticed his presence. Thankfully, neither made their observation of him public.

He listened for a few more minutes until Pastor Albert finished his sermon and led the closing prayer. Then Jake backed to the door before turning and exiting the church.

Ruby observed Mr. Lynton at the back of the church, standing stone still against the wall. He hadn't visited with the other churchgoers, hadn't spoken, and hadn't held her gaze but for the succinctest of moments.

What was it that had broken the man? Had Albert seen him? Would Mr. Lynton eventually take more than two steps into the church?

While she hadn't a clue what burdened Mr. Lynton's heart, the Lord knew. Ruby folded her hands, bowed her head, and prayed the Lord would mend whatever it was needing fixing in Mr. Lynton's life.

CHAPTER SEVENTEEN

RUBY OPENED THE OVEN at Wilhemina's and inhaled the delectable scent of cinnamon and nutmeg. She retrieved the pan and placed it on the top of the stove. "I believe I might just ask Papa to haul your oven home, Wilhemina. What a marvelous appliance!"

"Oh, yes, it is an extraordinary oven indeed. Hubert found it in the catalogue at the mercantile. It's a Charter Oak Stove, which cooks things more evenly than any other stove we've owned." Wilhelmina arched her eyebrows. "It has wire gauze oven doors."

Even if it didn't cook perfectly, the stove was a thing of beauty with its ornate finishes.

"Ooh, do you need a taste tester?" Lucy slid her hand toward a cookie.

A chorus of laughter filled Wilhelmina's kitchen. "Absolutely, Luce. Tell me what you think."

Lucy peeled a cookie from the pan and blew on it to cool it. Then she popped a morsel into her mouth. "Mmmm. Delicious. I think we all ought to feast on these for the noonday meal. The men have sandwiches and apple slices." She handed Mae a piece.

Mae chewed it slowly and closed her eyes as she did so. "I tend to agree with Lucy. Yes, let's save these for us."

"That would be acceptable, except I may have shared with Albert that Ruby was making her famous ginger cookies for dessert." A hint of a smile touched Velma's lips. "And unfortunately, sometimes Albert shares with others when there's information to be had about food."

Mama swung an arm around Velma's shoulders. "It seems the Shepherdson men do have a fondness for desserts. Timothy asked Ruby this morning if she was bringing ginger cookies, so he knows as well."

"And if Timothy had his way, he'd eat an entire plateful." Ruby nibbled on a piece of a broken cookie from the far corner of the pan.

"That's true," agreed Wilhelmina. "Where does he put all that food?"

"No one knows," said Mama. "He's just like Tyler and Albert that way. All three of them could eat nonstop and still be hungry."

"Hubert's the same way," declared Wilhelmina. "Although he clearly isn't a Shepherdson, what with that ample stomach."

That caused another round of laughter, for Hubert was most certainly not a slender fellow.

"Do you remember that time that all the cookie dough disappeared?" Mae asked.

Mama shook her head. "Just one time?"

"Well, the one time that we most easily recall," added Lucy.

"Oh, yes. Velma, did we ever tell you about the missing cookie dough?"

It was good to see Velma smile again, even for the briefest of moments. The loss of her baby had understandably devastated her. When she'd mentioned she'd rather stay home while food preparations were made for the men whitewashing the church, Mama had instead gently nudged her to join them. "It won't be the same without all of my girls there," she'd said.

Velma reluctantly agreed, and they all did their best to make sure she was loved, treasured, and cared for, especially during this painful time.

"I don't believe you told me that story," she said, taking a peek out the window, presumably to check on the children playing in the schoolyard.

"Once upon a time…" started Ruby.

Lucy finished placing the ham on a sandwich. "As Mama mentioned, it was more akin to once upon several times—"

"True," said Mae. She set L.J. on the floor and handed him a pan and a spoon. "Poor Albert. It would have all gone so well had he avoided getting caught."

Wilhelmina's already large eyes widened even further. "Oh, now you have me curious."

"Well," began Mama, "I had just stirred the ingredients for sugar cookies. I was still learning how to bake at that time."

Wilhelmina cast her a knowing glance. "And look how far you've come."

"Only with the help of you, Tabitha, and Augusta." She paused. "I was stirring the dough and left it to set for a few minutes while tending to Ruby, who had just awakened from her nap. When I returned, the batter was gone. Not one bit remained. At first, seeing as how, as the mother of an infant, I was deprived of sleep…"

Lucy tilted her head toward her sister. "I recall, Ruby, that you did not sleep well at night."

"Remember us begging Mama and Papa *not* to allow her to stay in our room?" asked Mae.

Ruby playfully nudged Mae. "I thought this story was about Albert."

"Oh, it is," said Mama. "Trust me when I say it is a story no one will ever forget, even though many have heard it countless times over."

Velma reached for another apple to slice. "While I suspect the culprit is my beloved husband, how did you discover what happened to the cookie dough?"

"Well, at first I thought I'd forgotten to mix it up since I was so exhausted from lack of sleep, but then I realized I *had* added the ingredients. I didn't suspect Albert in the beginning because he was supposed to be outside doing his chores. That, and he'd just eaten the noonday meal, so there was no way he should be hungry yet."

Mae placed the sandwiches in piles on several plates. "God is the Author of miracles for sure, seeing as how naughty Albert was in those days."

"Indeed. So I talked to Papa about it, and we searched all over for Albert, who by then had become our top suspect. We found him tucked away in the barn loft, his cheeks bulging with cookie dough. He swallowed the evidence posthaste, but within minutes was bent over complaining of a stomachache. Albert promised he'd never again eat batter after that episode, and to my knowledge, he hasn't. However, that hasn't precluded him from having his fair share of cookies."

A round of laughter ensued, and Ruby wouldn't give up the time spent with Mama, her sisters, Velma, and Wilhelmina for the world.

Lucy nibbled on a cookie. "Wilhelmina, did you tell Ruby about the disturbing article news?"

"Disturbing article news?" Ruby asked. "Luce, is there something you forgot to tell me?"

"I wasn't sure if Wilhelmina told you, but she and I both overheard a customer in the restaurant speaking about an article Lillian wrote."

Wilhelmina's brow furrowed. "I did forget to tell her. It was the most peculiar thing. I'd say it was a coincidence, but I don't believe in coincidences."

"Nor do I," said Lucy. "I was delivering some pies for Mama when Wilhelmina and I overheard two customers speaking about an article in *The Cornwall Courier* being suspiciously similar to one in *The Horizon Herald*."

"Really?" Ruby thought back to the time in Cornwall when she'd read an article that was exactly the same as the one Lillian wrote in *The Horizon Herald*. It had all but slipped her mind until Lucy mentioned about the customers. "Do you know who wrote the Cornwall newspaper article?"

Her sister shrugged. "Some person by the name of Murphy."

"Mr. Henry Murphy, perhaps?"

"Could be. If I recall correctly, it was about a horrific explosion in one of the canyons south of Cornwall."

"Oh, yes, I remember Lillian presenting that article to Mr. O'Kane. It was a tragic accident where eight men were killed and fourteen are missing, presumably still in the mine."

Wilhelmina nodded. "Yes, and Pastor Albert led the prayer for the families just last Sunday."

Ruby remembered Albert's prayer well, and she remembered the sorrow she felt for the families of those who perished and for those who were experiencing uncertainty about the missing fourteen. She had continued to pray daily for them.

"Do you think the articles are identical?" asked Mama.

"From what the customers mentioned, they are exactly the same with one exception," said Lucy. "The writer of *The Horizon Herald* article wasn't the Murphy fellow, but Lillian O'Kane. It was in her *Lillian's Horizon Happenings* column."

"Does anyone know anyone who subscribes to *The Cornwall Courier*?" Velma asked.

"Landon reads it from time to time when he's in Cornwall, but we don't subscribe," offered Mae.

Ruby chewed on her lip and glanced in *The Horizon Herald's* direction. Just who was stealing the articles? Mr. Henry Murphy or Lillian O'Kane?

Several minutes later, Ruby carried the tray of cookies to the church where the men were busy painting the exterior. So many from the town attended, including Papa, Timothy, Albert, Landon, Sheriff Zembrodt, Hubert, Mayor Trabert, the Lieutenant, and several others. One face she hadn't anticipated seeing among the volunteers was Mr. Lynton.

Papa announced the noonday meal had arrived, and the cluster of men crowded around the makeshift table Papa and Timothy constructed earlier that day.

"I'll say grace." Everyone folded their hands and bowed their heads, and Albert lifted their petition to the Lord. "Dear Heavenly Father, thank You for this day You have blessed us with. Thank You for bringing us all together and for the willingness of these men to contribute their time and wisdom to the repair needs of the church. Thank You also for the women who are preparing the noonday meal. Bless this day, Father, and help us to glorify You in all that we do. In Jesus' Name, Amen."

A chorus of amens followed. Mama and Lucy disbursed ham sandwiches, Velma and Mae checked on the children, and Ruby offered apple slices and cookies.

She conversed with her family members and the townsfolk but was unprepared for the last man who stood before her awaiting his portion.

A sharp inhalation of breath expanded her lungs. Mr. Lynton was here assisting with the church repairs? The cantankerous recluse who kept to himself?

Mr. Lynton had removed his hat, exposing plentiful unkempt dark brown hair. If he heeded more care for his appearance, he might not be such a sorry sight. As Ruby previously ascertained, he obviously was a younger man since no gray peppered his hair or beard and no wrinkles edged the corners of his eyes.

It was then that she realized she was staring.

Jake nearly returned home no less than three times on his way to the church. Only the fact that he'd promised Pastor Albert help with whitewashing the church kept him on the road to town.

Several horses and wagons waited near the church. A group of men stood just to the side, Pastor Albert among them. Jake sucked in a deep breath and dismounted.

"Jake, nice to see you here." Pastor Albert extended a hand and introduced everyone. Jake knew he'd never remember all of the names, but he did recognize Timothy as the young man who accompanied the newspaperwoman. Timothy must have recognized him as well because his eyes widened as he shook Jake's hand.

Jake gave it a firm shake and prepared to answer if Timothy asked to interview him again. Thankfully, that didn't happen.

An older man about Pa's age and presumably Timothy's father from the strong resemblance asked if Jake was the one who rescued the children as they both entered the church.

"Yes." Jake's clipped, curt response wasn't meant as disrespect, but he refused to allow this time of aiding Pastor Albert to become a discussion about things he would rather forget.

"Pleasure to make your acquaintance. I'm Tyler Shepherdson."

The sight before him reminded Jake of his time at church in Ingleville. Pa was an elder, and there was always need within the community for help and prayer. The men there shared a camaraderie, just as the men here appeared to. The tug of homesickness pulled at his heart.

Three men began repairing some of the pews—Jake, Mr. Shepherdson, and a man named Hubert, who was a round and chatty fellow. "Wilhelmina and the other women will be bringing the noonday meal soon," he said. "That's if they aren't too busy with their chit-chat. You know how they can be at times."

Prattling hens for sure, thought Jake, although, from the sounds of it, Hubert might possess that characteristic as well. Jake recalled how Ma and Dinah Jo could talk all day with their friends. Pa, Jake, and Corbin always waited patiently for them after church and social functions.

After restoring the pews, Mr. Shepherdson and Hubert joined several other men with removing weeds around the church, while Jake climbed on the roof and fixed some broken shingles. He could view the entire town from his position on the roof. Especially on this warm, sunny Saturday, folks bustled up and down the boardwalk. Several children played baseball and other games in the nearby schoolyard.

After the noonday meal, he'd start whitewashing the church.

Being away from the other men allowed Jake the opportunity not to speak and not to be asked questions. In his former life, as he now referred to it, he'd shared close friendships with a few men his age and welcomed conversation about farming, the weather, fishing, hunting, and crop prices.

Now he just wanted to do his part and return home.

Although Jake had to admit he enjoyed helping those in need and always cottoned to construction and repairs.

He looked up again in time to see a group of women emerging from the restaurant, some carrying basketfuls of what he presumed to be food.

"It's time for the noonday meal!" a man known as the Lieutenant bellowed.

The men ceased working and clustered around the makeshift table.

Jake's stomach growled in response to the thought of food. He stepped closer and took his place behind several other men in line.

And that's when he saw her.

The newspaper lady.

Her red hair, pulled up in some fancy coiffure, shimmered in the sunlight. She spoke to the woman beside her, a brown-haired woman carrying a baby on her hip. For a moment, he allowed the newspaperwoman to garner his attention. Her beauty drew her to him and her merriment amused him. Her words spoke of her being an educated woman.

Although she was bothersome with her insistence on securing an interview from him.

Ruby unloaded a basket onto the table and organized plates of cookies and apple slices. Jake presumed her to be near his age, and today she wore the same dress she'd worn when he'd first met her the day she'd driven off the road.

Not that he was in the habit of recollecting her clothing choices, because he wasn't.

If only he'd met her at a different time in his life, he might desire to make her acquaintance rather than attempt to avoid her.

Two women handed out sandwiches and glasses of lemonade. Ruby stood at the end of the line and laughed jovially at something Mr. Shepherdson said.

On the table was a plate of the very same cookies she'd recently delivered to his house. He unwittingly licked his lips, remembering how tasty the cookies were. He'd eaten the entire amount before supper that day.

"Mr. Lynton?" she gasped when he stood in front of her. "What brings you here?"

Timothy finished collecting a handful of cookies and attempted to juggle them with his sandwich, lemonade, and apple slices. "He's here to help with the whitewashing and other repairs, just like the other menfolk. You're such a featherbrain sometimes, Rubes."

Rubes. Must be a nickname her assistant referred to her by.

"Begging your pardon, Mr. Lynton. I just hadn't taken you for someone who was…"

"A charitable sort?" His eye met hers, and he wished he hadn't removed his hat and left it in the church. Jake figured his matted hair appeared even more so today, what with the hot Idaho heat.

Not that he cared about his appearance, because he didn't. Not in the least.

"Yes. I mean no. I mean I have no idea if you're charitable." A pleasing blush colored her lovely face and her eyes darted from the cookies to the brown-haired woman beside her with the baby. "Would you like any cookies, Mr. Lynton?"

"Don't mind if I do."

She deposited two cookies in his opened palm.

"Much obliged."

The woman twisted her mouth to one side as if debating her next words. "Have you given any more thought to the interview?"

"No. The answer is still no, and will always be no."

This time she pursed her lips in such a dramatic fashion Jake almost chuckled. With effort, he forced himself to remain stoic. "Thank you for these."

Ruby the newspaperwoman might exasperate him with her continual request, but for some reason, Jake found himself thinking of her more often as of late.

CHAPTER EIGHTEEN

JAKE HAD JUST FALLEN asleep when the sound of window panes shuttering and something clanging on the porch startled him. A high-pitched whistle blew through the unsealed chinks in the house, and Samson paced in circles, his toenails clicking on the wood floor. Jake rose and peered through the bedroom window. The tree branches bowed over and something—a piece of wood?—flew through the air.

"Samson? Come here, boy." The dog needed no further coaxing. He dashed to Jake, stood on his hind legs, and whined. Jake patted him, then lifted him into his arms. "I know you don't like storms, boy. I'm going outside to see what's clanging on the porch." He hugged the dog before returning him to the floor. "Keep an eye on things. I'll be right back."

Samson barked in response and licked at the air. His tail between his legs, he began pacing again. Jake gave him one more pat before donning his flannel shirt and a pair of trousers.

The harsh rushing winds slapped him on the face, the cooler air a stark contrast from the hot summer day. He gripped the lantern and gaped into the dark night, willing his eyes to adjust to the darkness. The moon cast an eerie glow interrupted by shadowy clouds drifting across it. The wind wrestled against him as he righted the overturned rocking chair. Bits of flying dirt scratched his face.

No rain. Only wind.

Wind that had the propensity to uproot fragile crops.

A dusty scent greeted him, and another flying piece of wood caught his attention and slammed into the side of the house. The barn door creaked open and slammed closed. Jake bounded in that direction, and once inside noticed the cow flicking her tail, bellowing, and stomping around with erratic steps. A hen escaped the coop and fluttered her wings while dizzily going in circles in a panic.

He peered up just in time to see a piece of roof dismantle and disappear—not the first to have done so. He calmed the cow, caught the hen and returned her to the coop, and fastened the barn door.

But the ongoing damage to the barn roof would have to wait.

An abrupt gust slapped at him as he returned to the house and sought refuge inside. He poured a glass of water from the pitcher and settled into the chair at the table, Samson perched in his lap.

There was no way he could sleep while the howling wind dominated the formerly peaceful evening.

In the morning, Jake woke from a cramped position with his head leaning on the table and Samson at his feet. The border collie's ears perked as he barked. Jake unfolded himself, stretched the kinks from his neck, and rolled his shoulders. He opened the front door and followed the dog to the porch. A piece of the railing had splintered, the crevice fixable only with a replacement piece of wood. Green leaves littered the ground along with numerous branches. An aspen tree was completely bent to one side. Fortunately, the wheat wasn't tall enough yet to be flattened, and the corn, while slightly bent, was largely untouched. But the barn roof was a different matter.

Holes now dotted the area where a solid roof once was. One of the windows was broken. Part of the corral succumbed to the fierce winds as well.

The damage would take some time to fix. Time Jake didn't have what with the other chores demanding his attention.

He inspected the exterior of the house and thankfully found no damage.

It could have been so much worse.

"Thank You, Lord." The words escaped his mouth before Jake could remind himself that he hadn't spoken to the Lord in some time.

He ate breakfast, plopped his cowboy hat on his head, commenced to handling the remainder of the morning chores, then headed to the fields. This evening, he'd tackle the barn and corral and assess the full damage. While discouragement lingered, Jake preferred to be grateful the damage wasn't worse. How had the townsfolk fared? Were the shingles he'd repaired on the church two days ago still intact? What about the parsonage? Pastor Albert and his wife didn't need further heartache.

Five hours later, he strolled to the house for the noonday meal, Samson on his heels. He removed his hat and swiped at the sweat collecting on his brow. He ought to consider a haircut, especially with the upcoming scorching summer days.

Samson barked and bolted to the road just as a rider on a horse rounded the corner. Who would be visiting him? He only knew of a few people who'd ever stopped at his home, one being for the interview he refused to give.

Jake started toward the rider only to discover it was Pastor Albert. Jake liked the man, although he was curious how the reverend had found his farm. Did he need help with damage to the church or parsonage?

"Hello, Jake." Pastor Albert extended a hand, and Jake took it in a firm shake.

"What brings you here?"

"Much obliged for all your help at the church the other day. Thank you."

"You're welcome. Glad I could be there."

Pastor Albert scanned Jake's farm, and storm damage notwithstanding, Jake felt a sense of pride for the place he called home.

"You've done a lot with the place."

"Thank you."

"How did you manage with last night's storm?"

"Lost most of the barn's roof and all of the windows. There was minor damage to the porch and corral. It could have been much worse."

"Yes, it could have been."

Jake shoved his hands in his trouser pockets. "How did the other townsfolk fare? The church and parsonage?"

"Minimal damage to Miss Greta's, which has already been rectified, but other than that I've heard of nothing else."

Pastor Albert perused the outside of the barn. "Looks to be abundant devastation."

"Yes. I aim to climb up there this evening and assess it."

"Hmm. Well, praise the Lord for His Providence during the storm."

A question formed in Jake's mind, one that he'd been mulling since he previously spoke to Pastor Albert about the Lord. "How long do you think it takes the Lord to forgive a transgression?"

"In 1 John 1:9, it tells us that if we confess, God is *faithful and just to forgive us our sins and cleanse us from all unrighteousness.*' In Psalm 86:5, we are told God is *'good and forgiving, abounding in steadfast love to all who call upon Him.'* God is not like we are. We hold grudges and take our time to forgive someone who has trespassed against us. We struggle with forgiveness, although we've been forgiven for much. God does not tarry in forgiving us when we repent. Where we might hold a grudge, He does not. And would not."

"Like my pa."

"Forgiveness is challenging. Sometimes we fear that if we forgive, that means the other person was right when that's not the case at all."

"But what if someone can't forgive because the offense was so painful and will never be forgotten?"

"Are you speaking of your pa after what happened to your brother?"

"Yes." Jake stared at the ground and scuffed at a half-buried rock.

"Have you considered speaking with your father?"

Jake returned his attention to Pastor Albert. Would he understand why Jake *couldn't* talk with Pa? "Seeing my pa again after my failure to keep Corbin safe…"

"Would be difficult."

"And what if he turns me away?"

"He could turn you away, but he likely won't."

If only Pastor Albert was correct in his assumption.

"It would be good to see him, Ma, and my sister again."

The reverend cupped a hand on Jake's shoulder. "And to make amends."

"If amends can be made."

"God desires reconciliation if at all possible."

Would Pa be willing to forgive Jake? Would he be happy to have his son return? Or did the pain run too deep to remedy all that was broken? "I'm not sure if reconciliation is possible or even if Pa—" The squeeze in his throat and the what-ifs prevented him from continuing.

"That's why we serve a God who not only created the mountains, the oceans, people, and animals, but who can make things we believe to be impossible possible. The verse in Matthew comes to mind about how with God, *'all things are possible'.* I will continue to pray that the Lord will lead you in your decision of whether or not to return home."

A semblance of peace niggled in Jake's heart for the first time since he'd separated himself from both his earthly father and his Heavenly Father.

No one but the banker, the two newspaperwomen, Timothy, and now Pastor Albert, knew where Jake lived. So why then were two wagons and five men on horseback driving toward his farm? He set his hammer on the fencepost and waited for them to draw closer. Perhaps they were lost. An easy thing to do seeing as how Idaho had numerous farms dotting its landscape. Or maybe the men were looking for someone. Maybe an outlaw had escaped after robbing the bank again.

No matter. He'd direct them and they'd be on their way, and Jake could finish fixing the corral before starting on the porch railing and barn roof.

The crisp morning air wouldn't last long, and if he wanted to complete all the chores beckoning him, he'd best be efficient.

Pastor Albert rode with Mr. Shepherdson, Timothy, and three other men in a wagon. The Lieutenant, Mayor Trabert, Hubert, Sheriff Zembrodt, and Mr. Bjorn, the barber, rode horses. Another man, whom Jake thought was named Landon—drove the second wagon with two passengers—one of whom was an older man from the deaf school if Jake recalled correctly, and the other was a man named Hans—and a stack of lumber.

Pastor Albert climbed from the wagon. "Hello, Jake."

"Is everyone lost?"

"Lost? No, we're here to help you fix your barn roof."

Jake worked his throat through a grainy swallow. They were here to help him? "I...uh..."

"Hello, Jake. Tyler Shepherdson. I brought some nails, and Landon has lumber in the back of his wagon. We thought you might need a hand."

Pastor Albert must have been concerned Jake would decline their offer because he hastened to begin unloading the lumber with the assistance of the other men.

"Where should we put this?" Timothy asked.

Still stunned, Jake attempted to find his voice. He pointed in the direction of the barn.

"The womenfolk will be by later with food," said Hubert. "Which I am personally grateful for." He rubbed his protruding stomach.

"You eat far too much," growled the Lieutenant. "Pretty soon we'll just roll you around to get you from place to place."

Hubert shrugged. "Not such a bad idea, is it?"

"With the hefty breakfasts Wilhelmina prepares, I'm surprised you're ever hungry." This from Landon who clapped Hubert on the back.

"She makes a fine meal. Just wish there were more of them."

Mayor Trabert, as skinny as Hubert was plump, chuckled. "Most folks eat breakfast, the noonday meal, and supper. Not Hubert. He eats breakfast, an after-breakfast meal, the noonday meal, an afternoon meal, high tea, supper, then an evening meal."

"High tea? No. Coffee, yes. Tea, no. Besides, how do you think I keep my slender figure?"

"Not by eating as much as you do," chuckled Timothy. He sidled next to Jake and whispered. "If you have any food in the house, best you hide it from Hubert."

"I heard that." Hubert playfully jabbed Timothy. "'Sides, I won't be doing any stealing today what with the sheriff in attendance."

Jake watched in amusement as the men joked with each other in comfortable camaraderie. He'd once had relationships such as these with Pa and Corbin and with some of the other men in town. A longing took up residence in him. Would he ever have a close relationship with Pa again? The conversation with Pastor Albert yesterday resurfaced in his mind.

Perhaps he should ride to Ingleville.

Within a half hour, the men were in place and working on the barn. Mr. Shepherdson unloaded a brand-new window. Pastor Albert must have noticed that needed replacement as well. "And don't worry about paying for any of this." He waved a hand at the items. "It was all donated."

Jake's jaw went slack. "I can't allow someone else to pay for..."

"No allowing about it," grumbled the Lieutenant. "As I see it, you don't have a choice in the matter anyhow. It's been bought and paid for and seeing as how some of it's already been hauled to the roof and nailed down, there'll be no returning it."

"Well, thank you."

Mr. Shepherdson grinned. "You're welcome."

Jake climbed onto the roof and together with the other men, replaced the broken boards.

The women arrived for the noonday meal. Jake spied from his place on the roof, hoping to see Ruby.

Which surprised him like nothing else ever had. For why should he anticipate seeing the pesky reporter?

Sure enough, she was among the women, many of whom were the same ones who provided the meal at the church. He climbed down the ladder, and he and Mr. Shepherdson carried his kitchen table outside. The men again lined up for the sandwiches, baked beans, and...ginger cookies.

"Care for a cookie?" Ruby asked when he reached the edge of the table.

"Yes, thank you."

"Does this mean you'll allow me to interview you?"

A suspicious glint sparkled in her green eyes. She smiled, pink dusting her cheeks and her dimple more prominent. Jake found it difficult not to return her smile, and he almost agreed to her request. They stood for a moment their gazes connected before Timothy jolted him in the arm.

"Did you save some cookies for the rest of us, Lynton?"

"Yes, yes I did, and no to the interview."

Ruby remained grinning as if undeterred by his most recent refusal. He reluctantly tore his gaze from her and strolled to stand beside Pastor Albert who was waiting to bless the meal.

There were three things Jake realized as he retired for the night and prepared to get some shut-eye. First, he'd started to make friends with some of the men in Horizon. Second, he would do as Pastor Albert suggested and return to Ingleville to make amends with Pa. After he visited the barbershop. After all, Ma would have his hide and then some if he arrived home looking as disheveled as he did.

And lastly, that a newspaperwoman named Ruby might not be so bad after all.

Ruby parked the buggy by the mercantile and plodded along the boardwalk to *The Horizon Herald.* It was a bittersweet day, but after much prayer and advice from her parents and Maribel, peace enveloped her.

It wasn't such a dismal thing not to work for the newspaper, was it? Yesterday she'd spoken with Tabitha about assisting at the mercantile when needed. She'd discussed with Miss Greta taking in some wash from the boarders. That would assist in helping Ma and Pa with expenses and paying her loan for the typewriter. This would also leave ample time to spend with her nieces and nephews and take Simon and Sherman for Velma if necessary while her sweet sister-in-law continued to heal.

Besides, not working for Mr. O'Kane and his spiteful niece would be a pleasant change.

Ruby offered a prayer heavenward for the Lord's guidance and to guard her tongue should Lillian be lurking about, and she opened the door to the newspaper office.

She watched as Lillian fluttered a piece of paper in front of Mr. O'Kane.

"Good job, Lillian. Our townsfolk here in Horizon are always glad to be apprised of happenings in Cornwall."

"Yes, Uncle, and especially this article. Can you just imagine the anguish of walking down the boardwalk in Cornwall and being assailed? To have four oversized men with their faces covered throw you to the ground and rob you for every last penny?" Lillian placed one hand against her bosom and pressed the back of her other hand against her forehead and wobbled as if she may collapse. "I would have fainted dead away if something like that were to happen to me."

She handed the paper to Mr. O'Kane, and his spectacles fell down his crooked nose as he perused the words. "Very well written, Lillian. Very well indeed. Set the typeset for tomorrow's issue."

"Certainly." Lillian flounced around and faced Ruby. "Oh. Hello, Ruby." Her nose twitched into a snarl.

"Lillian. Mr. O'Kane, might I speak with you in your office for a brief moment?"

Mr. O'Kane waved her to his office. "Do you have an article about the hero for me?"

"No, sir. Not yet." *Not ever.*

"And why not?"

"With all respect, sir, some things are more important than articles. Mr. Lynton does not wish to be interviewed, and I'll no longer press him for his story." She regretted that her voice wavered.

Mr. O'Kane steepled his fingers beneath his pointy chin. "I hadn't much confidence you could obtain the interview.

That was the thing about Mr. O'Kane. He always said what was on his mind.

"Be that as it may, I am annoyed to no end at the number of people who continue to stop in the office and ask why you are shirking your duties as a reporter."

"Shirking my duties?"

"Yes."

"But, sir, you…"

"Get to work, Miss Shepherdson. It's bad enough I've had people ask where you are and why you've been shirking your duties as a reporter."

"But, sir, you..."

"Don't argue with me. Just prepare some news for our customers. Do not take this as an indication that I'm retaining you as an employee unless you can provide me with the interview on the hero. But I will extend the deadline until next month if you will efficiently provide a few more items to fill the paper."

Ruby grasped the side of Mr. O'Kane's desk to prevent her from tottering over due to the shock of Mr. O'Kane being willing to allow her to continue to write for *The Horizon Herald*. But she must make one thing clear. "Mr. O'Kane, while I am appreciative of being able to provide more items for the paper, I must elucidate that I will not be obtaining an interview from Mr. Lynton. Not now. Not ever. However, I am honored to provide more articles on other subjects."

Indecision flickered in her boss's beady eyes. "Be that as it may, I do want you to endeavor to secure the interview. In the meantime, write an article or two for *Ruby's Horizon Happenings*."

Ruby wouldn't argue. "I'll be back tomorrow morning with an article."

"See that you are." Mr. O'Kane rose and gestured for her to take her leave. "You're dismissed."

She felt lighter than she had in some time, and so preoccupied with her thoughts and paying no mind to her surroundings that she ran directly into someone when she exited the newspaper office.

"Oh!"

Mr. Lynton righted her before she could topple over into a heap on the boardwalk and risk Lillian writing an article about her mishap.

"Hello, Mr. Lynton."

"Jake. You can call me Jake."

Was that a smidge of a smile on his hairy face? She squinted and dared to lean closer. Yes, it was a smile. A faint one, but a grin nonetheless.

She wanted to ask why the change of heart, but thought better of it. "Thank you. You may call me Ruby."

"I wanted to let you know I will allow you to interview me."

"Begging your pardon?" She might just have to replicate Lillian's actions and hold one hand to her bosom and one pressed against her forehead in an effort not to topple after hearing the unexpected news. "But you said…" A glance behind her indicated Lillian with her nose pressed against *The Horizon Herald*'s window. "Do you mind if we step aside to discuss this?"

Jake accompanied her down the boardwalk to the buggy. "I know I mentioned I wouldn't allow you to interview me, but I've changed my mind. I'm leaving town for a few days but will return next week. Is Monday agreeable?"

Ruby closed her suspended jaw and sought the words. "Yes," she breathed. "Yes, Monday would be perfect."

"Good. I'll see you after the noonday meal."

This time, he did offer her a full smile, and Ruby's heart stumbled at a frantic beat. A disturbing thought entered her mind as Jake assisted her into the buggy, his rough hand gently grasping hers. Was her heartbeat so erratic because she finally had the interview she sought? Or was it because there was something about Jake Lynton?

CHAPTER NINETEEN

JAKE FLIPPED THE TWENTY-FIVE-CENT piece between his finger and thumb and walked along the boardwalk to Bjorn's Barbershop.

He changed his mind when he arrived at the door. While having a haircut and shave seemed reasonable for the past three days and even as recently as five minutes ago, now Jake had second thoughts. Maybe he should continue being obscure. A man with long bushy hair and more whiskers than two men combined. Having what he'd termed his "disguise" kept folks from seeing the real man underneath.

The man who'd allowed both his brother and another man to perish.

He stood on the boardwalk, his hand clutching the doorknob. Jake could hear the conversation inside, although he couldn't comprehend the words.

But his mind wasn't on conversations anyhow. His thoughts were steeped in a memory.

"I heard it was the boy's fault. He did nothing to help his brother. Can you imagine? People are so irresponsible these days."

Mean Mrs. Litkey's voice sounded in his mind as if it were yesterday. Ma asked that he get a haircut before Corbin's funeral. Not that his hair then was anywhere near the length it was today, but if it was important to Ma, it was important to him.

He'd stumbled down the boardwalk, grief clouding his thoughts and slowing his movements. It was then that he'd heard Mrs. Litkey's shrill voice as she spoke to a group of women standing in a circle outside the new Ingleville millinery. He'd seen her point when he staggered by, hold up a hand just to the side of her mouth, and whisper none too discreetly her opinion of him.

"Such a disappointment for his family. One son gone and look at the one they have left—a careless cad. Everyone knows the younger brother needed guidance and supervision, and so Mr. Lynton asked his son to provide that. But did he? No."

Several gasps sounded from the other women, and Jake had choked back a response. A response that a man professing Christ shouldn't say—a retort that would have disappointed his parents, especially Ma, even more than they already were.

So instead, he'd turned on his heel and returned to his horse. If Mrs. Litkey and her group of gossipmongers thought so ill of him, what did the rest of the townsfolk think?

"You gonna go in or just stand there?" The deep voice behind him interrupted his thoughts, and he turned to see the Lieutenant.

Jake released his firm hold on the doorknob and stepped aside. "Not sure," he muttered.

"You ain't sure if you're gonna get a haircut or not?" The man's eyes squinted beneath his spectacles. "Looks to me like you should pay a visit to the barber. I haven't seen a beard like that in all my years."

Jake hadn't asked the Lieutenant's opinion of his appearance, but he didn't mention such. He inhaled sharply and gestured for the older man to enter the barbershop.

The Lieutenant continued. "Come on inside. I'll buy you a haircut and shave."

The older man didn't wait for Jake to argue. He gave him a little shove and followed him inside.

Jake stepped into the business and took a gander about the room. There were two barber chairs with mirrors in front of them on one side. To the right of one of the chairs, a compact ornate shelf in need of a thorough dusting hung on the wall with a myriad of tonics, shampoos, sticks of shaving soap, cigars, and other toiletries. Three regular wooden chairs lined the far wall.

"What can I do for you?" a gangly man with a Scandinavian accent asked as he puffed on a cigar.

Jake took a deep breath. Was it too late to change his mind? In answer to his question, the Lieutenant prodded him with a poke of his fleshy finger.

"Hello, Bjorn. This here man would like a haircut and shave." The Lieutenant moseyed to the chairs near the wall. A portly man with an overabundance of stark black hair peppered with liberal amounts of gray stood to shake his hand. The other man, just the opposite in appearance of the first, did the same. Then they all three lowered themselves into the seats.

"Just so happens I have an opening right now," said Bjorn. "Reckon you'll be needing a haircut and shave too, Lieutenant?"

"Yes, indeed. And I'll be paying for this here man's haircut and shave as well."

Bjorn nodded at Jake. "I remember meeting you before, but I'm afraid I don't remember your name."

A voice interrupted before Jake could answer. "That's right kind of you to pay his way." Is he your son?" The white-haired man's thick fuzzy eyebrows escaped into one of the folds on his forehead.

The Lieutenant shook his head. "Now you know as well as I do, Leonel, that I don't have any children."

The plump man clapped Leonel on the back, nearly knocking him off the chair. "How long have we known the Lieutenant? You know he and Miss Greta don't got kids."

Leonel hiked his shoulders into his lengthy large-lobed ears. "Didn't figure there was any harm in askin'."

"Rather obliging of you to pay for this man's haircut and shave, Lieutenant." Bjorn nodded at one of the empty barber chairs. "Have a seat right there." He unrolled his fingers from his cigar and rested it on the nearby counter, allowing the cigar to extinguish itself. Jake followed Bjorn's instructions and reclined in the faded black leather barber chair. He rested his feet on the footrest and peered over at the three men in the chairs watching him as if he were in the circus.

He hadn't figured he'd have an audience.

The barber draped a cloak around Jake's shoulders and then tapped his own clean-shaven chin as if wondering where to start.

The portly one pointed a finger at Jake. "Looks like you might a been needin' that for quite some time."

Leonel, with carefully slicked sparse black-and-white hair and a leathery face full of wrinkles, chortled, "'Bout time you came in, Scruffy. Bjorn here will give you a right good cut and shave, all for two bits."

"Don't mind them," said Bjorn, preparing his tools of the trade. "They're in here all the time. Once in a while I get my money's worth out of 'em."

Leonel chuckled. "You ain't hardly never get yer money's worth with my thinning hair."

"You still got whiskers once in a while, Leonel," said the Lieutenant.

"Ain't that the truth, but Bjorn don't give me much of a concession for just a shave."

"By the way," said the Lieutenant, "this here is Leonel." He thumbed the man on his left. "And this is Pablo on my right. They've lived in Horizon since Lewis and Clark ventured through the area."

"Funny, amigo. But Lewis and Clark weren't down this far south in Idaho and you know it," said Pablo. "Besides, you ain't but a few years younger than us, if that."

"He's younger? I thought he was older." The shocked expression on Leonel's pasty face caused Jake to chuckle. The three reminded him of some of the old codgers in Ingleville.

"Come now, gentlemen. This here is a new customer. Let's make his visit to Bjorn's Barbershop as comfortable as possible."

"Looks like he's been needin' to frequent this here establishment a bit more often." Leonel slapped his hand to his knee, then winced. "Ouch. Shouldn'ta done that with my rheumatism kickin' up and all."

"Remind me again—what's your name, son?" Bjorn asked Jake.

"Jake Lynton."

"I remember you when we were fixing the church roof and your barn. New to town?"

"He's that one that bought that ol' rundown Kountz place. Ain't that right?" Pablo scratched his head.

Jake attempted not to nod as Bjorn had already started cutting. The last thing he needed was a lopsided haircut. "That's the place."

Pablo grinned a toothless grin. "Ain't been out there in forever or longer, but good to hear someone's livin' there. Got yerself a wife and young'uns?"

"No, sir. Just me at the present."

"Ain't that a sorry tale. Well, maybe you'll find yerself a wife in this here town. I been married to my wife for near bouts forty years."

"Poor Maria. She never knew the heartache she'd face when she done said 'yes' all those many moons ago."

Pablo slugged Leonel in the arm. "She got herself a good man and you know it."

"Gentlemen, let's keep it peaceful-like in here. I want to be sure Mr. Lynton is a return customer." Bjorn continued to work his skill on Jake's hair.

"He'll need to come back a might more often than he done this time. No man should start lookin' like a curly-head when he comes to the barber." Leonel's comment caused him and Pablo to start chortling again, their old man chuckles filling the entire shop.

Jake stared at himself in the mirror. His appearance was so foreign to him from what it had been for the past few months. Sure, he'd neglected his appearance in the past months. But no more. Not with what Ruby had written in her notebook. For some reason, her opinion mattered to him.

Leonel craned his head to look out the lone front window. "Well, there goes Miss Ruby. She's a sight for sore eyes. Why don'tcha put some interest in that woman, Jake?"

Pablo's forehead wrinkled. "She's too nosy for my taste."

"She is real purdy, though. If I was fifty years younger, I might think about courtin' her."

"Leonel, you'd have to be a hunnerd years younger to even think about courtin' her."

Leonel ignored Pablo's comment. "Do you think she'd still consider a bachelor who's a bit beyond his years? I got me a nice farm and all." Leonel tossed a hopeful glance, first at the Lieutenant, then at Bjorn and Jake.

Pablo snorted. "Don't think so. She needs herself someone more her age. Like Mr. Lynton here."

Bjorn took more snips off of Jake's hair. "Never known you two to be matchmakers."

Jake figured this was as good of a time to weigh in on his own thoughts about their shenanigans. "Much obliged, for your matchmaking and all, gentlemen, but I have no interest in Miss Ruby. She's a feisty woman who doesn't listen well." Jake hid his smirk. Ruby *hadn't* listened well when he told her he didn't want to share his story. She kept coming around time after time hoping to persuade him, when he wanted nothing more than to be left alone and leave things buried in the past. But she'd sure listened the first and only time he said he'd allow the interview.

"She doesn't listen well? Then she'd make a good wife for Leonel for sure! He don't listen well either." This time, Pablo slapped his knee and winced. "That slapping the knee ain't something old fellows like ourselves should be doin'. Think I mighta broke my kneecap."

"Serves you right on your broken kneecap after what you just said. It ain't that I don't listen well, it's that my ears don't work as well as they once did."

Pablo elbowed Leonel. "I've known you for prit near forever and I ain't never known your ears to work well."

"I'm gonna pretend I didn't hear that. 'Sides, ain't no need to turn Miss Ruby away just because she don't listen well. Just means you have to speak up a bit more yerself."

"I hadn't heard that about Ruby," said the Lieutenant, "but I do hear a fair amount of gossip at the boardinghouse, just as Bjorn does here at the barbershop."

Bjorn paused with the scissors. "That I do."

Leonel picked at something on his arm. "We already got ourselves informed about the gossip here at the barbershop, but we's a bit behind on other gossip in Horizon. Whatcha got to tell us, Lieutenant?"

Jake thought of how the three sounded like a bunch of prattling hens. Some thought only women gossiped. They were sorely wrong.

The Lieutenant sat up straight and puffed out his chest. "Well, I heard the other day that Miss Ruby has been doing her best to try to convince some homely old curmudgeon to share his story with her."

Jake sucked in his breath. Homely old curmudgeon?

Leonel's eyes bulged. "You don't say?"

"That's what I heard. And the crabby codger won't even talk to her. Poor young lady. Working for that O'Kane and all, she's desperate for a story, but..."

"Sounds like the homely codger is a disagreeable man as all get out." Pablo shook his head. "Don't understand them kind of folks."

Crabby codger? Disagreeable? Jake tilted his head back and Bjorn nearly cut off more than he ought. "Might wanna sit still, Mr. Lynton, if you want a proper haircut and all."

"Me neither," said the Lieutenant. "I heard she drove all the way out to his place with Timothy and it was all, as my Greta said, 'for naught'."

"Don't make no sense that he wouldn't at least tell her his story for the newspaper. The advertisements and *Ruby's Horizon Happenings* is all I care to read about. Be good to have an interestin' story about the curmudgeon." Pablo drummed his fingers on his thigh. "Wonder why he won't tell her?"

"Seems he has something to hide."

Jake saw the Lieutenant look up at him in the mirror, and for a moment, Jake thought the man saw into his soul. But no, he couldn't possibly know the comely, crabby curmudgeon was him. Could he?

"But what could he be hidin'?" Leonel asked.

"All sorts of things. The man is probably a criminal." The Lieutenant shrugged. "It's a good thing Timothy accompanied her. No telling what this man is capable of. This is Horizon, but you never can be too careful these days."

"That's the truth," agreed Pablo. "This ain't the 1880s any longer."

Leonel cracked his knuckles. "Seems to me we oughta ask the sheriff if he has any wanted posters with the homely fellow on them. Could be we got ourselves a criminal in our town and don't even know it. Wouldn't that be a story for Miss Ruby to tell? I can see the likes of it now—old homely and crabby curmudgeon wanted for train robberies, bank robberies, horse thievin', disorderly conduct, vagrancy, drunkenness..."

"You forgot the time he bribed someone and cheated at cards in the saloon," added Pablo.

The Lieutenant adjusted his spectacles on his generous nose. "That ain't nothing compared to when he did all that cattle rustling up there in Wyoming."

Jake did his best not to twitch with each false accusation levied against the "homely and crabby curmudgeon". He would never do such things. Besides, to give any indication he was the topic of their gossipmongering would surely make the men aware it was him and secondly, he didn't need a botched haircut. But while he may have kept himself composed, his mouth had a mind of its own. "Maybe the fellow just wants his privacy," he said.

"Don't rightly think so." Leonel extended his skinny legs in front of him and crossed them at the ankles. "Seems to me someone ought to check that man out and be sure he ain't a menace to society."

Bjorn began the tedious task of first trimming, then shaving Jake's whiskers. The man was definitely earning his two bits today. Midway through, he stopped, set down his tools, and lit his cigar. "This is a job for two barbers," he grumbled.

He sat on the barber chair next to Jake and propped his feet up on the counter while he puffed on his cigar. "Can't say as I remember the last time I cut so much hair off one man. You going to wait another decade before coming in for a cut again?"

"No, sir." Jake's eyes flitted to the mirror. Behind him, the men were gawking at him, and he could see why. While all of his hair was cut, half of his whiskers remained.

After Bjorn resumed shaving Jake's mustache and beard, he stood back and allowed Jake to admire himself in the mirror. "What do you think, Mr. Lynton?"

Jake inhaled a sharp breath. He almost didn't recognize himself as the improvement was profound. "Thank you, Bjorn."

Bjorn swiped at Jake's chin where some of the shaving soap remained. Jake reached up and stroked his chin, then ran his hand across the top of his head.

"Why, Leonel, take a gander at that!" Pablo stood, his wobbly bowlegged legs barely holding him. "That ain't the scraggly man that first walked in here. I knew he was younger than us, but I'll be…I ain't realized he could be a great-grandson." He attempted to kick the pile of hair beneath Jake's chair with the toe of his boot. Why'd you keep all that hair and that unkempt beard all that time, Scruffy?"

The Lieutenant stood and his jaw went slack. "Almost didn't recognize you as the same man."

Pablo pointed at the floor. "Got ourselves enough hair there for a wig."

"I ain't never had that much hair. Got me more bald than hair these days." Leonel smoothed a hand over his thinning locks.

Pablo raked a hand through his own hair. "Some of us is just more blessed."

"You need all that hair on your head to balance your chubby body. Otherwise, you'd have a tiny head and a round body." Leonel, the Lieutenant, and Bjorn started laughing at Leonel's comment. Jake joined them.

It felt good to laugh.

"That'll be twenty-five cents," said Bjorn, interrupting Jake's thoughts.

The Lieutenant handed Bjorn the coin before Jake could reach into his pocket. "Much obliged, sir."

"You're welcome."

"Guess we can't call him Scruffy no more," declared Pablo. "'Cause he ain't scruffy no more!"

Pablo and Leonel broke into another fit of old-man laughter.

The Lieutenant took his place in the vacated barber chair. "This will be much easier for you, Bjorn."

Bjorn gave a nod of agreement. "Yes, it will." He paused and addressed Jake. "Have a good day, Mr. Lynton, and we'll see you next time you need a haircut and shave. And maybe don't wait so long next time."

CHAPTER TWENTY

JAKE TETHERED HIS HORSE and stood at the edge of the road that led to his parents' home. It looked much the same as it had a few years ago with the exception of the trees surrounding the cabin having grown much taller, and Ma's perfectly tended garden had expanded to nearly the barn.

He spied the corral where...

Maybe he should leave. What if Pa still blamed him for Corbin's death? What if he and Ma were thankful Jake had left town and their lives? What if...

He rubbed the back of his neck and sucked in a large breath. He had come all this way, had been so confident that it was the right thing to do. Had asked for prayer—and received it. He'd reconciled with his Heavenly Father and prayed for guidance.

So why, then, was it so difficult to make amends with Pa?

He stared at nothing for a lengthy moment as his emotions and thoughts jumbled within him. Hadn't he already thoroughly weighed his options?

Lord, please help me.

A man emerged from the house, and Jake recognized him immediately. He took a step forward, apprehension in the pit of his stomach. Pa's gaze connected with Jake's.

Jake held his breath.

Pa tilted his head to one side, then without hesitation, he leaped from the porch. "My boy is home! Do you hear that, Hester? My boy is home!" Without waiting for Ma's answer, Pa bolted toward Jake.

And Jake took to running, desperation to bridge the space between them consuming his every breath.

Pa embraced him. Emotion stung Jake's eyes as he returned Pa's hug.

"My boy has come home." Pa's muffled voice rang in Jake's ears.

He squeezed his eyes shut, his own breath catching in his chest.

Pa took a step back. "Is it really you, Jake?"

"Yes, it's me."

"I'm not dreaming?"

"No, Pa, you're not dreaming. It's really me." His father had grown older in the years Jake had been away. More wrinkles lined his face, he'd started to gray at the temples, and he was thinner than Jake remembered.

"You came home. I always knew you would. We prayed every night that you would. And you did. God is so good. He's just so good." Pa's chest heaved and tears filled his eyes.

They'd prayed every night?

Guilt consumed him. "Pa, I'm so sorry. I'm sorry for what happened to Corbin. I'm sorry for leaving like I did. And I'm sorry I waited so long to come back."

"It wasn't your fault—what happened to Corbin."

"But it was. I could have stopped him from riding Lucky."

Pa peered back at him with the blue eyes Jake had inherited. "Reckon Corbin was always one to do as he pleased, and once he set his mind to something, he'd proceed whether we tried to stop him or not."

The words Pa uttered from all those years ago reverberated through Jake's mind. *"Why didn't you stop him, Jake?"* He swallowed the bitter taste of regret. "But I thought you blamed me."

His father's strong shoulders slumped. "I'm sorry I ever made you feel like you were responsible. I know I asked why you didn't stop him. I—"

The pain in Pa's eyes gnawed at him. "You don't blame me?"

"No. Please forgive me for insinuating I did. I have no excuse for my careless words."

"And I have no excuse for leaving like I did."

Pa embraced him again. "I couldn't lose two sons. I couldn't. Praise be to our Lord for bringing you back."

"It's good to be home, Pa. I'm sorry I waited so long."

Pa released him and nodded toward the house where two women—Ma and Dinah Jo—stood on the porch. "They're giving us our space, but I know your mother and sister are anxious to see you again. And you're just in time for supper too. You do still like ham, potatoes, and shortbread, right?"

"I do."

Pa grinned, his smile temporarily replacing the pain formerly ingrained in his expression. "That's my boy. I know you're not an imposter after all."

"No, Pa, not an imposter. I'm your son through and through."

Ma and Dinah Jo both sobbed and once Ma hugged Jake, she didn't let go. "You don't know how long we've prayed. She took a step back, stood on tiptoe, and framed Jake's face with her hands. "It's so good to have you back. We've missed you."

The emotion squeezed Jake's throat. Pastor Albert had been right about reconciliation. But what if Jake hadn't listened? Had instead gone his own way? Had never returned to the family he loved?

And who loved him?

"I've missed you all too, Ma. It's good to be home."

Dinah Jo tugged on his arm. "How long are you staying?"

"For a couple of days, I reckon."

Of them all, Dinah Jo had changed the most since he'd last seen her. She strongly resembled Ma with her blonde hair and soft brown eyes.

When Ma finally released him and set about serving supper, Pa embraced him again. "I sure have missed you, son. We love you." Pa choked the words. "Never did we once stop loving you."

If Jake could apologize a hundred times over and over, it wouldn't be enough. "I never should have left."

Ma set a heaping plate of ham on the table. "That is all in the past." Her tender gaze reminded Jake again of how blessed he was to have his family. "I'm pleased that you look as though you've been getting enough to eat."

"Yes, ma'am. Although I have missed your cooking."

His mother beamed and offered him another hug. "Have as much as you'd like tonight. There's plenty."

Jake and Pa stayed up late into the night talking on the front porch. And on that day, God healed two broken hearts.

Ruby and Timothy rounded the corner to Jake's home. Would he be true to his word and allow her to interview him? Timothy doubted it, and truth be told, Ruby wasn't sure either. Guilt continued to assail her because she'd been so focused on securing this story, and there was obviously a reason, or multiple reasons, why Jake Lynton did not want to be interviewed.

She'd been convicted several times over that it wasn't really that important to keep her job at the newspaper. Certainly not worth pestering Jake and the Gholston family.

Today she would tell Jake Lynton that she no longer wished to write his story. While Mr. O'Kane still demanded it, Ruby wasn't as keen on working for *The Horizon Herald* as she'd once been.

Timothy assisted her from the buggy, and Ruby inhaled the pleasant aroma of the two pine trees on either side of the house. It really was a nice setting for a home with the plentiful fields and mountains in the distance.

"Here we go again," said Timothy.

Ruby raised a hand to knock, and the door opened immediately as if Mr. Lynton awaited their arrival. A clean-shaven man with short-cropped dark hair and a muscular and rugged exterior stood in the doorway.

"Hello, is Jake Lynton home?"

But just as the words tumbled from her mouth, Ruby realized this *was* Jake Lynton. Minus the abundance of plentiful hair and scruffy beard. "Oh!"

Her hand flew to her mouth and her jaw dropped. Were it not for the deep-blue eyes staring back at her, she would not have recognized him.

In a word, Jake Lynton was…handsome?

The heat climbed her neck and into her cheeks and settled there. Nearly incoherent babbling sounded in her ears as she spoke. "Hello, Mr. Lynton—hello. I didn't—well, I didn't recognize you at first. My sincerest apologies, Mr. Lynton—yes, the most sincerest of all apologies—that I failed to recognize you as the same man you were before."

A smile lit his face—a dapper one at that. Of course, with his abundance of facial hair, he may have smiled fully once or twice in the past, and she might not have noticed. But she *did* notice this smile.

Far too much.

Ruby diverted her attention to Timothy, who rolled his eyes before extending a hand to their host. "Hello, Jake."

"Timothy. Ruby." He directed his next words to her. "We can forego any formalities. Please call me Jake."

"Jake? Oh, yes, Jake. You mentioned before that I could call you Jake, and I must have somehow in my featherbrained—yes, featherbrained state—I had quite forgotten." Now she sounded like a bewildered ninny. Mr. Lynton had already told her she could call him Jake. Butterflies took up residency in her stomach. "You can call me Timothy, and this is my bro—assistant, Ruby."

Timothy's eyes widened and he chuckled. "What she means to say is that I am Timothy," he pointed to himself, "and she is Ruby."

"Yes, of course. That is what I mean to say."

Her brother leaned toward her and whispered none too quietly, "Rubes, this isn't like you. Are you feeling well?"

In response, she glared at her brother. "Don't be a nincompoop. I'm perfectly fine."

"You can take a seat there," offered Jake, pointing to a table with four chairs.

"Mr. Lynton, or rather, Jake, thank you for taking the time to allow us to interview you."

"You're welcome." Jake was in a much more pleasant mood than in the past. Could it be that when a man removed twelve pounds of hair and ten pounds of facial hair it made a difference in his disposition?

"However, I must admit that perhaps, as Papa would say, my persistence has surged to the forefront and has caused me to be somewhat vexatious. Such was the case in my attempts to secure an interview with you. After much prayer, I've been convicted of my error and have learned an arduous lesson about what is truly important. While I am grateful for you agreeing to speak with me, I no longer wish to share your story." There. She'd said it, albeit rapidly. And she meant every word.

"While I appreciate your candidness, I am still willing to share about what happened that day. If you'd like to hear it."

The decision weighed heavily on her. Yes, she'd have the story for *Ruby's Horizon Happenings*—perhaps her most outstanding article thus far. On the other hand, there were reasons unbeknownst to her why Jake hesitated so often to share about his heroic rescue. "I would like to hear it, but I am content not hearing it if it is painful to reveal."

Jake said nothing for several minutes, and the only sound was his dog's tail wagging against the floor and the ticking of the clock on the mantle. Finally, he spoke. "Reckon I'm fine with telling you what happened that day."

Ruby attempted not to stare at him as she rifled through her notebook. The man across from her at the table was so opposite in appearance than the man she'd known beforehand. So... dapper. "I always take notes so as to achieve the most accurate interview possible. Would you mind telling us how you came upon the children drowning in the river that day?"

"I should have done better."

She stopped writing and held her pencil midair. "I beg your pardon?" How could he have done better when four people now lived because of his actions?

"I should have done better. A man died because of me."

Pain radiated in the depths of his eyes. A pain so profound her heart broke.

For certain Ruby didn't need to tell this story after all. She closed the notebook and placed her pencil on top of it. "Mr. Lynton—Jake—I know that I have perhaps been overmuch in my quest to tell your story."

"That's true," muttered Timothy, and she jabbed him in the ribs, eliciting a low-throated yowl from him.

"As such, if you truly do not feel comfortable relaying your story, I'll not force you to do so."

Jake sat up straighter in his chair and clasped his large hands before resting them on the table. "No offense, ma'am, but no one has ever forced me to do something I don't want to do."

"Oh, I didn't mean that literally, I just..."

Jake held up a finger. "I don't want to tell this story for reasons you'll never understand and for reasons I'll not share.

However, I do know it's important for you to hear it or else you wouldn't have pestered me as you have these past weeks."

His candid words caused another round of guilt. "I ought not to have pestered you, Jake, and for that, I am truly sorry. I don't wish to compel you to tell a story you don't wish to tell or one that brings you great anguish."

"Even though you've been compelling me to tell it since the day you first found out it was me who saved the children?"

This was the Jake Lynton she'd come to know. The one who didn't mince words. Humility was a challenge at times, but when he'd mentioned having done better and a man dying because of him, it further changed her perspective. She prayed for guidance and prepared to stand. "I've been selfish in my tenacity."

"I'm surprised you are giving up so easily. This doesn't seem like the woman I've become acquainted with. The same one who drove off the road and lost her notebook. The same one who made sure children were able to keep raspberries illegally picked while trespassing."

Timothy snorted. Her brother was not helping matters. Not one bit.

Ruby inhaled a sharp breath.

"Please stay. I'll tell you my story, but I would ask to read it before you deliver it to your boss."

She worried her lip. His request *was* reasonable. And she *did* need this story. *And* she was already here. *And* she'd finally convinced him after all this time to share his story. "All right, Jake. We'll stay. Yes, you may read the article when I've finished it before I relinquish it to Mr. O'Kane."

"We have a deal then."

Ruby reopened her notebook. "Can you please tell me about that day?"

Jake had only recently begun discussing things with the Lord again. At first, his conversations with his Heavenly Father were stilted, but as the days passed, it had become somewhat easier. He'd prayed this morning for the words to say, for the grace to say them to Ruby, and for the ability to relive that day and not allow it to rehash memories of Corbin. He'd begged the Lord to forgive him for his failures, both with his brother and with the man he'd been unable to rescue.

The conversation he'd had with Pastor Albert had helped.

He was grateful for the lengthy talk he'd had with Pa and the pain and regrets they both shared. Only the Lord could have orchestrated that reconciliation. But while forgiveness had taken place, Jake still struggled with forgiving himself.

He cleared his throat and pondered his first words. "I was headed to Cornwall for a plow."

Suddenly, it was as though he was there again on the banks of the Cornwall River. The rain, subsequent hail, lightning, thunder, the relentless swirling of the water. The children's cries, Mr. Gholston's pleading. The threat of the dangerous waves overcoming him...

It was up to Jake and Jake alone. No one else could assist—not Gholston because he couldn't swim. Keeping him out of the water in his desperation to save his children was a battle unto itself. Mr. Strain—the man in the other canoe—was too far downstream in the river and too busy saving himself. No one else was around.

The current tugged at his weary body, but Jake pressed on. Now he realized it was only because of the Lord's mercy that more didn't perish, including Jake himself.

First the three boys, then the little girl whom he'd nearly forgotten if not for Gholston's desperate reminder. The dreadful swim back but gratitude because she was all right, despite slipping beneath the water.

Then the man.

The man Jake couldn't save.

Because he'd closed his eyes just for a moment to rest. He'd taken his thoughts from the rescue at hand.

Just a few seconds of rest as I continue through the water. In that moment, the man succumbed to drowning. In that instant with time being so very crucial, a life was lost.

"Jake?"

Ruby's voice returned him to the present.

"Uh, yes. Where was I?" It was then that Jake remembered he hadn't started telling his story at all. Perhaps he should change his mind again. "I..." he stared down at his calloused hands. "Ma'am, I'm sorry, I don't know if I can tell this story."

"That is fine. Please do not feel you must tell it."

When he looked up and his gaze locked with hers, he didn't see the tenacity and perseverance he'd seen every time she'd asked. Instead, only warmth and concern lit her green eyes. "I'm sorry." His voice sounded hoarse in his own ears. "I just can't."

Ruby leaned forward, and he caught a whiff of her lavender perfume and inhaled. "I once again wish to apologize. I had no right to continually pester you about a topic that has obviously been so painful. Will you please forgive me?" She blinked several times, and he saw the emotion that hovered close to the surface.

"I should be able to tell this story, but for some reason, I can't. And yes, I forgive you." He held her gaze, seeing the compassion and noticing again how truly pretty she was.

He attempted to force himself once again to share the details from that day, but Jake couldn't force the words that needed to be said.

"I can tell another story maybe," he muttered.

"You do have a sizable farm here. Do you have plans to grow other crops besides wheat?"

Farming he could discuss. Easily. He sat up in his chair. "Yes, I do aim to start growing spuds next year once I clear the far field. Near the raspberry bushes." He thought of the Aspinwall Potato Planter at the implement in Cornwall. If the crop was good this year, perhaps he could purchase the machine and his hopes of planting spuds next spring would come to fruition.

She offered a smile. "Oh, yes, the raspberry bushes. Did I ever tell you that the children made so many pies and preserves that if we were to fall on hard times, we'd surely remain well-fed?"

He returned her amusement. "Reckon I'm glad to hear that. I wouldn't want anyone to starve, even if they were trespassing."

"Trespassing or not, you ought to consider a raspberry farm."

That was not something he would consider. "With all due respect, wheat, corn, and spuds will be my crops of choice."

Their gazes connected again, and for a moment, he forgot that she was here to ask him about the details of that day in Cornwall.

"Ahem."

They both diverted their attention to Timothy, who had cocked his head to one side. "While we'd all like to sit here and chew the fat about raspberry farms, some of us have our own farms to manage."

"Oh, yes, that is true." Ruby tapped her pencil on her notebook. "Mr. Kountz, the previous owner of this farm, unfortunately fell ill. Because he rarely came to town except once in a while for church, folks regrettably didn't realize his illness was terminal. In the meantime, his farm fell under disrepair. From the appearance of the farm now, no one would be the wiser that it ever was in a dilapidated state. With your permission, I'd like to write a story for *Ruby's Horizon Happenings* about how you took a dilapidated piece of property and rehabilitated it into this..." She waved a hand around her.

"An article about the farm?"

"Indeed."

A prolonged exhale of relief left his lungs. "I could do that, although there's not much to tell. And there is more to be done. Of course, it wouldn't be the way it is now if the fine people of Horizon hadn't assisted me with the barn after the wind storm." He figured her story would be mighty short, but it surpassed having to share about the rescue.

Timothy inclined toward Ruby and lowered his voice. "Will Mr. O'Kane be amenable to that?"

The blush crept up her face and her dimple shone more prominently. Ruby shrugged. "Mr. O'Kane is not the author of the *Ruby's Horizon Happenings* column."

The Timothy fellow seemed a mite impatient, but who was Jake to blame him if he had his own farm to oversee? "Much obliged for the change in the topic of your article, but if your assistant needs to return to his farm, we can talk another day."

Timothy leaned back in his chair. "I am actually her…" He paused and peered over at the newspaperwoman.

"He's actually my brother."

"Ah, yes, that would make sense. I can see that now."

"You can?" Ruby's eyes widened. "We don't resemble each other much."

Jake thought of Corbin and how he and Jake were as opposite in appearance as two brothers could get.

"Let me guess. Farmer's instinct?" suggested Timothy.

"Farmer's instinct?"

Timothy folded himself forward. "Rubes here is always saying she has writer's instinct, which unfortunately is rarely correct."

Ruby jabbed him playfully in the arm.

"So, I always say I have farmer's instinct since I'm a farmer."

Jake chuckled. "So if you two are related, then Mr. Shepherdson is your pa, which makes sense, Timothy, because you look an awful lot like him only younger."

For the next hour, Jake answered Ruby's questions and shared about how he rode through Horizon one day—purposely omitting why he'd come here in the first place—and his dreams and aspirations for the Lynton Farm. He also declined to reveal his other hopes for the future. That of someday marrying and raising children on his farm, just as Ma and Pa had done on their farm in Ingleville.

When it was time for Ruby and Timothy to leave, Samson convinced Timothy to play fetch as Jake accompanied Ruby to the buggy.

"Thank you for the story." She peered up at him and for a moment, his heart stalled as her sweet smile drew him in. Perhaps now that he was getting his life back to rights, he could pursue a friendship with her.

"You're welcome. And thank you for not pressing me for more details." Standing there with her watching as Timothy threw the stick for Samson for what was probably the tenth time, he thought again of that day in Cornwall. "Please don't write this in a story, but I did rescue the four children that day. I was unable to rescue a man who was also on the river."

Ruby rested her hand on his arm, compassion in her eyes. "Sometimes we don't understand God's will."

"I'm realizing that, especially after spending time with Pastor Albert." Jake thought of the reverend and how he'd invited Jake to visit with him once a week for the next month or so. Jake found him easy to talk to, and Lord willing, the conversations would continue to help Jake overcome the pain and guilt.

"Thank you for risking your life that day. I know you don't want it to be written or for anyone to know. You have your reasons, and I promise to respect those reasons. However, I do want you to know that you are a hero, Jake Lynton."

Her words meant more to him than he could ever express.

CHAPTER TWENTY-ONE

LEAVE IT TO MAMA with her gift of hospitality to invite Jake to church and suggest he join them in their pew. Of course, with how the family had grown in recent years, one pew had become two pews, and Ruby found herself sitting next to Jake for the service.

Or perhaps her two sisters had participated in some scheming because when Ruby sat down that first Sunday Jake did more than stand by the back door, no one else sat beside her.

Not even her nieces and nephews.

Lucy and Mae were nothing short of obvious with their whispers and nods in Ruby's direction. Mama did her best to ensure everyone was scrunched together—everyone but Ruby, who might as well have had the entire pew to herself—and Papa avoided her eye. Velma pretended not to know anything about why there was a gaping space between Ruby and Mama, and Timothy had a suspicious smirk on his face—a more profound smirk than usual.

After church several weeks later when Jake asked if she and the children would care to join him in picking raspberries and apples on his farm the following Saturday, Ruby found it impossible to hide her anticipation. She readily agreed. The children would savor the opportunity to pick more raspberries for jam, and she would welcome spending more time with Jake. They discussed the plans. "And we will have permission to trespass?" she'd quipped.

"Permission to trespass." A glint sparkled in his eyes and he held her gaze. Ruby's heart pitter-pattered against her ribcage.

Now, on a hot and sunny Saturday, she and her eight nieces and nephews loaded into the wagon and met Jake at his farm.

Just the sight of him standing at the corral wearing a red plaid shirt accentuating his broad shoulders and trim waist drew her full attention.

"Right, Auntie Rubes?"

"Aunt Rubes is in a daydream, aren't you, Aunt Rubes?"

Someone tapped on Ruby's arm. "Yes?"

"Little Hans asked a question," said Becky.

"Pardon? Oh! I'm sorry. What was that question?"

"We can eat some of what we pick, right? 'Cause my tummy is growling up a storm." Little Hans rubbed his stomach.

"Yes, you may."

Jake strode toward them. "Hello, Ruby. Children."

"Hello, Mr. Jake," they chorused, with Polly and Hosea signing their greeting.

Jake climbed into the wagon beside Ruby. Her pulse skittered when his shoulder touched hers.

She was about to ask Polly and Carrie, who sat beside her on the buckboard, if they'd care to relocate into the back of the wagon as things had become overcrowded with Jake having now boarded, but the girls were laughing and signing and paying her no mind.

Jake flicked the reins. They veered around a corner and hit a rut, and Polly and Carrie inclined to the left with the movement, sandwiching Ruby into even closer proximity to Jake. His shoulders and leg rested against hers and the heat zipped up her neck and onto her face.

"Let's sing, Auntie Ruby."

It took her a moment to catch her breath. "What a brilliant idea! Do you have a suggestion, Pansy?"

"How about 'Blessed Assurance'?" asked Becky.

A chorus of yeses followed. All of the children and Ruby signed the words in addition to singing, their voices carrying on the pleasant breeze:

Blessed assurance, Jesus is mine!
Oh, what a foretaste of glory divine!
Heir of salvation, purchase of God,
Born of His Spirit, washed in His blood.
This is my story, this is my song,
Praising my Savior all the day long.

Jake sang too, his deep, husky timbre a pleasing sound. He faced her for a second and smiled. When he did so, Ruby nearly sang and signed the wrong words.

When they finished, Jake asked, "Why does everyone sign the words too?"

"We most often sign in addition to talking and singing. It aids us in learning the signs, makes Polly and Hosea feel included, and signing is marvelous to watch."

"I've been aiming to learn it. Until I moved to Horizon, I'd never even seen or heard of sign language."

They sang two more songs before reaching the raspberry bushes. The children piled out, buckets in hand. Jake assisted Ruby from the wagon, his hands remaining on her waist a moment longer after he'd set her on the ground.

"Thank you for agreeing to this," he said. He inclined toward her, and Ruby closed her eyes and held her breath. What would it be like to court Jake Lynton? For him to kiss her?"

He tenderly brushed her cheek while tucking a hair behind her ear that escaped from her chignon. "You're beautiful, Ruby Shepherdson."

She opened her eyes, his nearness causing her heart to pound and her knees to falter. She thought for a moment she might tumble haphazardly into his arms. "I—thank you."

"Are you two gonna stand there and stare at each other all day?" Simon asked.

"Reckon I could," answered Jake.

Ruby reckoned she could stare into Jake's eyes all day long too. She hazarded a glimpse from her side-eye to see Simon waiting expectantly, one hand grasping his pail.

Jake stepped back and challenged Simon to a race to the raspberry bushes. Never one to refuse a challenge, her nephew agreed.

As Ruby watched the two race to the others, a warmth stirred in her heart. Someday, if the Lord willed, she'd have a husband and family of her own.

And now, here he was. Racing Simon the lengthy distance to the raspberry bushes and wondering when he'd become such a slowpoke. Although his stride was more considerable, Simon's swift pace allowed him to outrun Jake. When they reached the raspberry bushes, Jake planted his hands on his thighs and simultaneously chuckled while also catching his breath. He hadn't run like that in years, not since he and Corbin would race out to the fields attempting to be the first to tell Pa it was time for supper.

Why Ma never saw fit to purchase a supper bell was beyond him.

He wasn't sure exactly when it happened, but Jake was beginning to have feelings for Ruby. After racing Simon to the raspberry bushes, he'd pivoted to look back at her.

Ruby Shepherdson was a beautiful woman. And not just beautiful, but also godly, kind, smart, and patient with her passel full of nieces and nephews. It had been worth it to suggest she and the children join him to pick raspberries and see her face light up with excitement.

Memories of Corbin would always fill him with a myriad of emotions, including grief and guilt, but God in His mercy was helping Jake day by day to overcome that pain and guilt.

It helped that Jake had paid a second visit to Ingleville last week to spend time with his family. He'd even shared with Ma that there might be a woman he fancied in Horizon. Of course, Ma had been ecstatic when she heard that news.

Little Hans tapping on his arm interrupted Jake's thoughts. "Can you lift me up to reach those apples?"

A tree, just to the side of the raspberry bushes, boasted several plump and juicy green apples. If the worms hadn't beat them to the fruit, they'd serve as a delicious filling for a pie. Jake hoisted Little Hans onto his shoulders.

"You're taller than my pa. This is fun!" Little Hans gripped just below Jake's forehead, temporarily blinding him.

Jake reached up and gently relocated Little Hans's hands to just above Jake's eyebrows. He held the little boy's ankles to keep him from falling. Jake strode to the apple tree where Little Hans's delighted giggles filled the air as he saw how many apples he could carry while still balancing on Jake's shoulders.

When the boy was finished, Jake lifted him to the ground, and Little Hans scampered off with an armload of fruit to add to the apple pail before joining the others to pick raspberries.

Jake invited Ruby to sit on one of the two upturned logs on the ground.

"I'm not sure there will be any raspberries left after today," she said.

He took in the sight of her with her red hair, several strands of which had escaped and were tousled around her face. She wore her green dress that enhanced her eyes, and she leaned forward and folded her hands in her lap. Pink stained her cheeks, and a sweet laugh bubbled from her full lips when she noticed Pansy's raspberry-covered mouth.

Jake was drawn to her in a way he'd never before been drawn to any woman. And to think he once thought her both an annoyance and a featherbrain. In truth, she was the opposite. She had an independent spirit, yet was completely loyal and devoted to her family. He wanted to reach for her hand, to draw closer to her as they watched the children pick the fruit.

Yes, he was a lovelorn fool.

"When is your family planning to visit Horizon to see your farm?"

"Next week. I'm eager to ask Pa some questions about the wheat and determine his opinion of the Aspinwall Potato Planter." He was fairly sure the farm implement was in his future. "I'm looking forward to having you meet them, especially Ma."

"And you have just one sister, but no brothers?"

He hadn't yet told Ruby about Corbin, but if he planned to have a future with her, he ought to share some about his brother.

"I once had a brother."

She raised a brow. "Is he estranged from your family?"

If only that was why Jake no longer had a brother. Estrangement would be far preferable to Corbin's death. He drew in a strangled breath. "No, Corbin passed due to a horse accident."

"Oh, Jake, I'm so sorry." She tucked her arm through his. "I had no idea."

"I don't speak of it much."

"Was that why you left Ingleville?"

The woman was perceptive. Of course, that's what made her a competent reporter. "Yes. It was my fault. Pa wanted me to make sure Corbin didn't ride Lucky, a half-broke horse that Corbin had his eye on."

"And Corbin didn't listen." She whispered the words, and he could see the sympathy in her countenance.

"No. He didn't."

She squeezed his arm. "I'm so, so sorry."

"Me too. If I hadn't relented, Corbin might still be here."

"But you couldn't force him to listen."

No, Jake couldn't have forced Corbin to do anything. "I don't often talk much of it, but I thought you ought to know."

"Thank you for sharing it with me."

The pain continued to crush him, but the melancholy had improved. "I've been talking with your brother, Pastor Albert, about things, and he's helped a lot."

"I'm glad to hear that. He does have a gift for providing wise counsel."

The regular church attendance and spending frequent time in God's Word had helped Jake return to the faith of his youth. Indeed, the Lord was changing his life for the better, including allowing him to meet a woman named Ruby Shepherdson.

Jake's haunted gaze and heartbreaking recollection about Corbin tugged at Ruby. If only she could erase the pain he felt. She'd always known there was something that had thrown Jake Lynton into a spiral of pain, and Ruby now understood his cantankerous demeanor when she first met him. The reason he'd launched into despair and had allowed his hair and beard to grow without tending to himself.

If anyone could help Jake, it was Albert. He had a gift for coming alongside those in need. A true miracle himself, her parents often said, given Albert's rough beginnings.

But the Lord was faithful. So faithful. And so good. Ruby knew He would heal Jake's broken heart.

CHAPTER TWENTY-TWO

AFTER HER FAMILY HAD retired for the night, Ruby scoured the stack of newspapers from *The Cornwall Courier* that Landon brought back with him from his most recent visit to Cornwall. If she had to choose between Lillian or Mr. Henry Murphy as the one engaged in article thievery, she would choose Lillian. Not that she knew the reporter for *The Cornwall Courier*, but from her investigations, all of the identical articles were first written in the Cornwall newspaper before being written in *The Horizon Herald*.

It was an awful lot of work for a dishonest individual to type the words of the former article; however, it was likely more efficient than interviewing subjects and penning an entirely new story from the beginning.

Of course, if Lillian was copying, she wasn't plagiarizing *all* of her articles. For no one else, besides Ruby and Mr. O'Kane wrote the Horizon articles, so those were her own. But the ones that also were found in *The Cornwall Courier*...

Ruby blinked her weary eyes. Staying up until all hours of the night examining clues was not for the faint of heart. She'd already found two potential articles, and now as she was about to close the page and turn in for the night, Ruby's gaze settled on a familiar, albeit short composition about

The Cornwall mine closing and leaving 158 men without employment. It was dated last month.

It was the very same article Lillian wrote for *The Horizon Herald* this week.

It appeared that not only did Lillian steal ideas, but she may also very well steal articles.

Ruby leaned back against the sofa and folded her hands in her lap. She wagered Miss Lillian O'Kane to be in a heap of trouble for her deceitfulness. To share the news with Mr. O'Kane would be fruitless as the man thought his niece did no wrong. However, asking Sheriff Zembrodt tomorrow morning before work to investigate would likely resolve any uncertainty about the deceptive journalism.

For the time being, Mr. O'Kane continued to allow Ruby to write sporadic articles for *Ruby's Horizon Happenings* along with other random news. While he'd been disgruntled and brusque when Ruby presented the article about Jake restoring the Kountz farm over a month ago, he'd allowed her to remain an employee. Ruby discerned it was likely for two reasons—because several of the townsfolk threatened to cancel their subscription if she did not remain employed, and because Lillian was frequently in Cornwall, supposedly interviewing people for articles.

Ruby was just grateful to have the additional wages to assist in paying for her typewriter loan and to help Mama and Papa with necessary expenses. Ruby scanned her articles one more time for accuracy. She was responsible for reporting births, marriages, and deaths. Perusing the next page, she ensured that all of the names in the *Town and Surroundings* section were correctly spelled.

All looked well. She proceeded to the Wanted Adverts, also her responsibility. Those who placed these types of advertisements were charged two cents per line per day. There was only one for today.

Wanted—an older lady to assist with the upcoming First Annual Horizon Ball, including washing dishes and general preparations not tended to by volunteers. Preference will be given to a woman with a pleasant singing voice who chews gum.

Lastly, she read through her article about the students at the Bennick Horizon School for the Deaf and how they were again planning to enter some of the crops they grew on the school grounds in the county fair this year. This would be the sixth article she'd written about the school since Mr. O'Kane hired her.

He'd rejected her articles at first and stated no one could possibly be interested in pieces about the deaf school. Ruby begged to differ, and after the first story garnered him the sale of several extra copies and requests for school updates, he'd been convinced. Ruby had silently rejoiced when allowed to proceed because the school was close to her heart since Polly and Hosea attended and Mae and Landon were such an integral part of it.

The advertisements she was responsible for securing were the most tedious of all. She loathed asking friends to place adverts in the paper week after week, especially at the rates of one square of ten lines for $2.50 and each additional insertion was $1. Fortunately, Mr. O'Kane did give a reduction to those who regularly advertised, but the price was still something most business owners struggled to include in their budgets.

She stepped through the door of *The Horizon Herald* and joined Mr. O'Kane and Lillian for the Tuesday morning meeting. She handed him her most recent articles for the week.

Mr. O'Kane adjusted his spectacles on his nose and flipped through her typed pages with bored nonchalance. "Ruby, have you finished securing some advertisements as requested?"

Ruby wanted to remind her boss that she had been hired as a reporter rather than a saleswoman, but to again do so would be to no avail. "Yes, sir. Mr. Kent at the livery and Wilhelmina at the restaurant both agreed to place advertisements this week."

As he always did when pondering a response, Mr. O'Kane stroked his fine-tipped mustache and nodded. "Would have been better to have secured more adverts than that, but alas, as a novice reporter, such will have to be sufficient."

It was the same retort he provided week after week. He peered at her through close-set eyes, awaiting her acknowledgment.

"Yes, sir." She didn't mention that some of the townsfolk who'd been friends with her family for years had resorted to turning and proceeding in the opposite direction when Ruby approached them for fear she'd attempt to wangle some funds from them in the form of an advert.

"And you, Lillian?"

"I was only able to secure five this week." Lillian pooched her lips and dramatically hung her head as if practicing for a part in the Boise City theater.

"Ah, Lillian. Five adverts does not disappoint. On the contrary, it proves your ability as a tireless worker and a loyal employee of *The Horizon Herald*. Well done." Mr. O'Kane firmed his mouth into a fake smile. "Your parents will be proud when I again tell them how well you're doing in your employ here."

They would not be proud of you if they knew you were an article thief, Lillian.

"Of course, they will." Lillian stood straighter and smiled smugly at Ruby. "You poor dear. Perhaps I can be a mentor of sorts and assist you as you continue to learn the newspaper profession."

"You're too kind." The words fell from Ruby's mouth before she could stop them.

Twin creases formed on Mr. O'Kane's forehead. "Lillian, that's quite benevolent of you. I'd never considered that you could mentor Ruby. It may have saved us much distress from her earlier missteps."

It was likely that Mr. O'Kane would never truly forget Ruby's faux pas with the one article that temporarily got her fired. But she for certain had no desire to be "mentored" by Lillian who could scarcely compile a logical thought on her own.

"Now, do tell me about the articles you are working on at present."

Lillian held her notebook to her chest. "I've been granted an interview with the grandson of Horizon's founder. He has stories to share that his grandfather told him."

Ruby pursed her lips. That story had been hers once upon a time, or rather, the idea had been. When she'd broached the topic with Mr. O'Kane two weeks ago, Lillian suggested she should be the one to instead interview the grandson, and Mr. O'Kane promptly acquiesced and assigned the story to Lillian. Such occurrences routinely happened, but this story had been more important to Ruby than the others since Papa had been the one to secure permission from the grandson.

"Don't you wish *you* could interview the founder of Horizon's grandson?" Lillian patted her glossy dark-brown hair to ensure it was still perfectly tucked in the tortoiseshell hairpin. "Perhaps after you've gained more experience, Mr. O'Kane will assign you the superior assignments."

"Perhaps," Ruby answered between gritted teeth. It wasn't easy to hold her tongue when it came to Lillian, especially since she'd bamboozled her uncle into believing Lillian was a gifted writer, when the opposite was true. If only Mr. O'Kane knew about the possibility of Lillian's shenanigans with the copied articles. Perhaps a story should be written about that.

"And you, Ruby?"

If only she could speak with Mr. O'Kane about her story idea without Lillian being present. The benefits would be twofold—she could ensure Lillian wouldn't be assigned her idea, and more importantly, she could rest assured Lillian wouldn't halt the proceedings because of her affection for gossip.

"Prattle on, Ruby. We haven't all day."

"I am working on an article about money being stolen from a business."

Mr. O'Kane inclined toward her, and Lillian's piercing eyes rounded. The other two employees stopped their work and stared.

"As in a robbery?" Mr. O'Kane asked.

"Perhaps. Thievery, an embezzlement, I'm not sure. All I know is that money has disappeared, and the owner would appreciate the public's help in finding out who the culprit is. However, due to the nature of the investigation, I prefer not to give further details at this time."

"I understand that you are being cautious about providing details, but…" Mr. O'Kane ushered Ruby and Lillian into his office and shut the door. "But as the owner of this fine newspaper, I do need to know details. Rest assured I will keep all particulars in confidence."

Ruby chewed on her lip. "Sir, I really ought not say until I have more facts. At this juncture, it is only a possibility."

"Nonsense, Ruby, as I mentioned previously, what you say will go no further than this office. Both Lillian and I are trustworthy."

Mr. O'Kane might know how to keep something confidential, but Lillian did not. Just a peek at Lillian's expression reminded Ruby of a crafty viper ready to pounce on and devour her prey. "Sir, with all respect."

"I'm flabbergasted by your lack of forthrightness, Ruby, especially given your prior blunder. Either tell us what you know or resign from your position as a reporter for *The Horizon Herald.*"

"Yes, sir." Ruby offered a prayer seeking wisdom and guidance because the last thing she wanted to do was speak any form of untruth.

"It's possible thievery from The Horizon Hotel."

Lillian gasped. "Are you certain?"

"I'm still investigating it."

Mr. O'Kane tapped his chin. "Who is your source?"

"With respect sir, a good reporter never reveals her source."

Lillian looked down her nose at Ruby. "Of course, it may be all a farse. Isn't your family close friends with Miss Greta and the Lieutenant?"

"Yes, but many people in Horizon are friends with Miss Greta and the Lieutenant. What would I have to gain by writing a story for *Ruby's Horizon Happenings* about a potential embezzlement at the hotel?"

Mr. O'Kane removed his glasses, then replaced them. "If you are friends with Miss Greta and the Lieutenant, you might perchance want to shed a negative light on the hotel since it is Miss Greta's competition."

Ruby's heart pounded in her chest. Perhaps she ought to have written the article first, then presented it to Mr. O'Kane. "Miss Greta has not lost much business due to the hotel. She maintains her clientele because most who stay at her boardinghouse do so because they want to stay longer than a few nights. Besides, a good reporter can report the news without bias."

Lillian placed a hand on Ruby's shoulder. "A good reporter, Ruby. A good reporter. You are not yet that advanced in writing for the paper."

The Lord often allowed Ruby to be tested when it came to Lillian. Mama had quoted 1 Corinthians 10:13 on more than one occasion and reminded Ruby that the Lord would not test her beyond that which she could handle with His help. The verse played through Ruby's mind: *"But God is faithful, who will not suffer you to be tempted above that ye are able; but will with the temptation also make a way to escape, that ye may be able to bear it."* Mama reminded Ruby that showing Christ's love to Lillian was the correct way to respond, even if it was grueling.

And it *was grueling.*

Downright impossible at times.

Lillian sidled closer and whispered, "Who is it that you think is embezzling?"

"Yes, you'll need to apprise us of that," added Mr. O'Kane.

"Because I don't wish to give any semblance of gossip, I cannot because I am still investigating the matter."

Lillian frowned. "Who is it?"

"As I said, I'm not sure who is stealing from the hotel."

Mr. O'Kane ticked off a list of potential suspects. "There is the owner, who resides in Missoula, Montana. There are three maids, a handyman, a manager, and kitchen staff. Then there are the customers. It could be anyone."

"Indeed, sir. And that is why we need to help the owner find out who it is. Sheriff Zembrodt has been notified of the situation and is also investigating. I have spoken to him as well, and he seeks the townsfolks' aid."

"Is he your source?"

"No, Lillian, he is not."

"Goodness me." Lillian placed a hand on her forehead. "I shall faint away just thinking about the fact that we may have a criminal lurking about the streets of Horizon. Uncle, you reassured me when I moved here that the town was without crime."

"You should consider acting," mused Ruby, accidentally verbalizing her thoughts.

Lillian firmed her hands on her hips. "If I wasn't a reporter, I *would* aspire to such a profession, but alas, I am needed as the only competent journalist at *The Horizon Her-*

ald. I could no more leave Uncle in a lurch than desire to be a maid."

"Thank you for your loyalty, Lillian. I knew when my wife suggested I hire you it was the right choice. Now, Ruby, work on the article and get it to me next week. Mention none of your suspicions, should you have any. Only that the hotel is seeking help in solving the crime."

Sheriff Zembrodt agreed to look into the potential article theft by Lillian. And since Ruby had always loved a good mystery, when she set out to seek more clues as to who was stealing from the hotel, she did so with vigor.

The first thing she did, notebook in hand, was interview a few of the employees at The Horizon Hotel. The first was the head maid, a soft-spoken, sorrowful woman younger than Ruby, with flaming red hair, a face full of freckles, and a troubled countenance. Ruby asked that they meet beneath the trees near the river where Ruby often took Maribel on their outings.

"Thank you for meeting with me today, Miss Jenkins. As you know, I write articles for *The Horizon Herald* and am aiming to write one about the hotel. It's been a welcome addition to Horizon for the past several years, and I believe it will be fitting for *Ruby's Horizon Happenings.*"

The woman folded her red, chapped hands in her lap. Her black-and-white maid's outfit was dusty, faded, and worn, and Ruby wondered why no one had offered her a new uniform.

"I can't stay long."

"I'll ask my questions posthaste. Have you noticed anything out of the ordinary at the hotel?"

Miss Jenkins dipped her head. "It's busier than usual."

Ruby jotted that information in her notebook and waited for Miss Jenkins to continue. When she didn't, Ruby prodded her with another question. "Do you ever receive money from the guests?"

"I do not. My job is to clean the rooms and assist the kitchen staff with dishwashing if I finish my room-cleaning early."

"Do you know where the money received from those staying at the hotel is kept?"

"I know it is kept behind the desk in the cash register, but I am not allowed to go behind there. Mr. Kuchel is firm in his rules."

"I see. If you don't mind me asking since the hotel is one of our larger employers in Horizon, do you make enough in wages to provide for yourself?"

"Yes, because I live with my family. If I were to live on my own, no. I have been there for three years, but have not yet received an increase in my pay even though I work hard."

That statement made Ruby ponder if the woman would be so desperate as to steal. But if she neither received money from the guests nor was able to access the cash register, then Miss Jenkins was unlikely to be the embezzler. Still, Ruby would list her as a possible suspect.

Ruby continued through the list of hotel employees, including two other maids, the handyman, and the cook. None of them offered any insight as to their involvement.

Tabitha's eyes enlarged to twice their size, and she rubbed her hands together after Ruby pulled her aside to ask some questions. "I'm so thrilled to be a part of an investigation. Can you tell me more about the story?"

"Regrettably, I cannot. Reporter's rules and all."

Tabitha's shoulders dropped slightly. "All right. I understand."

"You know I would if I could because I consider you like an aunt, but..."

"Oh, not a worry at all, Ruby. I know Mr. O'Kane is a challenging boss, so I'll not press further." She offered a genuine smile, and Ruby asked her first question.

"The mercantile does a fair amount of business in Horizon. Have you perchance noticed anyone purchasing more items than usual?"

"Well, at Christmastime, of course, we sell more wares, but seeing as how it's summer, there has only been one person who has bought more than he usually does."

"Oh?" Ruby held her pencil poised to write Tabitha's next words.

"Yes. Mr. Kuchel from the hotel. I'm not complaining that he has purchased—and paid in full for—additional more frivolous items. Usually, our townsfolk put items on account, and Mr. Kuchel did at one time, but lately, we have added no charges to his account."

This was interesting and just the stuff an avid reporter must investigate. "What sorts of things is he purchasing?"

"Well, he ordered two new suits. Now, don't get me wrong, Mr. Kuchel's job demands he wear presentable attire, but these suits and hats are beyond what he would wear at the hotel. He has also bought gift-like items in abundance."

"Such as?"

"Items ordered from the Montgomery Ward Catalogue such as a music box, an ornate tea set, an expensive pearl necklace, fancy women's hats, a bicycle, and a diamond ring."

It was to a reporter's honor to hide any revealing facial expressions when hearing something that may assist in the solving of a mystery. So she snapped her jaw closed, bit her lip, blinked her eyes so they wouldn't widen, and gripped her notebook to keep from tapping her pencil. "I see," she said, her answer sounding more like a breathless gasp.

"I know the hotel pays better wages than many of our Horizon businesses, but for him to be able to afford such extravagances?" Tabitha shook her head. "But I do not want to be a gossip, so please discern what you will, and I'll not say another word about my suspicions."

Ruby didn't wish to gossip either, but she did wish to solve this mystery, and speaking with Tabitha might just bring her closer to doing so. "One last question. Has Miss Jenkins, the maid, purchased more items than usual in recent days?"

"Miss Jenkins? No. She is such a dear girl and her family is struggling, what with her pa so ill. But no, the family only purchases the necessaries, never any frivolities."

"Thank you, Tabitha. I appreciate your help." Ruby bid her farewell, musings rapidly swirling through her mind.

When she began her quest to solve the embezzlement mystery, she had two suspects. While one had never really been a true suspect, it was to the benefit of an astute reporter to thoroughly investigate. Now that she had, there was only one true culprit.

The following day, Ruby delivered three of Mama's pies to Wilhelmina's. "These look scrumptious. Please tell your ma thank you."

"She'll be pleased you said so."

"Your ma has come a long way with her baking, but if one didn't know about her former cooking catastrophes, one wouldn't know, not with the delicious desserts she provides week after week."

"And she would humbly say that she has the Lord, you, and *Recipes from Augusta's Kitchen* to thank."

Wilhelmina smiled. "Well, it's always a huge praise when folks are properly fed."

"Especially Pa and Timothy. Both would wither away to nothingness if Mama hadn't learned how to cook."

Ruby was sharing a laugh with Wilhelmina when she heard someone with a familiar voice behind her. She turned to see Lillian with her hands on her slim hips.

"Do you think we could possibly get our noonday meal before suppertime arrives?"

There was much to notice about the ill-tempered Lillian. The scowl on her face, her haughty attitude, perfectly coiffed hair, fancy dress...

But what drew Ruby's attention was the intricate string of pearls around her neck. Such an item must have cost a fortune.

A fortune quite possibly secured through a convoluted embezzling scheme.

"Thank you for the reminder, Lillian. Your meal will be but a minute," said Wilhelmina, her voice always kind and charitable. "Thank you for the pies, Ruby." Wilhelmina rushed to the kitchen leaving Ruby and Lillian alone.

"Are you delivering more of your mother's pies?" Lillian pooched her lips and inclined her head slightly.

"Yes, I am. Perhaps Wilhelmina will bring you a slice for dessert."

"No, thank you. I prefer the apple crisp Wilhelmina makes." Lillian glanced around her before returning her attention to Ruby. "I suppose since we are coworkers, you could be the third to know a special secret only after Douglas and myself."

Ruby doubted she would care to know anything about a special secret Lillian might possess, but she didn't say as much.

"I know you're dying with curiosity, so I'll just tell you." Lillian presented her left hand, palm down, and fingers splayed. She wiggled her fourth finger. "Douglas and I are engaged."

The most elegant diamond ring graced Lillian's slender finger.

Much to her dismay, a gasp escaped Ruby's lips.

"Isn't it the loveliest ring you ever did see? It's real gold with three perfect diamonds. Aren't you just so jealous?"

"It *is* lovely. But jealous? No."

"You ought to be." Lillian wrinkled her nose. "Of course, maybe you're content being a spinster. Not everyone can find the man of their dreams as I have."

If Douglas Kuchel was the man of Lillian's dreams, those dreams were likely nightmares. But Ruby didn't voice her thoughts. "Congratulations."

Lillian waited as if she expected Ruby to say more, but the only thing on Ruby's mind now was how Mr. Kuchel managed to purchase the diamond ring, the string of pearls, and all of the other items at the mercantile on a manager's salary.

After delivering her article to *The Horizon Herald* and setting the typeset for the article Mr. O'Kane shockingly approved from last week, Ruby started down the boardwalk to the buggy. Thoughts of Lillian crowded her mind. While she'd never be envious of the woman, she might be a tiny bit jealous of her upcoming marriage. An image of Jake flashed through her mind. Perhaps someday, Lord willing, Jake would ask her to court him.

As she passed by the alleyway between streets, an arm reached out and jerked her so forcefully that Ruby nearly tripped. She jolted backward before being yanked into the hidden spot in the alley. Her heart pounded in her chest.

The arm released her, and Ruby wiped her sleeve where Mr. Kuchel's grimy hand once rested. "Mr. Kuchel! You frightened me."

"Stop interviewing my employees."

"I beg your pardon?"

"You heard me, Ruby Shepherdson. Stop interviewing my employees. And stop poking your nose where it doesn't belong."

"A reporter always asks a multitude of questions. You ought to know that being engaged to Lillian."

"Lillian doesn't ask people many questions, but you..." the man gritted his teeth, and his nostrils flared in and out with his angry breaths. "Do you understand me?"

"You're surely not threatening me, are you, Mr. Kuchel? Because if you are, I'll have no choice but to discuss this matter with Sheriff Zembrodt."

Mr. Kuchel fisted his hands at his sides. "Don't say you weren't warned," he growled.

The man was a scoundrel, but he'd not stop her from continuing her investigation.

Papa would tell her that it was necessary to inform the sheriff of Mr. Kuchel's brash behavior. And Papa, Timothy, and Albert might have a thing or two to say to the man himself for threatening her.

Head held high, Ruby pulled away from Douglas Kuchel and marched directly to Sheriff Zembrodt's office. When she entered, several other folks she did not recognize were speaking all at once.

"We already paid our hotel bill. There is no way we should owe again," said a short stubby man with a thick black belt that accentuated his ample middle.

"Why would they say we haven't paid when we did?" This from an older woman with cotton-white hair and a whiny, shrill voice.

A man with a bowler hat and an expensive suit interrupted both of them. "I have it on good authority that I already paid my hotel bill. Did the manager lose the money? If so, he should be aptly replaced."

A tiny woman with puffy leg o' mutton sleeves rapped on the desk. "I'll not pay twice. I shan't!"

Sheriff Zembrodt held up his hands. "Ladies and gentlemen, I hear your concerns, and I promise to visit with Mr. Kuchel at the hotel."

Could it be that this mystery was already solved?

Ten minutes later, with three additional promises to solve the matter, Sheriff Zembrodt ushered the visitors from his office. "Ruby, what can I do for you?"

"Sheriff, I have reason to believe Douglas Kuchel is embezzling from the hotel."

The next day, Ruby parked the wagon, and clutching her notebook and prized pencil in case she encountered someone with a story to tell, dashed into the mercantile. Mama's birthday was today, and nearly everything was in place, save for a few important items.

"Hello, Ruby! I'll be with you in a moment." Tabitha waved from the front of the store. Several customers examined the plentiful variety of goods, and Ruby secured a ten-pound bag of sugar while she waited for the proprietress.

Something caught her eye, distracting her from the task at hand.

The brand-new Montgomery Ward Catalogue beckoned her from its prominent place on the table near the sewing notions. It was a rare occasion that no one else flipped through the pages of the highly-anticipated book, so Ruby took full advantage of the opportunity. She hunched over and inhaled the smell of print. The year, printed in bold, was at the bottom, surrounded by a plethora of illustrations including clothing, tonics, a bicycle, musical instruments, and a sewing machine.

The very sewing machine Mama would be receiving this evening.

Ruby plopped her notebook, pencil, and bag of sugar on the table beside the book. She gasped at the realization that this volume contained 674 pages. Oh, but to haul the catalogue home and spend hours browsing through the fine wares! But Tabitha couldn't allow such privileges since so many townsfolk would desire the same thing, and it would be likely the book would be pilfered by a potential customer hoping to add it to their own personal library.

So instead, the catalogue remained at the mercantile on the special table awaiting those who wished to take an extended gander.

Ruby turned the first couple of pages to the table of contents. An illustration of a buggy was centered at the top, and the listings of numerous items in two columns filled the page.

If one couldn't find what they wanted in the Montgomery Ward Catalogue, they didn't need it, Tabitha was fond of saying.

Ruby concurred. Everything from books, stationery, trunks, buggies, furniture, hardware, toys, and clothing could be found within the pages. She first gazed upon the stationery on page twelve. In her mind, a girl couldn't have enough stationery, although some of the offerings in the catalogue were far too pretty to write on. She then turned to page seventy-two where the latest in women's fashions adorned the pages with plentiful shirt waists, all with their puffy leg o'mutton sleeves. Such sophisticated apparel!

While she typically didn't care about the latest fashions, when the opportunity to look at the lovely clothing present-ed itself, Ruby gladly took it.

Organs, pianos, and accordions followed, and an entire section of hall trees, mirrors, and tables covered the next seven pages.

"Ruby?"

She jumped at the sound of Tabitha's voice.

"Jimmie is ready to load your ma's present into the wag-on."

"Oh, yes, thank you." Ruby hastily grabbed the bag of sugar and hurried to the counter. Mae, Lucy, and Velma were waiting on the sugar to complete the desserts for tonight's festivities. And who knew how long Papa would be able to keep Mama away so the men could unload, unpack, and prepare the sewing machine.

"Paisley is going to be so thrilled when she sees her new gift. I've eyeballed it myself, truth be told." Tabitha flashed a smile at her husband.

"Yes, you've mentioned that." Mayor Trabert flashed an equally broad smile at his wife. "I'll hoist it into the back of the wagon for you, Ruby."

"Thank you, Mayor."

"That will be a dollar for the sugar and thirty-five dollars for the sewing machine for a total of thirty-six dollars."

Ruby opened her reticule and plunked a pile of money on the counter from everyone in her family's donation to Mama's sewing machine fund. Tabitha counted it out, and Ruby was about to conclude the purchase when she eye-balled the licorice. "I'll take eight licorice whips, please."

"Someone enjoys spoiling her nieces and nephews."

Ruby couldn't deny it. "We'll have two desserts tonight, but there's something special about licorice whips."

A half-hour later, Ruby rounded the corner to her parents' home. She couldn't wait for Mama to see her new present. Last year, Mama had stopped by the window of the mercantile every time they were in town just to behold the White Sewing Machine Tabitha had placed in the window on a table. She hadn't said a word to Papa about it, likely because she knew such an exquisite machine was far beyond what they could afford, but Papa knew she wasn't gazing at the farm tools like she hoped to lead him to believe.

With the entire family contributing to the very worthwhile cause, purchasing the sewing machine became doable.

And not only was Ruby ardently awaiting seeing Mama's face when she received her gift, but Ruby was also anticipating seeing Jake. She missed him in their days apart.

Her mind on Jake's broad shoulders and dapper smile drew her from the present and any sort of heedfulness, and she nearly ran plumb into Lillian as she exited the mercantile.

"Aren't you in a hurry," said her adversary, a hand on her svelte waist.

"Pardon me." Ruby did not have the wherewithal to concern herself with Lillian's condescending manner. Not when there was a birthday party to prepare for.

Mayor Trabert lifted the sewing machine into the back of the wagon next to the sack of sugar. "Tell your ma I said happy birthday."

"Thanks, Mayor. I will."

Several minutes later, Ruby parked the wagon beside the barn. Jake strode toward her, and for a minute she forgot to breathe.

In recent months, she'd grown fond of the man she'd once considered an irritable recluse. He looked exceptionally handsome today with his ruffled brown hair and blue plaid shirt. Would he someday ask to court her?

"Hello, Ruby."

"Hello, Jake."

His hands remained on her waist after he lifted her from the wagon, and a tingle zipped through her stomach as their eyes locked and he leaned slightly toward her.

What if Jake were to kiss her?

She dismissed the thought, for she ought not to entertain such notions since she and Jake weren't even courting.

Timothy cleared his throat.

Leave it to him to intrude on such a delightful moment.

"Not meaning to interrupt, but Lucy is asking about the sugar."

"Lucy?"

"Yes. You know, our older sister."

"Oh. Yes. Lucy. The sugar."

Jake's pleasing rumble of a laugh reverberated through the air, and his broad smile made her insides wobble.

Before she embarrassed herself further by sounding like a bumbling flibbertigibbet, Ruby took a deep breath and forced herself to avert her gaze from Jake's vivid blue eyes.

"And I should...uh...help with the sewing machine." Jake removed his hands and shoved them into his trouser pockets.

Timothy smirked. "Reckon we better unload the sewing machine and put it in the barn."

Polly, Becky, Carrie, and Pansy ran toward Ruby, holding hands, their braids bouncing. "Auntie Rubes!"

Ruby pulled her attention from Jake and focused it on her nieces. "Hello, girls," she spoke and signed for Polly.

"We found a baby bunny. Maybe you can write a story about that for the paper," suggested Becky.

Ruby doubted she could convince Mr. O'Kane to accept a story about a rabbit unless it contained something sensational or at least remarkably newsworthy, but she didn't mention as much. Ruby was about to comment that she'd love to see the bunny when a thought jolted her.

Her notebook.

Where was it?

She spun and searched the buckboard, the bed of the wagon, the crate with the sugar and licorice whips Timothy had taken to the house, then the buckboard again, praying it merely evaded her notice like the last time she thought she'd lost it.

"Is something wrong?" Jake asked.

"Yes. It's my notebook. I can't find it."

"I'll help you look for it."

Together they searched again to no avail. "Maybe it fell out as you were driving."

Ruby surmised she would recall if the notebook had flipped out of the wagon, and since there was no wind today, the possibility of that happening seemed even more remote.

CHAPTER TWENTY-THREE

RUBY RETRACED HER STEPS back to the mercantile. It was not at the counter, Tabitha had not seen it, and it was not near the Montgomery Ward Catalogue.

If someone were to abscond with her notebook, they would discover all sorts of important notes, including the one about Douglas Kuchel being the most likely suspect of embezzling from the hotel.

Lord, please help me find it, preferably before anyone has viewed it.

"I wish I knew what happened to it," said Tabitha. "You're sure it didn't fall out of the wagon on your way home?"

"I retraced my travels, and Jake didn't find it either." Her heart fell. The time writing notes and penning articles that she would later type could not be easily recovered.

"Not that it solves the problem with your notebook, but here's a new pencil." Tabitha handed her a pencil similar to the one that was with her notebook and was now lost as well.

Ruby hugged the older woman. "Thank you. If you see it, will you please let me know?"

"Yes. I'll send Jimmie to tell you."

Ruby bid her farewell and was walking toward the buggy when she spied a familiar person, head bowed, and crouched in the corner near the vacant building beside the newspaper office.

"Lillian?"

The woman jumped. "You scared me half to death, Ruby." She simultaneously slammed shut the raspberry-and-beige mottled marble cover with a raspberry-colored spine notebook in her hand and held it to her chest. "What is it you want?"

"Is that perchance my notebook?"

"I'm not sure what you are asking."

But Lillian's rapidly blinking and darting eyes belied her words. "You know full well, Lillian O'Kane, what I am asking. You are holding my notebook in your hands."

"I…" Lillian turned her head to the right, then to the left, all the while avoiding Ruby's gaze.

The woman had such audacity. Ruby hastily prayed for the Lord to guard her tongue. "Hand it over, Lillian."

Slowly and methodically, the woman released her clutch on Ruby's prized possession.

"How did you find it?"

"It was in the mercantile beside the Montgomery Ward Catalogue."

"And you thought it charitable to steal it?"

Lillian's dark eyes flashed. "I most certainly did *not* steal it. I was attempting to discern to whom it belonged. But after reading a mere sentence, I determined such lackluster and childish writing to be yours."

"Lackluster and childish?" The words seethed from Ruby. She had more to say, but it would not be the words of a woman who professed Christ. So instead she took a deep breath and prayed again. She opened her mouth to say something, thought better of it, and turned on her heel without bidding her adversary goodbye.

On Wednesday after visiting with Maribel, Ruby walked to the mercantile to retrieve something for Mama before continuing home to work on her article about the embezzled funds from The Horizon Hotel. Sheriff Zembrodt and his deputy were still investigating the matter, and Ruby had given them her information about whom she suspected.

She was about to enter the mercantile when she heard a voice call her name.

"Ruby?"

Lillian stood behind her on the boardwalk. "Yes?"

"I want to sincerely apologize for taking your notebook. I'm ever so sorry for saying your writing was lackluster and childish. That's not the case at all."

Lillian's syrupy voice was cause for suspicion, but Ruby knew she ought to show grace no matter how laborious that might be. Some struggles were only overcome with the Lord's help. Ruby sighed. "I forgive you."

"Thank you ever so much." Lillian clasped both of Ruby's hands in her own, causing her fancy reticule to swing on its chain with the motion. "I would like to atone for my error if I may."

Lillian was the most untrustworthy person Ruby knew—even more untrustworthy than Mr. O'Kane. But when Ruby saw the tears in the woman's eyes, she figured Lillian might be being forthright.

"Have you heard about Miss Amity Hicks, the circus performer?"

"The one who did somersaults on the backs of horses?"

"Indeed, she is the one."

Ruby had not only heard of the infamous Miss Hicks but had also read about her in *The Cornwall Courier*. When the circus came to the city ten years ago before Miss Hicks's retirement, Ruby had wished to attend, but circus tickets were pricey, and there was no train yet to Cornwall. Taking time from farming to travel to Cornwall was an impossibility for her family. "Yes, I've heard of her."

Lillian released Ruby's hands and inclined closer, the tears still fresh in her eyes. "She is here in Horizon visiting her relatives, but only for two days."

"Are you certain?"

"As certain as I am standing here in front of you."

"How did you chance upon this information?"

"I probably shouldn't tell." Lillian averted her eyes to her sleeve, which she brushed off with her other hand.

"Did someone tell you?"

"He—I mean—they did."

Ruby knew that a good reporter never revealed her secrets, but she was curious about how Lillian had discovered Miss Hicks was in Horizon. "Are you certain it is the *real* Miss Hicks?"

"I am certain." Lillian opened her reticule, retrieved a folded sheet of paper, and handed it to Ruby.

Ruby unfolded it and read the words:

Hello, my Dearest,

I will be in Horizon for two days and should like to visit with you. You mentioned that Lillian O'Kane from the local paper is interested in interviewing me. That is agreeable to me provided she arrives on Wednesday and doesn't tarry long.
Sincerely,
Cousin Amity

"Her relative presented me with this letter so I could show my uncle. You know how he is sometimes about not believing things."

Ruby wasn't sure *she* believed Lillian's claim. "I know nearly everyone in Horizon. What is her relative's name?"

"It's doubtful you know her as she and her family moved here from Montana last year. Her name is Lynn Olson."

Lillian was correct in that Ruby didn't know Lynn Olson. "Where does she reside?"

"One mile north of here in the old Thornton property. It's the cabin on the left side of the road just before the red barn."

"But today is Wednesday."

"Indeed. You'll have to visit with her today. Of course, if you haven't the time, I'm happy to do the interview. I just thought you might like to speak with her, and I wanted to show you I am sorry by offering this to you."

To meet Amity Hicks would be a dream come true. To interview her would be even better. "I would love to hear her story."

"Yes, as would I. So many were skeptical about her abilities. And now she's one of the most famous people in the entire United States." Awe transformed Lillian's countenance. "Can you imagine the stories she could share?"

Oh, Ruby could imagine all right. The questions were already formulating in her mind. "Thank you, Lillian. I will ride there posthaste." She'd retrieve the items for Mama on the way back through town so as not to miss the limited time the woman was available for an interview.

"It is half past two, so you ought to move along. I hear Miss Hicks has an early bedtime."

Ruby didn't figure being there long enough for the sun to set, but Lillian was right. She ought to go as quickly as possible.

CHAPTER TWENTY-FOUR

JAKE WAS LOADING GRAIN into the back of the wagon when he spied Ruby. He waved, and she halted the buggy beside him. Her beauty, as always, stole his breath. "How are you today?" he asked.

"I'm thrilled to be able to interview Miss Amity Hicks, the famous circus woman."

"I've heard about her. Wasn't she in Cornwall with the circus years ago?"

"She was. I heard from Lillian—oddly enough—that she is here in Horizon staying with relatives. She agreed to an interview, but only if it is done today as she will be leaving town soon."

Jake scratched his head. "Why isn't Lillian interviewing her?"

"She apologized for stealing my notebook and wanted to make amends."

"Are we talking about Lillian O'Kane?"

"I know, hard to believe. But this is amazing, Jake. I have always wanted to see Miss Hicks perform, and while I won't be able to do that, I *will* be able to talk to her and glean some fantastic stories for *Ruby's Horizon Happenings*."

Jake didn't want to damper Ruby's enthusiasm. "Where is she staying?"

"Her relatives live at the old Thornton property. It's one mile north and is the cabin on the left side of the road just before the red barn."

"I haven't been there, but are you sure you should go alone?"

"It's Miss Amity Hicks." Ruby's eyes enlarged. "Can you believe she's here in Horizon?" Ruby patted her notebook on the seat beside her. "I best be on my way before it gets much later." She smiled and waved, and Jake watched as she disappeared down the road.

Something didn't sit well with him about Ruby visiting Miss Amity Hicks on her own. Once he finished his errands in town, he'd ride out to the old Thornton place himself.

Ruby beckoned the horse as fast as safely possible. She was both nervous and excited. There was a lightness in her chest. Perhaps after Mr. O'Kane published her article, another newspaper would want it as well. After all, it wasn't everyday that someone could interview someone as famous as Miss Amity Hicks.

When Ruby arrived at the old Thornton place, she nearly rode on past as it was not what she expected. For someone related to Miss Hicks, shouldn't they have attempted better upkeep of the place? But instead, the logs were peeling, the porch was missing some slats on the railing, and several shingles were lacking on the roof. Perhaps Miss Hicks and her relatives had fallen on hard times. If that was the case, Ruby wished she'd brought along some bread and preserves.

She climbed from the buggy and watched her step as she ascended the stairs. An odor akin to a dead animal greeted her.

Something wasn't right.

Ruby spun and started to run to the buggy when a hand grasped her shoulder so hard she nearly tottered off her feet.

"Not so fast," a voice hissed.

The voice sounded familiar, but Ruby couldn't place it. A hand clamped over her mouth. "Don't scream or say a word. Come calmly with me or you'll regret it."

He dragged her backward into the cabin, and she nearly tripped on the stairs. When they entered the house, the man spun her again and kicked the door shut. "Now we talk," he growled.

And she knew at that moment who was holding her captive.

The very man she suspected of embezzlement.

Douglas Kuchel shoved her to the lone chair at the table and began pacing.

The dead animal odor was stronger in the cabin, and an inch of dust covered both the table and the floor.

This was clearly not where Miss Amity Hicks was staying.

And it was clearly not a place where her relatives supposedly lived.

How could Ruby have been so foolish and gullible? She folded her hands in her lap to hopefully ease some of the shaking. What would Mr. Kuchel do? Her legs felt weak and her heart raced. He could plan ill intent and no one would know. *Lord, please help me.*

Mr. Kuchel ceased marching and stopped in front of her. He lowered and positioned his head into her line of vision. A vein in his forehead engorged and his eyes were bloodshot. She'd never seen him as anything but a calm, yet pompous, businessman. His reddish hair stood at odd ends and puffiness beneath his eyes attested to his lack of sleep. "You will rescind it."

"Rescind what?" She heard the tremors in her own voice.

"What you wrote in your notebook."

"My notebook?"

Mr. Kuchel reached up and yanked on her coiffure. Her head snapped back, and a sharp pain reverberated through her neck. He drew his face to just inches from hers. From this close, she could see a furry patch on his chin where he'd missed shaving. "You will remove your accusation that I am the embezzler of the money from The Horizon Hotel or I will…"

What would he do? She shivered as her mind raced. He leaned closer, his musty breath foul and smelling of a mixture of boiled cabbage and something rancid Ruby couldn't define. She closed her watering eyes and attempted to hold her breath.

"Did you hear me?"

Tears spilled onto her cheeks from the pain radiating from the top of her head where he held a tight grasp on her braided bun to her tense shoulders. "Yes," she whimpered.

"Good." He released her hair and her head snapped forward causing her to wince. "You *will* tell Sheriff Zembrodt and that worthless deputy of his that I am not at fault. That it is Miss Jenkins."

"But Miss Jenkins is one of the maids." Ruby thought of the demure woman with sorrowful eyes and a troubled countenance.

"Yes, and that's who it was who stole the money." His voice rose a level and he yelled again, spittle landing on her cheek. "It was not me!"

Would he let her go if she agreed to tell the sheriff it was Miss Jenkins? It was worth a try. "I will tell the sheriff and his deputy it was indeed the maid if you will please release me."

Mr. Kuchel's nose twitched, accentuating the bump toward the top of it. He sniffled. "I don't know whether or not I can believe you, Ruby Shepherdson."

"You can believe me. As a matter of fact, now that I think about it, Miss Jenkins is the embezzler."

The man took a step back and tapped his toe on the worn floorboard. "What makes you say that?" He removed a gun from the back of his pants. Was he planning to shoot her?

Ruby had to think quickly. *Lord, forgive me for the untruth I am about to utter.* "Miss Jenkins has been wearing new and stylish dresses to church along with an elegant hat. She could not afford those items with her meager pay."

Mr. Kuchel's chin tucked into his neck. "You've noticed that?"

"I have. I never gave much thought to it until you mentioned she was the one. Now I see you are correct."

He stomped toward her again and gripped her shoulder so hard, she imagined the bruise forming immediately. "You better be telling the truth. I will not go to prison for the embezzling. Not when I have already proposed to the love of my life."

The pressure on her collarbone was nearly more than she could withstand. "I—I..."

Mr. Kuchel released his firm grip. "Yes?"

"I am telling the truth, and I'm so very happy for you and Lillian." Her voice wavered and she feared a sob might be forthcoming from the throbbing that now spread to her left hand.

"Yes, well, I have loved her for a long time. I only had to prove I was worthy. But you see, a man making the pathetic wages I make at The Horizon Hotel would not allow me to offer her much in the way of the finer things." He nudged the gun beneath her chin. "Now tell me again why I'm not the embezzler."

Ruby bit back the tears from the pain. "You are not the thief. I'm sorry I ever accused you of such. Miss Jenkins is the one who's been stealing the money."

"Yes, you are correct. It was Miss Jenkins."

Now that she had Mr. Kuchel convinced, she needed to escape. She covertly perused the cabin. Nothing but an old dented tin can on an otherwise empty shelf. But she could kick and hit and scream. She could bolt to the buggy and...

The door opened and Jake rushed through. "Leave her be, Kuchel."

Mr. Kuchel aimed his gun at Jake and fired.

The bullet grazed Jake's arm.

"Look what you made me do!" yelled Kuchel. He tucked the gun inside the back of his trousers and rushed Jake, attempting to tackle him to the ground.

Jake braced himself against the impact, ignoring the pain in his arm. When Kuchel drove his shoulder into Jake's midsection, he grabbed beneath the man's arms and pivoted, slamming Kuchel's body against the rickety log wall.

Kuchel released a string of profanities before somehow worming his way from Jake's hold and swinging for his face.

While Jake was a good head taller and had fifty pounds on the smaller man, Kuchel used his size to his advantage, darting about and taking cowardly shots, some of which glanced off the injury on Jake's arm.

Gritting his teeth against the burning, throbbing sensation, Jake returned a blow.

Blood dripped from Kuchel's nose.

Jake's bottom lip stung from a new cut.

They scuffled within the scant space, just barely missing Ruby, who tucked herself in a corner. Breath whooshed from Jake's lungs as Kuchel landed a punch with more power than he anticipated the puny man possessed.

A fleeting hint of satisfaction arose when Kuchel staggered back after Jake's fist connected with his nose. Again.

"You won't ruin my plans," Kuchel snarled, his voice nasally from his broken nose as he reached behind his back. "Neither of you will."

The bit of sunlight glinting through the grimy window caught the revolver's barrel as it aimed at Jake. "No one will ever know where you're buried."

Jake dove at Kuchel as the gun swung toward Ruby.

Something loud exploded near his ear as another line of pain streaked across his right shoulder.

The breath fled Jake's lungs once again when he crashed onto the floor, which creaked beneath his weight.

Kuchel stumbled out of the way and reaffixed the gun on Jake.

In a flash of welcome color, Ruby darted behind Kuchel and, holding the lone chair like a bat, swung the piece of furniture into Kuchel's lower back.

Kuchel jolted forward, wrath claiming his blood-streaked features.

Jake jumped to his feet and swung one final time.

Kuchel collapsed just after Jake's fist collided with the underside of his jaw.

"Hotel Manager to Stand Trial for Kidnapping, Assault, Attempted Murder, and Embezzlement"

By Ruby Shepherdson

Douglas Kuchel, the manager of The Horizon Hotel, is currently spending time in the Horizon jail awaiting trial for allegedly embezzling from the hotel in the amount of $500 over the course of several months. In his capacity as manager, Mr. Kuchel had ample opportunity to pilfer from the business and did so by recording inaccurate amounts in the ledger.

"Because the wages at the hotel were pathetic, it left me with no choice but to take matters into my own hands," Mr. Kuchel told Sheriff Zembrodt. "Wouldn't you do the same? Especially to win the heart of the woman you loved?"

Before Mr. Kuchel could continue providing quotes to *The Horizon Herald,* and in doing so perhaps mar his plea of not guilty, his attorney immediately intervened and provided the reporter with an abrupt, "No comment".

Mr. Kuchel is also accused of kidnapping The Horizon Herald reporter, Ruby Shepherdson of the *Ruby's Horizon Happenings* column, in an attempt to manipulate her into rescinding her accusation that he was the embezzler. Miss Shepherdson was working with Sheriff Zembrodt to solve the case of the missing hotel money. Mr. Kuchel is alleged to have physically assaulted Miss Shepherdson and to have shot Jake Lynton in the arm. Both Miss Shepherdson and Mr. Lynton are expected to make full recoveries.

"I cannot believe Mr. Kuchel would do such a thing," said Mr. Ferris, the owner of The Horizon Hotel. "He seemed like a decent man and quite unassuming. He was paid well, despite his claims. I reside in Missoula, Montana, but was on the first train to Horizon to ensure no further thievery at my business.

I am currently looking to hire an honest
manager to replace Mr. Kuchel."

Douglas Kuchel's trial is set for October
9.

Miss Lillian O'Kane will also stand trial
separately for her role as an alleged accom-
plice.

Who needed to search for stories to write when one had
grand adventures in which to write about? Ruby finished
typing the article and read it one final time. She praised God
for His provision over both her and Jake. According to Doc,
Jake suffered only flesh wounds that would heal in short
time.

She rolled another sheet of paper into her Smith Premier
typewriter, flipped the page of her notebook, and started her
second article.

"Lillian O'Kane Accused of Plagiarism"
By Ruby Shepherdson
Miss Lillian O'Kane of the *Lillian's Horizon Happenings* column in *The Horizon Herald*
is accused of plagiarizing articles from
The Cornwall Courier and stating they were
her own. On numerous occasions, she copied
directly stories first published in The Cornwall Courier and written by Mr. Henry Murphy.
She put her name as the author of the article
and insisted they were her own. She allegedly
traveled to Cornwall on numerous occasions to
obtain copies of the newspapers.

"Frankly, I'm disturbed by this," said Mr. Tupper, the editor for *The Cornwall Courier*. "I'm grateful for it being brought to my attention, and will do whatever is necessary to secure a conviction."

Mr. O'Kane of *The Horizon Herald* had this to say about his niece's alleged crime. "I always knew something wasn't right about Lillian, and I gave her the job only as a favor to my brother. I always knew there was no way she could have written such professional articles."

Mr. O'Kane was seemingly unaffected by the accusations leveraged against Lillian and was more lenient about the articles Ruby wrote for her column. While Lillian had received what she deserved, Ruby experienced no pleasure in Lillian's downfall.

CHAPTER TWENTY-FIVE

THE DAYS PASSED QUICKLY, many of them spent with Jake. He joined Ruby's family for their Friday suppers, sat beside Ruby in church, and accompanied her three times now on the outings with her nieces and nephews. Each time, Ruby was sure Jake had no idea what he'd gotten himself into. Especially when learning sign language.

It warmed her heart that Jake enjoyed spending time with the children and didn't disregard or ignore them. If he ever did ask her to court him—and she hoped he would—and then someday if they subsequently married—and she dared to dream they would—Jake Lynton would make a kind and doting father.

Pansy curled up in her lap, and the rest of the children sat in a circle for Jake's official sign language lesson. From the smirks on Polly's, Hosea's, Simon's, Carrie's, Becky's, and Sherman's faces, Ruby ascertained that his tutelage would include some shenanigans.

She was correct.

Due to the size of his large hands, Jake struggled somewhat with forming some of the letters of the alphabet—the first lesson taught by Polly and Carrie.

"Not sure I'm suited for this," mumbled Jake, his awkward finger formations anything but graceful.

"You'll grasp it soon enough," said Sherman, who then nudged Simon and they both folded over in laughter.

"It would be better if you were a kid," offered Little Hans.

Jake's eye met Ruby's and he leaned toward her. "Am I really failing that badly?"

"Not at all. It does take some time to learn. These children are fluent because they've been practicing for so long, especially Polly and Hosea, who both learned it when they arrived at the school. You'll do fine. It just takes practice."

Jake's gaze lingered, and Ruby's heart hammered at his nearness. How was it that she was falling in love with the man she formerly thought of as a cranky and irritable hermit? He was so close she could see the specks of yellow and navy in his brilliant blue eyes.

A tapping on her arm attempted to draw her attention from Jake. "Why are you staring at Mr. Jake, Aunt Rubes?"

"I..."

"Because he's staring at her, silly," said Simon, while simultaneously signing. Hosea slugged him in the arm, and they both started laughing.

"When I'm a big woman, I'm not gonna stare at people like that," declared Pansy. She folded her arms across her tiny body."

"You will if you're in love," said Carrie, her words eliciting giggles from her, Polly, and Becky.

Ruby felt a swoosh of heat flame her cheeks, and she focused her gaze on the mountains in the distance.

Little Hans's brow furrowed. "Are you in love with our Aunt Rubes, Mr. Jake?"

She dared peek at Jake from the corner of her eye. Red suffused his face, and his eyes widened. "Well, I reckon I might be."

Sherman shivered dramatically. "Eww. When I grow up, I'm never gonna be in love."

"Me neither," signed Hosea.

"I'm gonna be a missionary so I won't be falling in love," added Simon.

"Or me," said Little Hans. "Girls are weird."

"And boys are stinky," countered Becky.

Using her pointer finger, Polly turned it in a circle several times near her ear and then pointed to Ruby and Jake. All of the children laughed again, some with tears running down their faces.

"What does that sign mean?" Jake asked.

Ruby shook her head and attempted to hide her own amusement. "They're telling us we're crazy. You children are…" She pressed together her first two fingers, ran them down her nose, and then folded her hand in a fist with her thumb extended.

That elicited more giggles, but the loudest and most voracious laughter came when Jake attempted to copy Ruby's sign. "What does that mean, anyway?"

"It's the word for hilarious."

"Except you need to practice that one, Mr. Jake," said Pansy.

Jake grimaced as Ruby repeated the sign. "I think I'm a long way from learning that."

Another half hour of practice proved him right. He wouldn't be learning the sign for hilarious anytime soon.

Eight antsy children, who'd had to sit still for an extended time with their awkward pupil, started a game of tag. Ruby translated for Hosea. "They say you're it, Jake."

The children did their best to prevent Jake from catching them, even though he was a fast runner, especially with his long legs. Ruby watched with admiration until he turned and started running in her direction.

But honestly, she'd be just fine if Jake Lynton caught her. So she pootled along with lackluster ambition until he easily caught her. He swirled her around to face him and held her for a moment before releasing her.

His touch sent a shiver through her and her knees weakened.

Little Hans began to whine. "Are you two gonna stare at each other again or can we keep playing?"

Jake dismounted and wiped his sweaty palms on his trousers. He was nervous as all get out about the task he hoped to accomplish. Would Mr. Shepherdson say yes? Agree that Jake was suitable? Turn him away?

He spied Ruby in the distance, a basket on her arm. The sight of her stole his breath, and he stood unmoving beside his horse.

Like a dolt.

The breeze tousled strands of loose hair and a smile lit her face. Her green skirt swished around her ankles, the dress accentuating her slim waist.

Dinah Jo would say he was smitten, and Jake couldn't deny it. If he was honest with himself, he'd grown fond of her long before today. Would she agree to court him?

She waved and he offered a lighthearted wave in return. Was it too soon to care about someone the way he cared about her? Too soon to plot a future with the woman who consumed his every waking thought?

Romantic fool, he chastised himself. But where Ruby was concerned, that statement rang true.

He thought of just a month ago when he could have lost her to Kuchel's nefarious scheme. The fear in her eyes and the pain the evil man inflicted on her would haunt him forever. What if he hadn't arrived in time to help her? What if she hadn't told him where she was going? What if he hadn't decided to drive to the old Thornton place after finishing ?

God was good.

He thought, too, of how she'd whacked Kuchel in the back with the chair. Jake had heard Ruby was good at baseball and played every year for the deaf school's charity event, but he'd had no idea just what a powerful and accurate swing she had until a month ago. Yes, Jake saved Ruby's life when he arrived at the cabin, but she'd saved his as well.

"Hello, Jake. What brings you here today?"

The glow of her smile drew him in. If only he could ask her straightaway if she'd court him, then he'd have his answer before succumbing to the anxiety of asking her pa first. But he'd best not disrupt the proper order of things.

No matter how much he wished he could.

"Hello, Ruby." His gaze traveled to her full lips. He wanted to circle her waist and plant a kiss on those lips, but such notions would have to wait. "Is your pa here?"

Her shoulders slumped slightly. Was she disappointed at his question? "Oh. Yes. He's in the fields." She pointed in the direction where Mr. Shepherdson worked.

"Thank you. Reckon I'll wander that way."

But neither of them moved. Instead, they stood there in silence while Jake thought about kissing her. Of maybe someday asking her to be his wife. Of sharing a life together on his farm. *Their* farm.

You're a cad, Jake Lynton.

"Well. Thank you, then." Jake fidgeted with the button on his sleeve while Ruby pressed her hands along the front of her skirt. He needed to speak with Mr. Shepherdson and quit delaying.

A wisp of hair had blown across her cheek, and he took a step forward, gently whisked it from her face, and tucked it behind her ear. She closed her eyes and tilted her head.

He cupped her face in his hand and leaned toward her.

Time stood still with only the sound was his heartbeat pounding in his chest and the birds chirping nearby.

"I need to speak to your father," he said.

Her eyes opened, and he saw questions in their depths. "He's in the field."

Reluctantly, Jake dropped his hand and touched the brim of his hat. "I'll be on my way then."

The Shepherdson farm extended for acres, and from what Mr. Shepherdson said, ran adjacent to Timothy's on the south side. The walk gave Jake more time to think...and pray.

Would he be worthy of Ruby? Be able to provide for her if they did someday marry? Sometimes courtships were lengthy, and other times they didn't result in marriage.

Would Ruby be happy on his farm? Would she be amenable to being his wife even if it meant less time to write her articles? Would his family be surprised? He knew they already adored Ruby after meeting her, especially Ma.

If there was a drought or flood or damaging winds destroyed their house and crops, would they still be able to eke out a living? If they did someday marry, would their marriage be strong enough to withstand anything?

The insecurities piled on him, so he prayed again. Marriage was important to the Lord, and Jake knew God would guide them.

And God would guide Jake in the nerve-wracking task ahead of him. He surveyed the bountiful crops, an eagle flying in the blue sky above, and the snow-tipped mountaintops in the distance, all giving testimony of a talented Creator. A Creator Jake had turned his back on for far too long.

His renewed faith emerged stronger and more robust than ever, and peace overcame him. Whatever lie ahead, whether a courtship and subsequent marriage to Ruby, a life of farming, or both, God would be there.

"Mr. Shepherdson?"

"Jake. Good to see you." Mr. Shepherdson unfolded from his crouched position checking on a row of crops.

"Sir, I was wondering if I might speak with you."

"Is everything all right?"

"Yes, sir, it is." Jake rolled his shoulders, hoping to release some of the tension that settled there. "I'm fond of your daughter."

Mr. Shepherdson grinned. "Reckon I could see that."

"And I was wondering..." A forceful swallow worked his dry throat. "Well, it's like this..." He normally wasn't one to mince words. Why then did he stammer like a bumbling ninny? He rubbed the back of his neck and cleared his throat.

"Yes?" a smile tugged at Mr. Shepherdson's mouth.

"Suppose I could just ask it plainly." He kicked at a pebble in the dirt. "Matter of fact, it's like this..." He tried. He really did, but the words lodged in his throat. He thought of Ruby and her beautiful smile, the way her sparkling eyes lit, the dimple in her chin that became more prominent when she was determined about something, and how pretty she was in her green dress. Her kindness and compassion for others. Her lovely voice when she sang. Her love for the Lord. Heat infused his face. If only he still had his whiskers to mask his embarrassment.

A bumblebee buzzed by and the breeze blew through the cornstalks. Best quit lollygagging or it would be suppertime before he uttered another word. "I am fond of Ruby," he finally said. Then chastised himself. Hadn't he already declared as much?

"You're fond of Ruby, and you'd like to..." The corners of Mr. Shepherdson's eyes crinkled as he gestured for Jake to complete his sentence.

"I'd like to be fond of her. I mean—" He removed his hat and scratched his head. He couldn't recall a time he'd been more tongue-twisted in his entire life. "I'm not one for asking hard questions, sir." His excuse sounded weak in his own ears.

"You'd like to court my daughter, am I right?"

The breath he'd been holding rushed from his lungs. "Yes, Mr. Shepherdson. I'd like to court Ruby Shepherdson."

Of course Ruby Shepherdson, you ninny. There's only one Ruby in Horizon, and besides, her pa ought to know of whom you're speaking.

"Yes."

"And as such, if you're worried about..."

"Yes. You have my permission to court her."

"I do?"

Mr. Shepherdson chuckled. "Reckon I don't know what it's like to have to ask a girl's pa that question as my Paisley's father wasn't alive when I sought to marry her."

"Sorry to hear that, sir. But you did say yes, right?"

"Yes, I did. You have my permission. But you'll have to ask her to be sure she's amenable. You and I both know Ruby is a bit strong-minded."

A whole additional set of nerves attacked him like a swarm of bees attacking someone disturbing their hive. "Oh, yes. I will. I'll ask her. And you can be assured that if we marry, I'll love her."

"I do hope so."

"I mean, I already do love her. But I'll also care for her always."

Mr. Shepherdson clapped him on the back. "You're a good man, Jake Lynton. I know you'll do right by my daughter."

Ruby watched as Jake strode to the fields in search of Papa. His broad shoulders stretched the gray-and-black shirt he wore. Jake was not only a dapper man, but he was godly and kind, and the more she'd come to know him, the fonder of him she'd grown.

Her family liked him too, and he, Papa, and Timothy had spent a fair amount of time talking about farming, fishing, and hunting. Jake and Albert had become close friends, and Jake confided to her that God had used her brother to bring him back to the Lord.

The man filled her thoughts more than any article ever had. Lucy and Mae teased her continually about having feelings for Jake, although Ruby couldn't really blame them. She'd been persistent once upon a time in teasing them about Hans and Landon.

Mama would say she was woolgathering, and she would admit that she was.

Ruby had hoped to spend a few minutes with Jake, but he seemed anxious to find her pa. Was everything all right at his farm? Had Papa asked him to assist with something here? Would she see him again before he returned home? Or should she invite him for supper?

She shifted the basket of clean linens. She really should stop dallying and deliver them to the house. Mama was at Maribel's today, and Ruby was assisting in the house.

Ruby finished the laundry and was putting away dishes when she heard a knock on the door. She wiped her hands on her apron and turned the doorknob to see Jake standing on the stoop. "Jake, is everything all right? Is Papa all right?"

"Everything's fine. Everything is." He cleared his throat and stared at the floor before his gaze captured hers. He shoved his hands in his pockets.

"Are you sure?"

"Yes, I'm sure."

They stood in the doorway, and Ruby attempted to peer around him. Why was he so nervous? She dared allow her imagination to wander. What if...

"Ruby Caroline Shepherdson, would you do me the honor of courting me?"

Her answer exploded from her the moment her mind comprehended the question. "Yes!"

A grin crossed his handsome face. "That's good news." He reached for her hand and tugged her from the house and onto the porch. "I just asked your pa for his permission."

Jake continued to hold her hand, his large calloused thumb gently rubbing the back of her hand. Time stood still as the mere touch caused her stomach to swarm with butterflies. "Care to go for a stroll?"

He offered his elbow, and they meandered past the barn and corral. The day was perfect for a walk, especially with Jake. Ruby's mind buzzed with the reality that he'd asked her to court him.

"I'm hoping to plant spuds next year and save up to purchase an Aspinwall Potato Planter. I saw one in Cornwall, and that would save a lot of time." His eyes lit with the talk of his plans for his farm, and Ruby couldn't help but be drawn to his enthusiasm.

"Until you mentioned it, I hadn't heard of such a machine."

"Neither had I." Jake explained to her all the aspects of the invention that would save time and produce more crops. "How is your job at *The Horizon Herald*?"

"Mr. O'Kane has reduced the number of articles I'm assigned and has been writing many of them himself since we discovered Lillian's plagiarism."

Jake covered her hand with his and the warmth flooded through her. "I'm sorry to hear that. I know how much writing the column means to you."

"Thank you. I do love writing, but I've been thinking of other ways to accomplish my article goals as of late."

"Such as?"

One of the things she appreciated about Jake was his support for her writing dream. She chewed on her lip and prepared to tell him the plan she'd not yet shared with anyone but the Lord when she'd prayed for His direction. "I've been contemplating publishing a book. I'd have to seek a publisher who'd be interested, of course."

"I do not doubt that with your ambition and the Lord's guidance, you'll be able to achieve that."

His confidence in her made all the difference.

CHAPTER TWENTY-SIX

DAYS LATER, EXCITEMENT RIPPLED through her at her most recent assignment. Who would have thought she, Ruby Caroline Shepherdson, would be selected to write an article about the orphan train arriving in Horizon?

Not that Mr. O'Kane could choose anyone else for the position. Not when Lillian was now in jail.

But still...

Albert, Lucy, and Mae had arrived in Cornwall on the orphan train years ago. The commendable and worthwhile venture of linking orphans with new parents was the reason the three knew about the love and care found in a forever home.

Maybe someday Ruby and Jake would adopt a few children of their own.

Jake. She never would have anticipated she would have someday courted the less-than-affable man who'd once refused to share his story: the man who'd rescued her from the abominable Mr. Kuchel. Or the man who'd rescued her the first time she'd met him. Or the one who'd caught her and the children picking raspberries on his property.

Just the thought of him caused butterflies to flutter in her stomach. She would see him tonight for supper at Wilhelmina's, but it wasn't soon enough.

Thoughts of their time together consumed her thoughts. She recalled the warmth of his kiss and the way he'd recaptured her lips for a second one.

An accidental jolt from a small child running through the crowd returned her attention to awaiting the train's arrival. Several other folks meandered along the platform, likely awaiting the orphans who would arrive on the two o'clock train.

This was the first time the orphan train would visit Horizon. Would all of the remaining children find homes? Ruby prayed it would be so.

The whistle blew, and she stood on tiptoe. A plume of smoke rose above the trees as the train entered town.

"Here it comes!" shouted a tall, lanky man whom Ruby did not recognize.

Commotion ensued, and several people pushed forward. Would this be the day children and their new parents would be united? Ruby's heart pounded in anticipation for the families that would be created today. She clutched her notebook in hand, experiencing the anticipation buzzing in the air around her as several folks spoke at once. A man beside her squeezed his wife's hand. "It won't be long now until we meet the children. Might even be that one of them is *our* child."

Ruby smiled their way. Several people arrived from nearby towns when they heard the news about the event. *Lord, I don't know the couple beside me, but I pray You have a child in mind just for them.*

The train slowed to a stop, its engine still huffing and puffing from its recent journey. The townsfolk stepped back and allowed the passengers to disembark. Many were travelers returning home. But at the very end of the line, a woman slightly older than Ruby with brown hair fastened in a haphazard bun, and a couple—presumably the reverend and his wife—descended the stairs behind a passel full of children of all ages. The woman carried an infant wrapped in a blanket, and the reverend's wife hoisted a wayward toddler of about two who boasted a sleepy frown. He rubbed his eyes and buried his face in the woman's shoulder.

Another little boy of about four carried a tattered bag and wore a pair of too-short knickers and a faded brown shirt. His gaze connected with hers, and Ruby's heart lurched. She squinted to see the piece of paper pinned to his shirt as they neared. Gus. His name was Gus. Who was this child and what was his story? Would he be the one whom the couple beside her would adopt? Ruby made a note to converse with some of the children. Surely their stories would be fascinating, although likely laced with heartbreak. Perhaps by arriving in Horizon, Idaho, today, they would find their happily ever afters.

Albert hurried along the boardwalk to the orphan train group. "I'm Pastor Albert Shepherdson. Thank you for coming to Horizon."

"Reverend Weberling, and this is my wife, Mrs. Weberling." The man paused and pointed to the young woman carrying the tiny infant. "And this is Miss Schroeder."

"Pleasure to meet you all. This is my sister, Miss Ruby Shepherdson, and she will be writing an article for our local newspaper about your arrival."

The Reverend, his wife, and Miss Schroeder greeted Ruby.

"We'll meet at the church," Albert said. "Is there anything I can do to help?"

"We have a few bags," the reverend gestured toward the train. "Much obliged for your help and for the gracious hospitality."

"You're welcome. We're glad to have you here." Albert slung an arm around Ruby's shoulder. "I can't wait to read your story about this event."

"Thank you. I'm highly anticipating it." She lowered her voice to a whisper. "Do you think all the children will find homes?"

Something flickered in Albert's eyes. "That's our prayer."

Ruby attempted to imagine her older brother as a young child on the orphan train. The fear. The uncertainty. The apprehension he must have felt. Had he worried no one would adopt him? She rested her head on his shoulder. "I sure am thankful Mama and Papa adopted you, Lucy, and Mae."

"Me too, Rubes. Me too. God is good and faithful and truly cares about those with no home."

When the crowd finally cleared, Albert rushed inside the train to procure the bags for Reverend Weberling. Several minutes later, Ruby followed the entourage of eleven children and three adults to the church. Gus, the little boy with the too-short knickers, continually glanced back at her. And while she had no way of ascertaining his thoughts, she noticed sorrow and reservation in his countenance. Ruby prayed someone would adopt him posthaste.

Folks crowded into the church, some eager to adopt a child and others merely curious. Miss Schroeder hung back, the infant now sleeping soundly. She smiled wearily at Ruby, and exhaustion tugged at the corners of her eyes where a few fine lines had formed. Perhaps Ruby could interview her later. Oh, the stories she could tell from her travels!

"Ladies and gentlemen, thank you for coming today. Reverend and Mrs. Weberling and Miss Schroeder have accompanied these eleven children from New York. They've had many stops along the way and are now hoping to find families in Horizon and the surrounding towns. The children have their names pinned to their clothing, and the reverend, his wife, and Miss Schroeder are available to answer any questions you may have. Velma baked a cake this morning, and we've set up a table outside. Please visit with the children and see if one or more of them would be a fine addition to your family."

Gus slowly backed toward the door. Miss Schroeder gently reached for his hand while holding the infant and tugged him beside her. She smiled at him. "We'll have cake in just a moment, Gus, but please do remember to stay in the churchyard."

"Might I help?" Ruby asked as they walked outside.

"Thank you so much. Would you mind holding the baby while I speak with Gus for a moment?"

Ruby took the sleeping baby girl and held her close. Oh, but to be a mother! Besides being a wife, it was the deepest longing of her heart—even more so than being a writer. Ruby kissed the top of the baby's head. If she and Jake were already married, they'd adopt this sweet one in an instant. With so many nieces and nephews, Ruby had vast experience caring for little ones.

Would Jake agree to adopt a child someday?

Miss Schroeder crouched to Gus's level and spoke calmly and tenderly to him. Gus scowled and nodded, but the suspicious glint in his eyes insinuated he did not agree with the woman. "Yes, ma'am," he muttered.

"All right then, go ahead and enjoy some cake."

Gus did not need to be asked twice. He took a piece from Miss Greta who was serving it, and stalked off.

Couples—including the one at the train station—conversed with the children, the group of which consisted of three older ones above the age of ten.

Simon and Sherman were having seconds of cake, but attempting to be secretive. Velma strolled in Ruby's direction, and while she attempted to be cheerful, Ruby knew her sister-in-law struggled to hide the pain that still lingered after the loss of Baby Albert. Ruby's heart hurt for her as no one should have to lose a precious baby.

"Hi, Ruby."

"Velma, hello." With her free arm, she hugged her sister-in-law.

"What a sweet baby," Velma reached for the infant, and Ruby somewhat hesitantly released her. Oh, but to snuggle a little one for hours on end! To sing to her, tell her stories, and plant kisses on her soft forehead.

Velma held the baby close and rocked slightly back and forth. She closed her eyes and a tear hovered on her long lashes. Was she thinking of the baby boy she and Albert lost? If only the Lord had allowed their son to live. Velma and Albert were godly, wonderful, loving, and caring parents.

Why would the Lord see fit to take their baby home so soon after his birth? Ruby dabbed at the tears forming in her eyes. There were some things she would never understand.

With effort, she tore her gaze from the endearing scene before her. She best jot some notes or she'd never be able to deliver a story to Mr. O'Kane. She held up her notebook and angled her pencil to write something when Albert welcomed Velma and the baby into a hug. He pulled them near, and the tears that only seconds before threatened to fall, now slid haphazardly down Ruby's cheeks.

"I think she might need a home," Velma said, her voice muffled and thick with emotion as the tears cascaded down her face.

Albert reached a finger to Velma's cheek and gently wiped the tears. "I believe she may have found one."

Velma's shoulders slumped in defeat, and Ruby found her own doing the same.

"She has?" Velma whispered.

Ruby should step aside and forego interrupting this private moment between her brother and his wife. But her feet remained rooted in place.

"Yes. She has…"

Ruby heard Velma's audible gasp. "I'm not sure I can give her up."

"You won't have to because I believe she's found her new family as a Shepherdson."

Velma visibly inhaled as her shoulders shook. She took a step back and searched Albert's face. "Do you mean it? That she is ours?"

"I believe God put her in your arms at just this very moment in time for a reason."

Velma quietly sobbed as she fell once again into Albert's arms. The baby girl, now awake, wiggled and squirmed.

"Shall we complete the appropriate paperwork and make her ours forever?"

"Oh, yes. Yes, please."

Albert reached for his wife's hand and as they walked away, Ruby noticed unshed tears in her brother's eyes.

She swiped at another of her own tears, for how could she even contemplate writing an article after such a poignant moment? Grasping her pencil, she wrote the words at the top of the page in her notebook: "Happily Ever Afters Emerge When the Orphan Train Arrives in Horizon."

And while she knew the baby girl could never replace the child Albert and Velma lost, she also knew that the orphan had found her own happily ever after.

"Where's Gus?"

Miss Schroeder's words interrupted Ruby's musings and she startled. She ceased writing the key points of her outline for the orphan train article and scanned the area around the church.

"He was just here a minute ago." Miss Schroeder wrung her hands. "He has to be here somewhere."

"Perhaps he's near the trees." But an efficient perusal indicated nearly every other child playing tag beneath the canopy of trees—all but Gus.

When a cursory glance in the immediate area revealed no Gus, and the boy didn't respond to those calling his name, Albert led a prayer seeking God's guidance.

Clamor arose amongst the numerous townsfolk, children, and visitors in the churchyard and surrounding vicinity.

"He was just here a moment ago."

"He couldn't have wandered far."

"Again?"

"Where could he go?"

"Did someone check the church?"

"Is he in the outhouse?"

Ruby hurried to the creek near the church. It was higher than usual this year, and a boy as young as Gus could easily drown. Her heart pounded. *Lord, please let us find him.*

Thankfully, Gus was not near or in the creek. Nor was he in the church, the outhouse, or the nearby houses. The Lieutenant had fetched Sheriff Zembrodt, and a search party was formed. Papa, Albert, Timothy, Landon, Hans, and many others determined to go in separate directions in the hopes of finding the little orphan boy who'd wandered off.

Miss Schroeder, the preacher, and his wife were clearly out of sorts with having lost one of the children. Ruby couldn't blame them. She was worried and she didn't even know Gus. She couldn't imagine the panic and concern those who cared for him must be feeling right now.

After assisting in the search, she rushed to *The Horizon Herald*. With the latest occurrence, her article would be delayed, and while she didn't care to have to tell Mr. O'Kane, it was necessary to warn him it may take her a day longer to complete the task.

She found her boss inside setting type.

"Ruby Shepherdson. Where have you been?"

"I'm covering the orphan train arrival, sir." Was Mr. O'Kane being snarky or did he truly have a faulty memory?

"Oh, yes. That's right. Is it finished?"

"No, but I have taken thorough notes and have completed my outline. I will need an additional day to finish it, however, because of an unforeseen circumstance."

Mr. O'Kane turned from setting the type and folded his arms across his skinny self. "You are chronically in need of additional time, Miss Shepherdson. Were this any other job, you'd be dismissed from your position posthaste."

She resisted temptation and contained her thoughts to forego reminding Mr. O'Kane that she was now his only reporter. In addition to Mr. O'Kane himself, of course. Although he had taken to writing even more articles since releasing Lillian. And no one answered his repeated "Help Wanted" adverts in the paper to write for *The Horizon Herald.*

He glowered at her, the horizontal lines in his pasty forehead becoming more prominent. "You'd better have a valid excuse for needing more time for such an important article."

It hadn't been an important article when she'd broached the suggestion with him, but Ruby didn't say as much. "I do indeed. There is another story I will be covering as well, which is the reason for the orphan train article necessitating an additional day."

"I'm listening."

Ruby chewed her bottom lip. She for certain did not want to sound as though a gossipmonger. "Unfortunately, a young child has gone missing from the adoption gathering at the church."

Mr. O'Kane inclined his head sideways. "You don't say. So we could write an article about the negligence of those involved in organizing the orphan train." He stroked his chin. "Perhaps folks ought to know that children are not safe under the care of such individuals."

Ruby gasped. "No. No, Mr. O'Kane, that is not it at all. No one is at fault. There was much commotion—happy commotion—as nearly all of the children have been adopted today. The blame should not rest squarely on anyone's shoulders. The boy merely wandered off and is now lost."

"I like my perspective much better."

"While perspectives have their place, truth is always the best option." The words jumped from her mouth without thought, but Ruby would not allow Mr. O'Kane to blemish the reputations of the hardworking and compassionate people who sought to find children forever homes.

"Finish the orphan train story immediately and write the one about the missing child as well. Both are due in two days. Our faithful readers are depending on us to produce quality articles in an efficient manner."

"I will do my best, but I do want it to be accurate."

Mr. O'Kane shook his head. "You do whatever it takes to have those articles to me. While yes, we do want them to be accurate, ensuring they are printed promptly is far more critical. Now, I must be on my way. My wife has scheduled a supper event for us. Close the door when you leave."

Without another word, Ruby's boss turned on his heel and left the business. She sighed. Working for *The Horizon Herald* didn't muster much joy for her these days. If it wasn't for her love for writing articles such as her pending ones about the orphan train, she'd quit tomorrow.

She watched as Mr. O'Kane gallivanted out the door and down the street in the direction of his home. Ruby sighed and was about to exit the building herself when a muffled thud in the closet behind Mr. O'Kane's desk caused her to jump. Was someone in the newspaper office? No, an adult was too large to cram themselves inside, especially with the abundance of supplies.

Perhaps it was just something falling from a shelf. Mr. O'Kane was known for stacking things far too high.

A rustling sound followed, and Ruby froze. Something was in the closet. Perhaps a dog had gotten locked inside. It might even be hungry. She recalled when Landon found Beans and what a blessing he had been to their family. She tiptoed closer. "Hello?"

Something crashed to the floor then, and Ruby opened the door. A little boy zipped past her but not before a broom handle thumped her on the side of the head.

"Come back!" she yelled, running after him while simultaneously nursing the pain from the broom handle.

Gus ignored her and bolted across the office, causing loose papers to shuffle off Mr. O'Kane's desk and flutter to the floor.

Ruby grabbed his arm. "Gus, please stop!"

Gus tugged and pulled, attempting to break free from her grasp.

"I'm not going to hurt you. I just want to talk with you."

"I'm not goin' back."

"Going back where? To the orphan train?"

He spun and twisted, hoping to yank his arm from Ruby's hold.

"Please, Gus. I'm not going to hurt you," she repeated.

The boy slightly settled and narrowed his blue eyes. "I'm gonna go live by myself on my own farm. I don't need no family.

"How old are you?"

"Six and that's plenty old enough to live on my own farm." Gus firmed his mouth in a straight line and glowered at her. "Ain't no one gonna stop me neither."

Gus did *not* look to be six years old. Scrawny and puny, Papa would say he was just knee-high to a grasshopper. "You want to be a farmer?"

He angled his head to one side and eyed her. "Yeah. Gonna have cows and chickens and the like."

"Sounds like a wonderful plan. Will you have a dog? Horses? Maybe a goose or two?"

"A dog, yes. And three horses. Two to pull my wagon and one to ride. But no gooses. They's mean."

Ruby could attest to the fact that geese could be mean-spirited because she'd once been bitten by one when she was just a girl. The goose chased her, bobbed its head up and down, then launched the attack. "I understand that. I wouldn't want to have a goose either. I once was bitten by one."

Gus's eyes rounded. "You were?"

"I was."

"And you lived to be a grown-up lady?"

His question amused her. "I did."

They stood for a moment in silence, and Ruby prayed God would guide her next words. "Everyone is so worried about you. Miss Schroeder and Reverend and Mrs. Weberling are looking for you."

"I don't wanna go back."

"But what if a family wants to adopt you?"

"They won't keep me."

His matter-of-fact statement broke Ruby's heart. "Why wouldn't they want to keep you?"

Gus kicked at the floor. "They never do." His shoulders bowed. "One time they even found a child they liked better."

If what Gus was saying was true, it was no wonder he refused to be adopted.

"And the other time they just plain didn't like me and gave me back to the o-fen-ege."

Ruby kneeled to the boy's height. "I'm so sorry, Gus."

"Like I said 'afore. That's why I want to live by myself on my farm. Now if you'll 'scuse me, I'll be on my way." He started to back away from her.

"Are you hungry?"

Gus wrapped his thin arms around his body. "Maybe. I guess I kinda do like baked beans."

"Wilhelmina makes delicious baked beans at her restaurant. As a matter of fact, I was planning to go there myself this evening for supper. Maybe you would care to join me."

"I might wanna. But I ain't goin' back to no o-fen-ege. Not ever." He stuck his bottom lip out, defiance written on his face.

"That isn't up to me to decide, but I do know that if a family wants to adopt you and make you their forever son, they won't be able to find you hiding in a closet or on your farm."

Gus's blond brows knitted together. "I 'spose not."

Ruby held out her hand. "Let's go let Reverend and Mrs. Weberling and Miss Schroeder know that you are all right. They've been worried about you."

Something flashed in Gus's eyes. Something akin to regret. "All right, but if they make me go back, I'll just run away again."

CHAPTER TWENTY-SEVEN

JAKE RODE INTO TOWN after a full day of work to take Ruby to supper at Wilhelmina's with the plan to propose to her. His heart thrummed overtime in his chest. Would she agree to be his wife? Would he be worthy of her?

One thing he hadn't expected was being asked to help find a missing child.

Mr. Shepherdson cornered him as he strolled down the boardwalk. Apparently, a little boy from the orphan train wandered off. "He has blond hair and blue eyes, and his name is Gus," said Mr. Shepherdson.

"I'm happy to help."

"Thank you. In about ten minutes, a group of men are preparing to disperse to different areas of town and surrounding farms. We'll meet by the livery." A glint in Mr. Shepherdson's eye replaced his concerns over the boy for a brief moment, and he jabbed Jake playfully in the rib. "Are you ready to ask her?"

"I just hope she says yes."

"She will."

Jake hoped the older man was correct, but it helped ease some of his anxiety knowing Mr. Shepherdson had readily given his permission for Jake to propose.

As he continued down the boardwalk, his mind returned to the lost child. Why had he run away? Had they found him yet? There were hazards for someone the boy's age to be by his lonesome. Evening would soon be upon them and the chances of locating the child would be much slimmer by that time.

In all the commotion, he hadn't had a chance to talk with Ruby and postpone their supper. After he checked a few more places where he thought the boy would hide, he'd find Ruby and see if Monday evening would suit them better.

He passed by *The Horizon Herald*, then did a double take when he saw Ruby and a little boy through the window.

Jake retraced his steps and entered the building. "Ruby?"

"Hello, Jake. Would you mind telling Mrs. Weberling, the reverend's wife, that we found Gus? She remained behind at the church in case Gus returned."

Jake had a million questions but figured those could wait until he alleviated everyone's concerns about Gus's safety. "Yes, I'll let her know. Will Gus be returning to the church soon?"

The small-statured boy with pale hair and large round blue eyes shook his head with such vigor it nearly knocked him off his feet. "I ain't going back nowheres."

Ruby opened her mouth, likely to correct him, then must have changed her mind for she instead patted him on the shoulder and focused her attention on Jake. "Thank you for letting Mrs. Weberling know. Would you mind returning here afterward?"

"Will do. I'll be back."

Gus hugged himself tightly and scowled at Jake. Poor kid. What must he have been through to not want to return to those who managed the orphan train?

Mrs. Weberling was sitting inside the church with Velma, who was holding the tiny baby girl in a stained pink dress. Tears brimmed in Velma's eyes, and she looked up with a hopeful glance when Jake entered.

"We found him, ma'am."

"And is he all right?"

"He is. Seems to be a bit obstinate but in healthy condition all the same."

"Oh, thank You, Jesus!" She held a hand to her heart. "We were so worried."

"I see the sheriff and some other men have just arrived. I'll let them know as well."

Mrs. Weberling bobbed her head. "Yes, that would be most appreciated. Thank you."

Jake nodded at both he and Velma and located the sheriff, Pastor Albert, Mr. Shepherdson, Reverend Weberling, and several other men a few moments later. Reverend Weberling gripped Jake on the shoulder. "It's truly a miracle we found the boy."

"Has he run off before?" Mr. Shepherdson asked.

"He has. He'd boarded a train unbeknownst to us the last time. Were it that we were five minutes later, we would have lost him forever because the train was leaving and no one knew he was aboard."

Jake shook his head. "Glad he's been found. He's with Ruby at *The Horizon Herald*. I reckon he'll be returned to you soon, Reverend, although he didn't seem any too thrilled about that prospect."

A pained expression crossed the man's weary features. "No, I don't suppose he was. Poor child has been through a lot. The missus and I are staying at Miss Greta's tonight. Would you mind returning him there?"

"Yes, sir."

But Jake had a strong feeling that returning Gus to the reverend and his wife wouldn't be as easy as one might think.

Miss Schroeder arrived at Wilhelmina's just as Ruby, Jake, and Gus took their seats. "May I speak with you briefly?" she asked.

Meanwhile, Gus tucked himself beneath the table. "Don't let her see me," he mumbled.

Ruby followed Miss Schroeder out the door and onto the boardwalk. "Thank you so much for finding him," the woman said. Tears glistened in her eyes. "We thought we'd lost him for good this time."

"You are welcome. I'm so glad I was in the newspaper office when I was. I abhor the thought that he might have stayed there overnight all alone. He says he ran away because he didn't want to be adopted again."

"Sadly, this isn't the first time."

"He insinuated no one wants him."

Miss Schroeder sighed. "I can fully understand why he would arrive at that conclusion."

Ruby waited for the woman to continue. She'd discovered in her interviewing experience that when she paused and allowed the person to speak in their own time, they most often did.

"Twice before he has experienced rejection. Thrice if you consider the story behind how he first came to the orphanage."

"Was he a baby?"

"A foundling, yes. From what I was told, the doctor assumed him to be about three months old at the time. We named him Gus, or Gustav, after the doctor who found him. When Doc opened his office for the day, there was Gus on the porch, wrapped in a dingy, dirty blanket and sleeping in a basket. The doctor noted he was malnourished and conjectured that he'd likely been born early and with some health issues. Unfortunately, Gus did not thrive at the orphanage although they did their best with limited resources. There was never enough food to go around."

"I'm so sorry." Poor Gus. No wonder he didn't want to return.

"Yes, it's been a heartbreaking story from the beginning. The orphanage was lacking in studies, and there were too many children and not enough teachers. Gus's grammar has suffered due to this. We've tried during the train rides to instill in him not only polite behavior but also grammar skills. His fear and despondency have prevented him from listening to much of what we say."

Ruby again thought of Albert, Lucy, and Mae. Had they suffered in the orphanage they once resided in before coming to Horizon? "How old is he?"

"He recently had his sixth birthday. When the orphanage contacted Reverend and Mrs. Weberling about him last year, it was decided he was a befitting candidate for the orphan train. So last year, we included him with the rest of the eligible children."

"Last year?"

Miss Schroeder nodded sadly. "Yes, and after a family chose to adopt him, they brought him back the following day just as we boarded the train. They said they'd changed their minds, but offered no further details."

Ruby gasped and held a hand to her mouth. "How disheartening."

"Indeed. Gus was the only child who returned to New York with us. He was returned to the orphanage until we again planned our next journey this year."

It made sense now to Ruby why Gus hesitated to go with another family what with having been rejected. "So he didn't want to entertain the thought of that happening again."

"And it had. When we stopped in Missouri on this journey, we thought God had answered our prayers when a kindly farmer and his wife agreed to adopt him. They were about to finalize their decision when they noticed one of our other boys who was taller, stronger, and two years older than Gus. They claimed they hadn't seen him before." A tear lingered at the corner of Miss Schroeder's eye. "They said they could only adopt one child, and so they vehemently returned Gus and took the other boy. A blessing for the other child, but another rejection for Gus."

"Poor little boy. He seems so sweet."

"He is. Brokenhearted and understandably so. But sweet, curious, funny, and energetic."

Ruby peered back through the window to see Jake and Gus engaged in conversation. Or rather, Gus talking and Jake patiently listening. "I know that because he ran away, folks were unable to take a proper look at him, but did anyone express interest in adopting him?"

Miss Schroeder shook her head slowly. "No. And now all of the townsfolk and those visiting from other places have left. I'm sad to say that Gus will again return to the orphanage."

"Do you think if he did have a home he would recover from the pain and rejection he's felt?"

The woman shrugged a slim shoulder. "We aren't sure. We certainly do hope so. But I'd rather call upon my favorite verse in the Bible when He says that with Him, all things are possible."

Ruby chewed her lip in contemplation. "What if there was a family who might be interested?"

"They would have until tomorrow to make their interest known. Of course, we don't want someone adopting Gus merely because they feel sorry for him. Gus is a special child. He's capable and smart and loving, but without the right family, it's doubtful he would ever reach his potential."

It gave Ruby much to consider and to pray about. "Jake and I will bring Gus to Miss Greta's after supper."

Miss Schroeder offered a tired smile. "Thank you for your kindness."

As Ruby turned to leave, she thought of another question. "Miss Schroeder?"

"Yes?"

"Were all of the children adopted this time?"

"All but Gus."

Gus proved to have a voracious appetite. Not only did he order baked beans, but Wilhelmina convinced him to try meatloaf and a hefty piece of rhubarb pie, which he nearly inhaled.

Jake wondered if they fed him enough at the orphanage. Maybe that was why he was so small.

"Is this how you got so big, Mr. Jake? Because you ate a lot of baked beans?"

Jake scooped up another bite of beans. "I like them fine enough, but I like steak better. My ma always said I ate enough for the whole family."

"I ain't got no ma, but iffin I did, I reckon she'd say I eat enough beans for our whole family too." Gus rubbed his stomach. "When I have my own farm, I'm gonna grow beans and eat 'em everyday. 'Course, it's a good thing I'll be livin' alone on my farm if I eat that many beans!"

Jake caught Ruby's eye and they both laughed. While Jake anticipated an evening with Ruby, he couldn't deny that in the short time of knowing Gus, the boy had grown on him.

The Lieutenant and Miss Greta entered the restaurant with a boy of about twelve.

"I know that boy. He's from the the o-fen-ege."

The Lieutenant spied them and ushered Miss Greta and the boy to their table. "Ruby and Jake, you gotta meet our new son." The man beamed with pride. "This here is August."

Jake and Ruby greeted the boy.

"Hi, August. So you don't gotta go back to the o-fen-ege?"

The skinny black-haired boy shook his head. "No, I went and got myself adopted."

Miss Greta dabbed at her eye, and the Lieutenant squared his shoulders and stood taller.

"What about you?" asked August. "Are these your people your new parents?"

Gus dropped his head. "No, they ain't my parents. I ain't got no parents."

Watching the boy now morosely poke at the remnants of his meal, Jake prayed Gus would find the family the Lord had in mind for the little orphan.

That evening after Ruby and Jake returned a somewhat defiant Gus to Reverend and Mrs. Weberling, they spent time talking in the wagon before disembarking.

They discussed Gus, how grateful they were that Ruby had found him in the closet, and how the orphan train had been instrumental in placing nearly all of the children with Horizon and surrounding area residents. Albert and Velma had adopted their little girl, and the Lieutenant and Miss Greta now had a son.

While there were many happy endings tonight, one story had not ended well. Gus's story. Ruby's heart broke for the little boy who yearned for a home.

Jake leaned against the barn and reached for Ruby's hands. It had been an eventful day, but she didn't want it to end. Stars sparkled and the moon cast a pleasing glow. The air smelled of fresh hay and impending fall. She stepped into his welcoming embrace and rested her head against his chest. He buried his face in her hair. "I love you, Ruby."

"I love you too, Jake."

She remained in his arms as the seconds ticked by before he gently released her and bent to one knee. "Ruby Caroline Shepherdson, will you do me the honor of being my wife? I promise to love you forever."

"Yes, Jake Lynton, I would be honored to be your wife."

He stood, lifted her, and spun her around causing them both to be dizzy before he teetered and set her back on her feet.

"Have you spoken to Papa yet?"

"Already handled."

Ruby released the breath she'd been holding. Not that she doubted her parents wouldn't allow her to marry Jake, for she knew they would. They'd grown fond of him as well.

She placed her hand in the crook of his arm, and they moseyed to the front door.

"It was quite something seeing Pastor Albert and Velma adopt that baby girl today," said Jake.

"She is absolutely precious. Velma said they named her Gloria." Ruby couldn't wait to spend more time with her newest niece.

"And the Lieutenant and Miss Greta. Who would have imagined that?"

Ruby shook her head. "That was an utter surprise. August will do well with them."

They stood on the porch, and Jake put his arm around her.

"Are you thinking what I'm thinking?" she asked.

"That there is a little boy who needs a home?"

"Indeed."

Jake exhaled as he surveyed the beginnings of a breathtaking sunset. Never in those pain-filled years had he imagined standing with the woman he loved—the woman he'd marry, reconciled with God and his family, and planning to adopt a lonely little boy whom God brought to Horizon just for them.

Yet here he was.

"What are you thinking?" Ruby asked.

"That sometimes blessings come from unexpected places." He kissed the top of Ruby's head, grateful she was one such blessing. *Thank You, Lord.*

EPILOGUE
ONE YEAR LATER

RUBY CLIMBED FROM THE buggy and held the brown, wrapped package to her chest. Her stomach jolted, and she tenderly placed a hand on it.

"I know, little one, I'm excited to tell your pa and brother too."

The baby kicked again in response as Ruby hurried to the barn where Jake and Gus were fixing the wagon.

Jake stood and circled her waist. "Did you retrieve the important item from the post office?"

"I did."

"Is it bunches of candy?" Gus asked.

Both Ruby and Jake laughed. "Not candy, but something even better." Ruby hugged the package to her chest before peeling back the paper to expose the contents.

It looked even lovelier than she could have imagined, and the happy tears flooded her eyes as joy bubbled within her. "Oh, Jake. I can't believe it's really true." Her eyes settled on the words on the cover:

Ruby's Horizon Happenings: Life in a Small Town in Idaho
By Ruby Caroline Lynton

"That's better than candy?" asked Gus.

She ruffled his hair. "Much better."

Ruby cast a glance to the sky and thanked the Lord for Jake, for Gus, for their new baby to be born, for her family, and for the book that included all of her articles and had taken the place of writing for Mr. O'Kane. When the publisher accepted it, the advance paid had provided Jake with the new Aspinwall Potato Planter.

She stood on tiptoe as Jake's lips captured hers in a passionate kiss. So many hopes and dreams had all come true and there were so many more to come.

READ A SNEAK PEEK FROM

WILL HORIZON GIVE HER
THE FRESH START SHE NEEDS?

Love on the Horizon

Sneak Peek

THE BEST DREAMS WERE the ones that came true.

And Mags Davenport's dreams were about to come true. She could feel it in her bones, as old Mrs. Fryman used to say.

She took a step back and scanned the bustling city. Hadn't she read in a discarded newspaper that Chicago had reached half a million people? Yes, her decision to travel West would be a good one.

The train depot beckoned her, and she entered the stately brick Dearborn Station with its enormous clock tour. Folks hurried in every direction. Hopefully with twenty-some railroad lines and over a hundred departures, one of those departures would surely lead her to the new life that awaited her.

No one would be the wiser that a twenty-three-year-old woman would be boarding for free.

For what could she do? The two dollars she'd saved would only be for absolute necessaries.

The lines to purchase tickets meandered through the building. Mags stood on tiptoe to seethe departure signs when she noticed a wealthy couple in front of her in deep conversation.

"While it's not my favorite place, I anxiously anticipate seeing our grandchildren again," the woman, who wore an elegant dress of the latest fashion, said.

"Yes, well, I'm never fond of visiting Horizon, but I know how much it means to you, and it's been all of two months since we saw the grandchildren.

"Indeed, Bertram. I miss them the second we board the train for Denver, and this time having been in Maryland, I miss them all the more. Besides, Horizon is such a lovely place,and the people are so kind. I've actually made a few friends there."

The man named Bertram, in the finest of silk hats, grunted. "Yes, Gladys, we all know you've made friends in Horizon."

The topic of which Bertram and Gladys spoke intrigued Magnolia, and she inclined closer. Horizon sounded like just the place she'd like to live, especially if people were kind.Goodness knows she'd had her share of spiteful and cruel people in Chicago—many of whom were related.

Gladys leaned her head back, the purple lilacs and other foliage atop her extravagant hat nearly poking Mags in the eye.

"Oh, dear me. I'm so sorry." The woman nodded in her direction then returned her attention straight ahead.

Feeling suddenly tattered and disheveled in her dress, Mags resisted the urge to lower her head and stare at her worn and holey shoes. But not this time. Her curiosity had been piqued about this Horizon place. She tapped on Gladys's shoulder. "Ma'am, if you don't mind..."

"What is it?" The woman's voice wasn't unkind, but it was clipped, and wariness filled her countenance. Perhaps she thought Mags would be asking for funds like so many beggars did—like Mags had numerous times, especially in her childhood.

"Might I ask about this place known as Horizon?"

A smile lit the woman's face, and the starch in her frame dissolved. "Our son, his wife, and our grandchildren live there." She handed her leather reticule to Bertram and opened the golden locket at her neck. "If you look closely, you can see our four grandchildren. The older ones are Polly and Hosea. The two little ones are Pansy and L.J."

Mags squinted to see the tintypes of the four children. Their smiles lit up the frames. Such happiness! What would that have been like?

"Oh, yes. They are lovely children."

"Indeed. So that is why we visit. What else would you like to know?"

"Is Horizon in Montana? California? Colorado?"

"Idaho."

That wasn't the answer she'd expected. "Idaho?"

"Yes, it really is a bit backward and primitive in my opinion, but it is improving. They now have a hotel, although we don't stay there. We stay with our son and his wife when we visit."

Bertram cleared his throat. "Must you make friends with everyone you meet, Gladys?"

Gladys's perfectly shaped brows dipped. "Yes, I must."

"Thank you for the information. Horizon sounds delightful."

And that was just the place Mags would go, provided her plan worked. And provided the porter failed to realize she hadn't purchased a ticket.

It wasn't the most ideal of situations, but when had she ever let that stop her?

Mags raised her chin and took a deep breath. Yes, she would go to Horizon. Find a fresh start, escape her past, and maybe, just maybe find a place where she belonged.

If you want to be among the first to hear about the next Horizon installment, be sure to sign up for Penny's newsletter at www.pennyzeller.com. You will receive book and writing updates, encouragement, notification of current giveaways, occasional freebies, and special offers.

A
WYOMING
SUNRISE
NOVELETTE

Author's Note

Dear Reader,

Thank you for taking a return trip to Idaho with me. I'm often asked what character in a book I liked best. In *Beyond the Horizon*, the choice was difficult, so I can honestly say it was a tie between Ruby and Jake.

It was so much fun to write Ruby's character and create a woman with a love for writing (who may or may not share some character traits with someone we know), who cherished her nieces and nephews, and who sought to do what was right, even when it was a challenge. Sharing the struggle with Jake as he sought the Lord's and his pa's forgiveness—and the struggle to forgive himself—was at times a tear-jerking journey.

As with all of my historical romances, I conducted an enormous amount of research. There were some fictional liberties taken in *Beyond the Horizon*, including the speed with which Ruby's book was accepted by a publisher and published. However, much of what you read was real or inspired by real items or events.

The White Sewing Machine was a real thing. It did cost $35 according to some advertisements, and sugar cost $1 for a ten-pound bag. Some years of the Montgomery Ward Catalogue really did have 674 pages and everything listed in the book was really included within its pages. An advertisement in 1888 mentioned the catalog boasted 3,500 illustrations.

And speaking of the Montgomery Ward Catalog, you may have noticed an alternative spelling in *Beyond the Horizon*. "Catalog" spelled the way we are now accustomed to seeing it, rather than "catalogue" as was used in the book, was not commonplace until 1895. In that year, "catalog" was known as a new spelling for the word. Since the book takes place in 1895 and rural Idaho would undoubtedly be a little bit behind the times, I kept it as "catalogue" for purposes of the story.

The Charter Oak Stove was a much-sought-after oven, and the Smith Premier was a real typewriter. As a matter of fact, it was one of the most popular typewriters at that time and was advertised regularly in numerous newspapers.

The Aspinwall Potato Planter was real and was an amazing invention. It saved time, and advertisements claimed it could "plant five to eight acres per day...and will do the work of eight men" (*The Columbia Herald*, 1893). Stedge's Tonic was real and there truly was a Buffalo Bill's Congress of Rough Riders Wild West Show. Cork vests were a forerunner to our modern-day life jackets, and a man truly did attempt to swim the Niagara River using a cork vest.

Hamburg steak was a real food item, and was not a typo for "hamburger".

There really was a wanted ad seeking a woman to assist with a fundraiser. The prerequisites were that she could sing and chew gum. Prices for ads in *Beyond the Horizon* were accurate prices found during that time period.

Miss Amity Hicks in the book was inspired by real-life circus performer, May Wirth. An Australian native, Miss Wirth was an acrobat in the Barnum and Bailey Circus in the U.S. She could perform somersaults while proceeding from one moving horse to another. Her claim to fame is as one of the top female performers for Barnum and Bailey.

The mine explosion was based on a real occurrence in the State of Washington. Ketchum, Idaho, is a real place and was first named Leadville in 1880 before the name was later changed to Ketchum after a trapper named David Ketchum.

Some of the most time-consuming research when writing historicals is to ensure that words were used at the time the story takes place. Words that were and weren't in use always interest—and sometimes—surprise me. Case in point: the words terminal, faux pas, top-notch, and locks (as in locks of hair), were all in use at the time of *Beyond the Horizon*. The word close-knit was not in use until 1926, so that word was removed and replaced.

The saying, "When I'm a big woman", said by Pansy in the book, was inspired by my own two daughters. When they were little, they wouldn't just say, "When I'm a grownup" or "When I grow up", or "When I'm a woman" but instead would always add "When I'm a *big* woman..."

Authors find names for their characters from a variety of places, and the names we choose must fit the characters (in our minds, anyway!) Ruby's name was inspired by one of my adopted grandmothers who also had red hair. Gus's name in the story was inspired by a tiny baby who lost his life. I'd been following his story and fervently praying for God's healing. Sadly, he did not survive.

For those of you who have been with me for awhile, you may recall the most humorous blooper in one of my books—John Mark in *Dreams of the Heart* going to the salon instead of the saloon. Thankfully that was found in the final round of edits! In *Beyond the Horizon,* two bloopers stand out: "he plopped his cowboy on his head" and "Mr. Greta" rather than "Miss Greta." Thankfully my eagle-eyed editors found both before the book went to print. Although sometimes no matter how many rounds of editing a book receives (and books receive many!) there can still be some sneaky errors that find their way into the final book.

I hope you enjoyed reading about the Shepherdson family, Jake, and the other delightful characters who call Horizon, Idaho, their home. I can't wait to share Timothy's story with you in 2025. We'll revisit our old friends and also meet a few new ones including Mags, the main female character.

As always, thank you for being a devoted reader. Until next time, happy reading!

Blessings,

Penny

Acknowledgments

As with writing any book, such a feat would not be possible without the help of many.

Thank you to my family for encouraging me in this crazy dream I call writing.

Thank you to my Penny's Peeps Street Team. Thank you for spreading the word about my books. I appreciate your encouragement and support!

Thank you to my readers. May God bless and guide you as you grow in your walk with Him.

And, most importantly, thank you to my Lord and Savior, Jesus Christ. It is my deepest desire to glorify You with my writing and help bring others to a knowledge of Your saving grace.

About the Author

Penny Zeller is known for her heartfelt stories of faith-filled happily ever afters and her passion to impact lives for Christ through fiction. Her books feature tender romance, steady doses of humor, and memorable characters that stay with you long after the last page. While she has had a love for writing since childhood, Penny began her adult writing career penning articles for national and regional publications on a wide variety of topics. Today Penny is a multi-published author of over two dozen books and is also a fitness instructor, loves the outdoors, and is a flower gardening addict.

In her spare time, she enjoys camping, hiking, kayaking, biking, bird watching, reading, running, and playing volleyball. Penny resides with her husband and two daughters in small-town America and loves to connect with her readers at her website at www.pennyzeller.com, her blog, www.pennyzeller.wordpress.com, and her Facebook page at www.facebook.com/pennyzellerbooks where she posts faith, funnies, writing updates, and encouragement. All of her socials can be found at https://linktr.ee/pennyzeller.

HORIZON SERIES

WYOMING SUNRISE SERIES

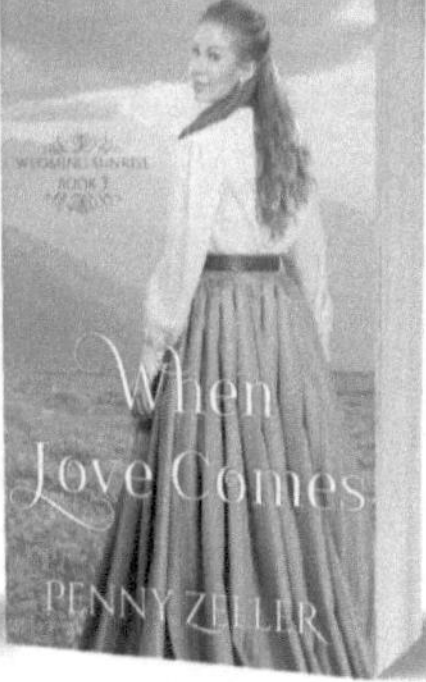

HOLLOW CREEK

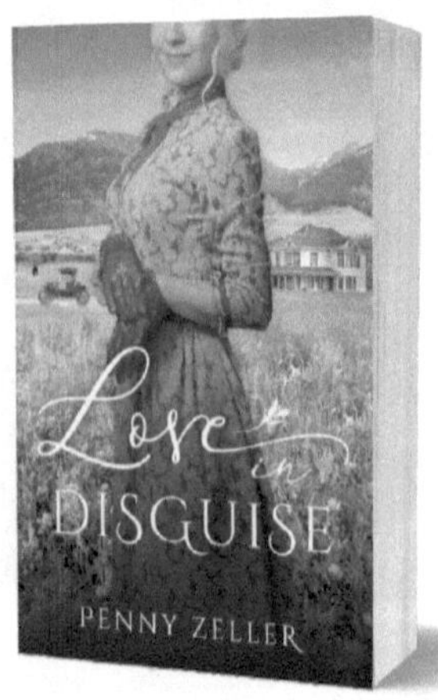

LOVE LETTERS FROM ELLIS CREEK

PENNY
ZELLER
Love
FROM AFAR

PENNY
ZELLER
Love
UNFORESEEN

PENNY
ZELLER
Love
MOST CERTAIN

STANDALONE BOOKS

MOUNTAIN JUSTICE

SMALL TOWN SHENANIGANS

Chokecherry Heights

www.ingramcontent.com/pod-product-compliance
Lightning Source LLC
Chambersburg PA
CBHW021242190726
48289CB00005B/1446